The Girl on 30A

Deborah Rine

Deborah Rine

The Girl on 30A is a work of fiction. The characters, incidents, and dialogue are drawn from the author's imagination and are not to be construed as real. Any resemblance to actual events or persons, living or dead, is entirely coincidental.

ISBN-13: 978-1981114382
ISBN-10: 1981114386

This book is dedicated to the sugar-white sands and turquoise waters of the Emerald Coast and the delightful people who live there.

Books by Deborah Rine

Banner Bluff Mystery Series:
THE LAKE
FACE BLIND
DIVERGENT DEATHS

Contemporary Novel:
RAW GUILT

Deborah Rine can be contacted at:

www.deborah-rine-author.com
http://dcrine.blogspot.com/
Face book and Twitter

To be creative means to be in love
with life.
You can be creative only if
You love life enough that you want to
enhance its beauty
You want to bring a little more music
to it,
a little more poetry to it,
a little more dance to it.

Osho

Chapter 1

Claire left Christmas Day. Her mother stood at the open front door twisting a dishcloth in her hands. Tears streamed down her face. Dad sat on the porch steps, a cigar squashed between his lips; a glass of Scotch cradled in his hands. Jeremy was in the living room where she'd left him, staring blindly at the floor.

#

They'd had the usual roast beef and Yorkshire pudding followed by a raspberry trifle. Aunt Rose and her family had left right after dessert. Her brother Timothy, his wife Beth Ann, and their four rambunctious kids headed out the door a few minutes later. They were having another Christmas dinner with Beth Ann's family across town. Two of the kids were screaming as the door banged shut. Suddenly the house seemed very quiet. Claire helped her mother clear the table and load the dishwasher. They chatted about Timothy's kids. Like every year, the nieces and nephews had ripped open each gift, tossed it aside and then torn into the next one.

"I don't know if Bobby and Aiden really liked the video games we bought," Claire's mom said, scrubbing the roast pan.

"Don't worry, Mom. I'm sure they loved everything. They were just really excited." Claire put the last dessert plate in the dishwasher. She didn't mention that she thought those kids were spoiled rotten.

Her mother looked up, frowning. "I think Lucy would have liked a Barbie doll instead of a baby doll. But I thought she was too young."

Claire put an arm around her mother's thin shoulders and gave her a hug. "Let me finish washing the pans. You prepared the entire meal."

"No, no you've helped enough. Go relax with Jeremy. I think he's looking for you."

Claire suppressed a sigh. Of course, he was.

Claire went into the empty living room and collapsed on the sofa. The night before, she'd been on the phone with her boss until almost midnight. Christmas Eve and he was nattering on and on about sales numbers and projections. She'd almost fallen asleep with the phone clutched to her ear.

Now exhaustion poured over her. She closed her eyes and leaned back against the sofa pillows. She and Jeremy would stick around a little longer and then they would head home. The thought of the long weekend ahead, depressed her. Jeremy had it planned out hour by hour. She sighed and then snuggled down and was drifting off, when she felt a cold hand on hers. Her eyes flew open and she sat up with a start.

"Hey, honey, didn't mean to give you a shock." Jeremy was on his knees in front of her. Looking down at him made her feel silly. She wanted to extricate her hand but he held on tight.

"What's up, Jeremy?" She tried to keep annoyance from creeping into her voice. He was looking down at something in his hand. She could see his spreading bald spot.

"Claire…uh…Claire." He swallowed and then looked up. He was holding a little black velvet box. "Will you marry me?"

She was speechless. They had been living together for two years. Each time Jeremy brought up marriage, she had put him off: "I'm not ready," or "Let's talk about it next week." Now Jeremy had jumped the gun and bought a ring.

She stared at the little box and shook her head. "Jeremy, I don't know. I just don't know."

"How can you not know. I love you. You love me. We've been together for four years. It's time to get married." He spelled it out in his precise manner. She could tell he was annoyed. Then he said, "I want to get it over with so we can move on with our lives." He dropped her hand, reached down, and fumbled with the box. Inside was a small diamond ring. "I checked your other rings. I know this is the right size." He removed the ring from the box. With those cold hands he began to push the ring onto her finger.

"No, Jeremy. I'm not ready." She felt as though she was suffocating. She gulped for air. "No. Please, no." She wrenched her hand from his grasp, then slipped the ring off her finger and dropped it in his palm.

He looked up at her, frowning. "Claire, what are you doing? This is so childish. Come on, put on the ring."

She stood and pushed him aside. He fell backward onto the pink flowered ottoman. She felt as though a dam had broken inside her. Tears filled her eyes, tears of anger and deliverance. Not until that moment had she admitted to herself that she could escape; escape Jeremy, escape her life, escape her job.

A movement in the hallway caught her eye. Her mother was hidden around the corner, listening. Jeremy had probably told her he was going to propose.

Claire stood in the middle of the room, her hands in tight fists, her arms held straight against her hips. She shouted so the whole house could hear. "Jeremy, I'm not ever going to marry you. Not ever. I'm sorry…but it's over. I'm… leaving."

She turned and ran into the hall. Her mother was there, looking small and frail. Claire hugged her briefly.

3

Then she picked up her old brown leather purse from the entryway table and ran for the door.

Outside, her dad looked up from his porch chair and smiled. "Way to go baby girl. It's about time."

She leaned down and kissed his cheek. "Thanks Daddy."

Her car was parked right in front. Before pulling open the door, she waved back at her mother. "Sorry, Mom." Then she got into her car and pulled away.

Chapter 2

Claire and Jeremy shared a two-bedroom apartment. It was on a nice, tree lined street with parking at the rear. When she opened the back door with her key, she was immediately assailed by the odor of Jeremy's aftershave. Like Jeremy it permeated the apartment. She'd never been able to tell him how much she hated the smell.

Claire walked down the hall. She used the second bedroom as an office and dressing room. She switched on the light and slid open the window. Fresh, cool air blew in. She took several deep breaths; then got to work. At the back of the closet were two large suitcases and a smaller valise. She placed them on the floor and began pulling clothes off hangers, stuffing them willy-nilly into the suitcases. From the bureau she added underwear. When the bags were full, she zipped them shut. In the bathroom she swept her make-up, toothbrush and various tubes and bottles into a duffel bag.

Claire caught a glimpse of herself in the mirror. She stepped back and took a long, hard look. She had always thought of herself as average: five foot seven, dark blond hair, blue-grey-green eyes depending on the weather; size six dress, size eight shoe. Pretty, but certainly not gorgeous. But the Claire in the mirror looked thin, washed out and grim. She turned from the mirror and went back into the bedroom.

Her computer and charger were in her briefcase beside the desk. Packing had taken all of fifteen minutes. She walked through the apartment one last time. There was nothing she would miss. She bequeathed it all to Jeremy. The truth was, she had never liked the furniture, the dishes or even the bathmat. In every decision, she had acquiesced to Jeremy's preferences. Not anymore.

In the kitchen she tore off a sheet of paper from the pad she used for grocery lists. Jeremy insisted they organize their shopping trips with a carefully prepared list of items. Claire wrote with a marker in big black letters. *I'm sorry, Jeremy.*

Outside, it was already dark. It took two trips to lug everything down to the car. As she slammed the trunk shut she saw a car turning into the far entrance of the parking lot. Could it be Jeremy? Quickly she slid into the driver's seat. Gunning the engine, she careened between parked cars and out of the lot.

Once on the street, she started to laugh hysterically. What was she doing? What had come over her? It was as though she had been taken over by a tsunami of emotions that had propelled her out of the life she'd known for the last five years. She was leaving it all. It wasn't just Jeremy. No, she was leaving her job and her family along with her boyfriend. Hallelujah! She couldn't stop laughing. It was totally nuts.

The streets were empty and peaceful. Everyone was celebrating Christmas with their loved ones. There were gifts under the tree, carols around the piano, roast turkey and pecan pie. But she was leaving it all. The thought of being alone was incredibly delicious.

After driving for ten minutes, Claire pulled over and stopped the car. She plugged in *Panama City Beach, Florida* on the GPS. Then she pulled back onto the street. It took about twenty minutes to reach the highway. She followed the entrance ramp onto I-85 South. She was on her way.

It would take about five hours to get to the Gulf coast. She wouldn't need to stop except for gas and maybe some coffee. The drive on the highway was a breeze. There was little traffic. She put some country music on the radio and sang along as she drove. Jeremy hated country. Jeremy was right, she was being childish as she blasted Garth Brooks and Carrie Underwood.

She settled down and drove steadily in the right-hand lane. Feeling more relaxed, she began to deconstruct what she'd done. The truth was, she had been ruminating about this escape for the past three months. The idea had lurked in her brain, but she had refused to acknowledge her thoughts. Busy with a new project at work, she'd barely been home these last few weeks, which made it easier to avoid any decision.

Claire worked for Safetynaps, a British-based firm that sold adult diapers. In the UK, they called diapers "nappies," hence the company name. Before that, fresh from her MBA in marketing at Duke University, she'd worked for a cosmetics company. Then Safetynaps offered her a managerial position and a lot more money. When she started, they had an infinitesimal slice of the market. In the last five years, the company's market share had quadrupled, partly due to Claire's efforts. She had reorganized the department and developed a strong sales force. The latest advertising campaign had struck the perfect note, promising senior citizens comfortable and invisible protection. She had received several raises and increased responsibility. But her boss, Randal Cunningham, was a slave driver. He called any time, day or night. Basically, he felt she owed her life to the company.

Jeremy seemed to think this was just fine, which should have warned her. An accountant with a large and prestigious firm, he traveled quite a bit and worked long hours. Between his job and hers, he and Claire weren't home together on a regular basis. Likely, that had kept her from realizing that he was a slave-driver as well. He was primarily interested in accumulating money for their eventual marriage.

"We need to earn and save as much as possible," he'd said more than once. "Then, when we have our two children, you can take off four years and we'll be fine. I'll want you back in the work force once the second kid goes to preschool."

At the time, she'd said nothing but she'd privately smiled at Jeremy's naiveté. He thought he could plan their life with the precision of an accountant balancing the books.

He'd wanted to pool their money together. Thank God, Claire had insisted on keeping her own separate investments and savings account. Now she could sail off into the sunset free and clear.

An hour of driving got her across the Georgia state line and into Alabama, where she stopped for gas and coffee. As she slid her credit card into the slot at the pump, she became aware of someone standing behind her. She looked over her shoulder. A scruffy guy was leaning against her car. He was of medium height and dressed in jeans, a hoodie and cowboy boots. Under the bright lights of the filling station, his dark eyes glittered beneath greasy blond hair.

"Can I ask you where you're going, miss?" He scratched an acne-pitted cheek with a dirty fingernail.

Best say as little as possible. "South." She turned back to the pump, pulled her credit card from the slot, and stuffed it in her pocket. Then she reached for the nozzle.

"Could you give me a ride? I'm going south." He was standing much too close. She could smell cigarettes and booze.

"Sorry, no." She didn't look up.

"Come on. Don't be a hard ass. I need a ride." His breath was foul.

She flinched. "Please, get away from me."

"Please, get away from me," he mimicked.

"Yes. Please." Her voice wavered.

He slurred his next words. "Man, you're one hell of a bitch."

Just then a man came around from the other side of the pump. "Is this guy bothering you, miss?" he asked.

Claire looked up with relief. The newcomer was dressed in a suit and tie. He must have been six foot six and he towered over the other guy.

"Yes, as a matter of fact he is. He wants a ride and I don't take hitchhikers," Claire said.

"You better move on, dude. This lady is not going to give you a ride." His voice was even but his tone was steel.

"All right, all right. Just cool it, okay? I'll find someone who'll help a guy out." The hitchhiker moved away.

Claire smiled. "Thanks for stepping in. I think that guy is smashed."

"No problem. He won't bother you anymore." The man was handsome in a rugged way. He didn't look like a suit-and-tie sort of guy. He smiled and went back around to his own car on the other side of the pump.

After Claire finished pumping gas, she drove over to the convenience store. Inside, she decided to skip the coffee and bought a diet Coke. Once back in the car, she pulled out and looked over at her savior. He was standing by his car, talking to someone. Claire waved and he waved back. As she pulled onto the highway, she tried to remember what the freaky guy looked like. The encounter had taken place so quickly. She put it out of her mind and headed on down the road.

Chapter 3

Somewhere after Columbus, it hit her that she had made a monumental decision without much forethought. Was there still a job for her? Would she have to turn around and go back to Jeremy and Safetynaps with her tail between her legs?

#

It had all started last September. She'd received an email from Lucca Silva, a foreign exchange student from Brazil she'd met when she was in grad school. They'd dated for a couple of months and then he moved on to new pastures. Lucca was incredibly handsome and utterly charming. He dated a lot of girls but he managed to leave them as friends. You just couldn't hate Lucca.

In his email, he asked if they could get together. Claire was going to be in New York the following week and so was he. They agreed to have dinner, and Lucca said he had a business deal to propose. When she entered the glitzy Asian-fusion restaurant, she spotted Lucca in a booth with a gorgeous Latina. He stood up and gave Claire a kiss on the cheek. Then he introduced her to Gabriella, his Brazilian fiancée. The woman wore a smashing red dress with a plunging neckline. Claire felt dowdy in her grey suit.

They chitchatted about old times, drinking Caipirinhas. Then Lucca made his pitch. "What are you doing these days, Claire?"

"I'm marketing manager at Safetynaps. It's going very well." She took a sip of her drink.

"Adult diapers? Give me a break! You have to get out of that world. Talk about depressing. I think it's time for a change."

"What do you mean?" Claire looked over at

10

Gabriella, whose eyes were dancing. There was something special about those Brazilian girls. They vibrated energy.

"Here's the deal." Lucca gave her his most engaging smile. "We've got a great line of purses…"

"Purses?" Claire couldn't help repeating. She was taken aback.

"Yes. They are beautiful, made in Brazil of full-grain leather. A cousin of mine runs the factory, so you'll deal directly with him."

"Me?" Claire said.

"Yes. I'm offering you a great opportunity to make a lot of money, selling a beautiful product that you'll love. It'll be perfect for you," Lucca said.

"They're the latest fashion. Women are crazy about them. I'm telling you. They're hot," Gabriella chimed in.

"Yeah. Gabriella is working down in South Florida. She's having fabulous results," Lucca said.

Gabriella pulled out a catalogue with the various product lines. The company's name was: *Letízia*, named after Lucca's grandmother. Claire had to admit that the purses were special. There were traditional black and brown bags made of lovely smooth leather. She liked the fashionista backpacks in electric colors, too. But the line Gabriella was selling with such success consisted of adorable smaller bags in bright colors: pink, yellow, turquoise or blue. They were cleverly constructed with zipper pockets and small pouches ideal for stashing cell phones, lipsticks, credit cards or cash. The catalog also displayed a selection of colorful scarves that picked up the tones of the purses. They could be worn at the neck or tied through a gold loop on the purse. Gabriella claimed they were selling themselves from Key West to Miami to Palm Beach.

After they'd viewed the catalogue, Lucca told Claire

what he was proposing. He needed someone to cover northern Florida, stretching from Pensacola to Jacksonville and down to the Orlando area. She would receive a small salary at first, augmented by a commission. Eventually she would be reimbursed one hundred percent on a commission basis.

"I've been thinking about you in recent months. You were a creative and high-energy person back in school. I think you could bring those qualities to this position. We'll be there to help you, but I think you would do a fabulous job." Again, Lucca flashed her his special smile.

Claire didn't know what to say. Working on her own and developing a plan was both exciting and scary. But to never again receive midnight calls from Randall Cunningham would be phenomenal.

"I don't know what to say. This is so far from what I'm doing right now." She smoothed back her hair and sat up straight. "Of course, I'm flattered that you considered me. But I don't know much about retail." Her voice trailed off. Then, she looked down at her worn-out, brown leather purse that was tucked under her chair. She picked it up and showed it to them. "I'd have to start by treating myself to a new bag. This is about a hundred years old." They all laughed.

She explained that she was in the middle of a major project. They agreed she would think about the job and get back to them by the end of the year. She'd heard from Lucca a couple of times in October and November, but hadn't responded. She'd been uncertain and afraid of Jeremy's reaction. Now here she was, heading for the Florida Panhandle on December twenty-fifth, assuming the job was still there.

A few minutes later, she found a spot to pull off the road and dug out her phone. There were several calls and texts from Jeremy but she ignored them. She texted Lucca: *I'm on-board and I'm on my way to Panama City Beach.*

Seconds later she received a response: *Fantástico! We'll talk on Monday.*

She laughed out loud. She was on her way to a beautiful, new life.

Chapter 4

It was eleven o'clock at night when Claire arrived in Panama City Beach. She'd never been down to the Gulf coast, although she knew friends who vacationed there. The highway followed the coastline and she could see white sand and sparkling water in the moonlight. She found a motel, booked a room, and fell into bed. Minutes later, she was fast asleep.

When Claire woke up, the sun was pouring through the slit in the curtains. For a while, she lay there feeling totally relaxed. She had nowhere to go, no one to see. She felt incredibly liberated. She stretched and then sat up and reached for her phone. Immediately her mood changed. The screen was covered with Jeremy's texts. Poor Jeremy. She owed him a call. But if she told him what she had done, he'd try to talk her out of it. She could hear his snide voice. "Sell cheap purses from a Third World country? I'm sure they're superficially attractive, but how long can a job like that last? Don't do something you'll regret. Come home and we'll talk this through." The truth was she might capitulate if she talked to him. She texted him instead: *Please don't contact me. I will call you when I'm ready.*

Phew, that was done. Next, she called home.

"Claire?"

"Hi, Mom."

"What happened, honey?"

"I can't explain it all now. I'm fine. I'm in Panama City Beach, Florida. It's a beautiful day."

"Florida?" She could almost hear her mother's headshake. "This is not very mature...running away. You have responsibilities."

"I'm fully aware of my responsibilities. I'm also an

14

adult and I can make my own decisions."

"Are you depressed? Are you on drugs? I don't understand."

That made her laugh. Her mother saw the dangers of drugs everywhere. "No drugs. I'm perfectly well-balanced. I just realized I needed to change my life."

"What about Jeremy? You broke his heart."

"He'll recover, Mom. Listen, I'm sorry to upset you. I'll call you next week and explain everything."

Claire heard some background noise. "Oh, here's your dad."

Her father came on the line. "Hey, baby girl, are you all right?"

"Yeah, Dad. Everything is fine. I'm in Panama City Beach. I've got a new job down here and I'm excited about it. I'll tell you about it next week."

"Well, good. I'm glad you're taking your life into your own hands."

Something loosened inside her, as if a tight knot had unraveled. "Thanks, Dad."

"Keep in touch. You know your mom and I love you and want the best for you."

"I know, Dad. I'll call next week. Okay? And thanks again for believing in me."

He chuckled. "Always have, always will."

After a shower, Claire dressed in shorts, a tee-shirt and a sweatshirt. Outside it was seventy degrees with a light breeze. It didn't feel like December twenty-sixth. According to the weather gurus, this was the warmest winter yet. She began to walk towards a place called Pier Park. Last night the desk clerk had told her it was about a mile away down 30A. Highway 30A was the main drag that went along the coast. A mishmash of houses and massive condominiums lined both sides of the road. As she walked, she glimpsed the water between the buildings, sparkling in the sun. When the landscape opened up, she had a fabulous view of a sugar white beach and turquoise water. She took a big breath. She couldn't believe she was here.

Ahead was the entrance sign to Pier Park with a large sun motif. She turned down the road, on a hunt for a Starbuck's. She passed several outdoor cafés and a bunch of cool shops. She found Starbuck's a couple of blocks down the charming little street. It was located by a small park. After treating herself to a latte, she went outside and sat in the sun. The other tables were occupied by seniors and a young couple with a baby. She was tempted to look at her phone out of habit, but she resisted. She knew she had to call Randall Cunningham and give him the news. He would go ballistic. In fact, he would be justified, as she'd left with no notice. On the other hand, she'd completed the latest project before Christmas. Her assistant Curtis could take over without a problem. He knew as much as she did about the workings of the department.

Claire smiled to herself. She had felt that familiar stress, thinking about Randall. Then thinking about Curtis gave her relief. She was an emotional bouncing ball. Maybe she needed some of those drugs her mother had mentioned. She looked up as a shadow fell over the table. A chubby girl with a pretty face smiled down at her. "Hey, ya'll. Could I sit here?" The girl gestured to the other chair pulled up to the table.

Claire looked around. All the other tables were taken. "Yeah, sure. I'm just sitting here enjoying the sun."

The girl sat down and plopped a bag on the ground beside her. On the table, she placed a large Frappuccino covered with whipped cream and a drizzle of caramel. In her other hand, she carried a blueberry scone. "I'm Amy

Sullivan. Thanks so much for letting me sit here. I won't bother you." Amy had a pleasant Southern drawl. She was blond with big blue eyes and hair pulled back in a messy ponytail. She wore a blue patterned shirt over beige cropped pants. Though somewhat over-weight, she carried it well.

"Oh, you can bother me. And my name is Claire, by the way."

"You on vacation?" Amy took a bite of her scone.

"Not exactly. I'm going to move down here and start a new job. But today, I'm taking a break." Claire sipped her latte, eyeing the scone. It looked delicious.

"Hey, do you want a bite?" Claire was about to say no but Amy divided the scone in two and handed Claire half on a napkin. "So where are you from? You don't sound like you're from around here." Amy munched on the scone.

"I drove down from Atlanta. I just got here last night. But I'm originally from Chicago."

"Where are you going to work?"

"Well, it's kind of complicated." Then something clicked in Claire. She didn't have that many girlfriends. Between work and Jeremy there hadn't been enough time to keep up with friends. Sitting here in the sunshine, she felt as though she were in another world altogether. Sharing her irrational escape from Atlanta with a stranger she'd likely never see again might just be what she needed. She told Amy about her job at Safetynaps, about Jeremy, about Lucca Silva's job proposal, and about her rash decision to skip town.

Amy asked a lot of questions that spurred her on. Halfway through, Claire went inside and bought another latte and a scone. She split it in two and handed half to Amy. They both giggled, and Claire felt as though she'd made a friend.

Chapter 5

When Claire finished her story, she and Amy sat together companionably without talking. Then Amy said, "So you've left this guy Jeremy for good? You've left your corporate job and now you're going door-to-door selling purses. I've got to tell you, that sounds crazy." They both laughed.

"I know…but the way my friend Lucca explained it…these purses are fabulous." As she said it, Claire felt herself beginning to waver again. Had she made a totally ridiculous decision? At least she hadn't called Randall yet. She could still drive back to Atlanta by Monday and go back to work.

Amy's face had taken on a more serious expression. "Can you show me these purses online?"

"Let's see." Claire took out her phone and typed in *Letízia*. The company logo came up and then a selection of bags. She scooted over next to Amy and together they looked at all the purses.

Amy took a long time eyeing each bag. When they hit the small colorful ones with the matching scarves, she studied them intently, using her fingers to enlarge the images. Then she looked at Claire with raised eyebrows. "Those are cute. What are you selling them for?"

"I don't know anything yet. Lucca said he'd call me on Monday. Why?"

Amy moved her chair so she could look Claire in the eyes. After taking a last sip of her melted Frappuccino, she leaned on the table, her arms crossed. "I work in a boutique called Beach Mania. There are three Beach Mania stores in the area: one in Panama City Beach, one in Seaside and another in Destin." They're eclectic, upscale gift shops. You know, nice things more expensive than the usual tourist emporiums."

Claire's eyes opened wide. "And do you carry handbags?"

"We carry all sorts of things. Anything that's special and will sell. And…" Amy paused.

"And?" Claire leaned forward.

"I really like your collection. But more importantly, I think Alexa will love these pebbled bags with the scarves."

"Who's Alexa?" Claire was thinking she might have a sale before she even started.

"Alexa Cosmos owns Beach Mania as well as three children's shops, Baby Beach Bunny Shops. They're also along 30A. The stores specialize in kids' clothes and toys. Unique merchandise priced in the higher margins. A lot of grandmothers frequent these stores and they'll spend a lot for a cute outfit for a new baby or a three-year-old granddaughter."

Claire sat back in her chair. "Could you set up a meeting with Alexa? Maybe at the end of next week? I'm talking to Lucca on Monday. I'll need a few days to figure out what I'm doing. I want to talk to Gabriella, the girl selling in South Florida, to get some tips. I don't know much about retail. This is totally new."

"Alexa's gone until after New Year's. She's got some family back in Greece and left for ten days. We'll set up something in January."

Claire was grinning like a Cheshire cat. "That would be wonderful. Gosh, Amy, thanks so much for helping me out."

"Hey, listen, if we can sell your handbags, it will be wonderful for Beach Mania, too."

Claire and Amy talked for the next couple of hours. Amy had dealt with many sales reps who came into Beach Mania, and had some great ideas for introducing a product and convincing an indecisive shop owner to buy. "I've turned away a lot of people, partly because of a second-rate product but also because of the rep's spiel."

Claire nodded. "So Amy, you know everything about me. What about you? What's your story?"

Amy looked down at her hands, clasped together on the table. "Oh, there's not much to say about me. I'm from around here…Panama City. My parents got divorced when I was a kid. I lived with my mom who had a lot of issues…drinking being one of them. I've been on my own since I was seventeen."

"That must have been hard."

"I moved out, got a job and took care of myself. Actually, I worked two jobs for a long time until I met Alexa. Now, I officially manage the Seaside store but I'm sort of Alexa's assistant. So I do other stuff for her as well." There was a hard edge to her voice as though she was defending herself.

"Wow! Good for you. To do so much on your own is admirable. I've worked hard, but I've always had family to fall back on. You must be proud of yourself."

Amy blushed and smiled shyly. Then she changed the subject. "Where are you staying?"

"I'm in a motel about a mile away, The Crystal Sands. I pulled in there last night, half dead from exhaustion."

"I've got my car here. Would you like to go for a drive up 30A? I could give you a little tour of the area."

"Would you? That would be great. But what were you planning to do today? I don't want to put you out."

"I drove down from Grayton Beach specifically to spend an hour at Starbuck's. I was dying for a frappuccino. I don't have anything else to do today."

"Amy, I can't tell you how glad I am I met you." Claire felt incredibly happy.

Chapter 6

Amy had a blue Prius filled with stuff. She tossed a sweater and some plastic bags into the back seat so Claire could sit down. They headed west on 30A. As they drove, Amy expounded on the restaurants, shops and condominiums they passed. She had a lot of favorite dining spots and a critical view of competing tourist boutiques.

Claire noticed all the For-Rent signs posted in front of houses and condos. "I've got to find an apartment. It looks as though there are a lot of places to choose from."

"The beach houses and condos along here are looking for short-term rentals. In the winter, you can find a place for a month or two at a somewhat reasonable rate. That's what a lot of seniors do. But everything changes in the spring. The owners make a killing during spring break in March and then during the summer months. They won't want to rent to you for a year."

Claire thought about this as she looked out at all the signs. "Where do you live, Amy?"

"I've got an apartment on the second floor of a house in Grayton Beach. My landlord lives downstairs…or rather, my landlady. I call her Aunt Irma. She and her husband, Al, moved down here from Michigan some thirty years ago. Al passed away about five years ago. That's when she decided to rent the top half of her house. It's just the perfect size for me and I like Irma. We're buddies." She turned to smile at Claire.

Claire smiled back. "Where do you think I could find a place?"

"It kind of depends how much you want to spend. Plenty of people who work down here can't afford to live on the strip. They live inland on the other side of 98." Amy

21

drummed her fingers on the steering wheel. "I know this guy who might be able to help you. I'll text him. Maybe he'll have some ideas."

They drove through a lovely town called Rosemary Beach that looked like Claire's idea of an Austrian village. Large shade trees lined a boulevard that opened up to a park skirted by timber-framed buildings. Italian-style porticos and outdoor cafés lined the streets. Amy parked on a side street and pulled out her phone. She texted, her thumbs going a mile a minute. Looking over at Claire, she said, "I asked Randy what he knows about long-term, reasonable rentals. You want furnished, right?"

"Yes, I guess I do. Or else I'd have to go out to IKEA and buy the basics."

"Around here, there are a lot of furnished rentals. Let's see what Randy finds."

Amy pulled back onto 30A. A few miles down the road, they drove through Alys, a little town that made Claire think of a Greek island with its startling white Cycladic architecture. Framed by the blue, blue skies, the flat-topped buildings made Claire feel as though she were on the island of Mykonos. "These towns are so beautiful," she said.

"You haven't seen it all yet. These are planned communities, each one with a different feel."

A few miles further, they came to a place called Seaside. Amy turned right, away from the water, and parked on a wide horse-shoe shaped road. In the middle was a large, grassy bowl with a bandstand. The other side of the street backed on the gulf and contained shops and restaurants.

"Come on, I'll show you around. Our store is right over here." They crossed the road and walked up to a pink and mint green painted shop. Claire noted *Beach Mania* painted in curlicue script on a wooden sign over the entrance. Amy pushed open the door and they went inside. "Hi, Heather," Amy sang out as they entered.

"Hey, Amy. What are you doing here? You're supposed to be taking the day off." Heather was tall with dark brown hair and a statuesque build.

"Heather, this is Claire, my new-found friend. She just moved down here and I'm showing her around."

"Hey." Heather stretched out her hand. "Welcome to our little part of heaven." Then she turned to Amy. "I'm glad you stopped in because something came up this morning. Could you come in the back and I'll show you?"

"Sure thing," Amy said.

While the two women went into the back room, Claire wandered around the store. She noted the attractive displays. There were some bathing suits and cover-ups as well as a variety of dresses and shirts. On another wall, she found jewelry, books, hand cream and cute hostess gifts. While she looked around, a group of women came in. They seemed charmed by everything they saw.

"Look at this adorable straw hat with the flowery ribbon. I've got to get it," one woman gushed.

Another beckoned to the hat lady. "Sandy, just come over here and look at this pearl-grey sweater."

"It's elegant." Sandy's eyes searched the boutique. "I wonder if they have any purses? I'd like something for spring." She turned to Claire, who was listening to the chatter and wishing Letízia purses were already on display. "Miss, do you carry purses?"

Claire shrugged. "Sorry, I don't work here. The salesgirl is in the back. I'm sure she'll be right out."

When Amy came back, she helped Heather ring up the women's purchases. After the customers left the store, Claire told Amy about the woman who was looking for a spring purse. "You would have had your first Letízia customer. How cool is that?" Amy said.

"Very cool!" Claire beamed.

"Listen I'm starving. Do you want to eat? We could go across the street to The Great Southern Café."

"Sure, but let me treat you to lunch."

They each had a glass of crisp white wine and a plate of crab cakes with fried green tomatoes. Claire had never eaten anything so delicious in her life. They chatted for a long time and then headed back to the car.

As they crossed the street, Claire looked over at the grassy knoll nearby. A man was sitting there, staring right at her. A chill went down her spine. She recognized those glittering, dark eyes. She'd seen them last night at the gas pump up in Alabama. The guy nodded and gave her a wide grin. It was an evil grin, like a monster before it devours its prey. Then he looked over at Amy.

Amy frowned. "Hey, do you know that guy?"

"No. No, I don't." Claire walked faster towards the car, leaving Amy in her wake.

Chapter 7

When they were in the car, Amy looked over at Claire. "Hey, are you all right?"

"Yeah, I'm fine." She could feel perspiration pearling on her forehead. "Maybe too much sun."

"We can keep on driving or I can take you back to the motel," Amy said.

"No, let's keep going. I'm so glad to have a guide." Claire pulled out a tissue and wiped her forehead.

"Well, if you're sure." Amy observed her, frowning. "I was going to take you up to Grayton Beach where I live and then to the end of 30A. We can drive back on Highway 98. It's ten times faster."

A mile further down the road they came to another development called Watercolor. Amy drove up and down the streets. The houses were Southern-style with wide screen porches. A man-made stream gurgled its way down one avenue, complete with fountains and waterfalls. It was peaceful and idyllic. At the corner was a restaurant called The Wine Bar. Amy told her they had a great selection of wines and sometimes you could get a carafe for the price of a glass. They both agreed they would have to come back there soon.

They drove across a bridge over a lake. "These are salt water lakes. People boat on them, but they say not to swim. Apparently, someone pulled a ten-foot alligator out of here recently," Amy said.

Claire shivered. "Can alligators really live this far north?"

"I don't know. Maybe it has to do with global warming."

Further on, they went by several shops and

25

restaurants. Among them Claire noticed a curious building that resembled a Japanese pagoda. Shortly after, Amy turned down one street, then another. She pulled up in front of a yellow two-story house surrounded by a white picket fence. A woman was sitting in a rocking chair on the porch with a bowl on her lap.

"Hey, Aunt Irma. I've brought a new friend," Amy called out as they made their way up the front walk.

The woman put down the bowl, wiped her hands on her apron and stood. Bright blue eyes glowed in her deeply wrinkled face. She pushed strands of white hair off her forehead and smiled broadly.

Amy introduced Claire and then turned to the far end of the porch. Claire hadn't noticed another woman sitting there in the shadows. "That's Françoise. She's a famous artist." Amy said.

Françoise wore jeans and a black tee-shirt. Her skinny legs were twisted together like a corkscrew. She held a cigarette, her elbow balanced on a bony knee. "I *was* a famous artist," she said, in a heavy accent. "Now I'm a, what is the word, a has-been." She blew a puff of smoke and picked a bit of tobacco off her thin upper lip.

"Now Françoise, you are very talented. You've just hit a low point." Irma turned to Claire. "Françoise has paintings hanging in museums in France, New York, and San Francisco."

"I would love to see some of your work," Claire said.

Françoise shrugged and sighed. "There is nothing to see. My palette is dry."

Amy spoke up. "Come on, you've got paintings you'll be selling at the Arts Festival."

"When's the Arts Festival?" Claire asked.

"The first week of February. It's an eclectic event

26

with artists, writers, poets and musicians. It brings people from around the country."

"Yes, for four days, Seaside is very busy. Then it all dies down again until spring break," Françoise grumbled.

"Can I get you girls a glass of sweet tea?" Irma asked in a cheery voice.

"We just had lunch, but tea would be nice," Claire said.

Amy waved a hand. "Sit down, Irma, I'll get it."

While she was gone, Claire talked a little about herself and explained that she had just moved down to the area. She was interrupted by Françoise who began to cough uncontrollably. After a sip of iced tea, the artist patted her mouth. "*Excusez-moi.* Smoking is bad, but I cannot stop. It is my only pleasure in life."

For a moment this depressed woman's outlook on life quashed Claire's ebullient mood. Not everything was perfect in this little part of heaven.

Chapter 8

Sunday morning, Claire slept late again. The sun was pouring through the slit in the curtains when she awoke. Another day in beautiful Panama City Beach. She extended her arms over her head, pointed her toes, feeling the stretch through her entire body. She sighed with pleasure. Amy had dropped her off in the early evening and she had fallen asleep the minute her head touched the mattress. Yesterday had been a winner. She had a new friend and her new career seemed promising.

Claire reached for her phone. There were texts from Jeremy and several calls from Randall. He wanted to know why she wasn't picking up. He also wanted to discuss tomorrow's meeting. At some point today, she had to give him a call. A wave of anxiety poured over her but she pushed the feeling down.

Then there was a text from Amy's friend Randy. Currently, he knew of only two possible long-term rentals in her price range. He left the necessary contact information. Claire called both numbers and made appointments for that afternoon, one at two and one at four. That meant she had several hours free. In the bottom of one bag, she had stashed her running gear. She hadn't been out running for years, but she'd hung on to the shorts and shirt.

Ten minutes later she was out the door. A block away there was an entrance from the road to the shore. She jogged down the wooden walkway and onto the beach. Near the water the sand was compacted from the outgoing tide and she began to run. Within five minutes she was huffing and puffing and had to slow down to a walk. Once her heart rate slowed down, she started running again. She kept that up for a half-hour and then turned and headed back toward the motel. She noticed other walkers and joggers out getting exercise. Families with young children were digging holes and building sand castles but no one was in the water. It wasn't hot enough for that.

By the time Claire opened the door to her motel room, she was drenched with sweat and felt invigorated. After a shower, she put on a blue flowered sheath and some sandals. She picked up her purse and checked it out. It looked old and tired. She needed to buy a snazzy new bag. This one would not do when she was out visiting clients. She needed something fabulous to catch people's eye.

Once in the car, she drove west on 30A like she'd done yesterday with Amy. Both of the rentals were in that direction. As she drove, she noted boutiques that might be prospects for Letízia merchandise. With cars behind her, she couldn't slow down, but in the weeks to come, she would have to catalogue the various shops along the road.

Twenty minutes later she arrived in Rosemary Beach, the little European-like town. She parked on a side street and decided to walk wherever her fancy took her. A farmer's market was being held in a park and she wandered through, looking at the bright red tomatoes, leafy greens, and jars of jam, honey and olive oil. It all looked delicious. Once she had found a place to live she would come back here and shop. Further on at the corner, she turned down a crooked street towards the beach. She spotted a cute café on the right called Cowgirl Kitchen and decided to stop for brunch. The friendly waitress recommended the Mexican tacos with eggs, chorizo and cheddar, which were delicious.

She spent a little more time sightseeing, but made sure to arrive right on time at the first appointment. The address was just a few blocks off 30A in a neighborhood of older homes. Claire pulled up to a ranch house encircled by a chain-link fence. Two enormous German shepherds growled as she arrived at the gate. From a screen porch, she heard a woman yell, "Tiger, Rory. Stop that." The screen door opened, and a skinny woman in jean shorts and a sleeveless shirt came to the gate and held the dogs by the collar. Her lifeless bleached-blond hair hung straight to her bony shoulders.

"Come on in. Don't be afraid of these two. They won't bother you."

Claire hesitated. "Hi, I'm Claire Hall."

"Lucile." The woman opened the gate and yelled over her shoulder. "Clive, the girl's here to look at the room."

Claire went up the walkway. She could feel the dogs sniffing at her heels. A big man in a wife-beater and shorts opened the door. He had a bottle of beer in one hand. Small eyes squinted at her under a bush of wild red hair. He looked her up and down, lingering on her breasts. "Come on in. I'm Clive. I'll show you the room."

Claire followed him into the house. They went through a cluttered living room and down a dark hall. The dogs kept pace behind her. Clive opened a door into a musty room and stepped back to usher her in. Her heart sank. Spotted grey wall-to-wall carpeting covered the floor. To the right of the door was a queen-sized bed covered with a thin orange and brown bedspread. On the left, against the wall, stood a small table with a scratched wooden chair. Next to it was a small refrigerator with a microwave on top. An armchair of an undefinable color sat under the curtained window.

"How do you like it? Pretty cozy, right?" Clive was standing way too close. He smelled of beer and old sweat.

"Yes, cozy," Claire repeated.

He placed his hand on her arm. It felt warm and damp. "Here's the bathroom." He led her across the hall.

30

The tile flooring was cracked. There were rust stains in the sink and the shower curtain was torn.

Claire glanced around. All she could think about was getting out of there. Between the dogs and Clive, she felt uneasy. She smiled at Lucile, who was hovering in the hallway. "Thank you so much for showing me around."

"You could move in any time, even today," Clive said. He was literally breathing down her neck. She felt a nudge as one dog sniffed her butt.

"We're flexible," Lucile chimed in, looking at Claire hopefully.

"I'm, uh, looking at several places. I'll have to get back to you. But thanks for showing me around." Claire backed down the hall as she spoke. At the end of it, she turned and flew through the living room, down the steps and out the gate. The dogs followed her and began to bark as she got in her car and turned on the engine. As she glanced back at the front steps, she saw Lucile waving and Clive scowling.

Chapter 9

Claire clutched the steering wheel as she drove down 30A. Thank God, she had a second rental to look at and didn't have to move in with Clive and Lucile. That room was unbelievably depressing and Clive gave her the heebie-jeebies. She felt a massive sense of relief as she left the place behind.

Five minutes later, she arrived in Seaside where she and Amy had eaten lunch the previous day. A parking spot opened up and she pulled in. After locking the car, she went for a stroll. Across from the horseshoe drive and grassy bandstand, there were shops and restaurants by the water. Claire noted several shops that sold beach bags, flip-flops and t-shirts. Maybe they would be interested in Letízia purses.

She crossed the street and wandered into the Sundog Book Shop. It had been years since she'd had the time to sit down and read for pleasure. There was always work and responding to Jeremy's demands. A friendly young woman with kind blue eyes and auburn hair in a messy bun was organizing a table display. "Can I help you?"

"I haven't had a chance to read for years. What can you suggest?" Claire asked.

The young woman thought for a moment, holding a pencil to her lips. "This has sold well." She handed Claire a copy of *The Woman in Cabin Ten*.

"Oh, I've heard of this book. It's a mystery, right?" Claire said.

The woman nodded and reached for another book. "Yes, a mystery with a twist. Here's one we're reading with our book club. It's a very different read but engrossing." She handed over a copy of *Mothering Sunday*.

Claire held the two books to her chest. "A book club? I've just moved here and I don't know anybody. I'd love to join a book club." She held out her hand and introduced herself.

The woman responded, "I'm Kate. You're certainly welcome to attend. We have a nice eclectic group. We meet on the first Thursday evening of the month."

Outside, Claire felt elated. She had only been in Panama City Beach for thirty-six hours and little by little her life was coming together. In the car, she typed the address of the rental in Lemon Cove into the GPS. It was only ten minutes away. She would arrive there a little bit early.

Claire drove west again on 30A, through Watercolor and Grayton Beach. Lemon Cove was a development along the water squeezed in between Grayton Beach and the National Forest. She turned left off 30A on to Lemon Drive. It twisted and turned among a forest of pine trees. Back among the trees, she could see large houses with wide porches. Nearing the Gulf, the street opened up and Claire followed it to the right. The houses on the left backed onto the beach. They were painted bright, Mediterranean colors and stood on stilts, raised above the sand. She caught glimpses of the sparkling water. Then there were no more houses, just the sea, the sand, the dunes and the open sky. The breeze had picked up and sand blew across the windshield. She glanced at the GPS. The address was up ahead. The road twisted around a dune and a stand of windblown trees. Beyond them lay a massive house, standing alone. A tall metal fence marched across the front of the property. Attached to the fence was a large stainless-steel plaque with the words *Citrus Haven* engraved in thick letters. Through the open gates she could see a black Mercedes in the driveway.

33

Claire drove through the gates and pulled up behind the Mercedes. She got out of her car and gazed up at the house. The front door seemed dwarfed by the building above it. To the right were three stainless steel garage doors, with three more to the left at an angle. Above them was a coach house. Lemon and orange trees in large stone pots flanked each side of the entranceway.

As she studied the façade, the front door opened and Harry Potter's double walked out. He came over, his hand outstretched. "Are you here about the rental? Daniel Rutherford." Like most everyone she'd met down here so far, he spoke with a drawl.

She couldn't help smiling. "Hi, I'm Claire Hall."

He caught her expression and grinned back. "I know, Harry Potter, right?"

"Yes, and particularly with the round glasses. But Harry Potter with a Southern accent." Claire smiled.

"To tell you the truth, I kind of play it up. People remember me and they generally have a positive view of Harry Potter, so…it works." He gestured to the door. "Come on in."

Claire liked this guy. He seemed completely genuine. She stepped into the entryway.

"I'll show you around the house, then show you the coach house. The owner wants someone on the premises to check on things periodically. Would you be open to that?"

She paused, thinking about what that would mean. "I suppose I could do that." She glanced around the entryway. The flooring was black-and-white tile, and there were hooks and cubbies to stash shoes and beach paraphernalia, and a set of wooden oars hanging among the oversized umbrellas, beach balls, and floaties.

Daniel showed her around the ground floor. A laundry room held two industrial washers and dryers. Next door was a long hallway. Daniel pulled open one door that led to a utility room with cleaning products, a vacuum cleaner and brooms. "I'm told you're welcome to use the laundry facilities and the cleaning supplies if you want," He gestured down the hall towards a padlocked door. "The owner stores personal stuff in that storage area. It's off-limits." He smiled.

They peeked into the garages, which were enormous and empty. Across from the entrance to the garages was an elevator. Daniel pushed the up button and the doors opened. Claire gasped in startled delight. Inside, shimmering blue-green paper covered the walls decorated with glittering fish that seemed to be flittering by. It was like being under the sea.

The elevator doors opened onto a wide foyer. Across the marble-tiled expanse was a huge great room. As they entered the room, music throbbed from powerful speakers. Claire noticed several groupings of sofas and armchairs. The kitchen was granite and steel. A counter with ten stools underneath divided it from the living room. Picture-sized windows framed spectacular views of sand, sea and woods.

Claire looked up at a TV screen over the fireplace. The screen showed the driveway and her car. Then it flashed to a view of her and Daniel standing near the kitchen counter, then to the entryway, then the garages; on and on. "Security cameras?" she said.

Daniel nodded. "The guy who owns this place is really into techy stuff. He actually turned on the music and the air conditioning remotely when I told him you were coming this afternoon. This house has all the bells and whistles."

They walked up the stairs toward the third floor. She was aware of Daniel trudging up behind her, but unlike with Clive at the previous rental site, it didn't make her nervous…even though they were very alone, and it probably should have. After all, she didn't know this guy. She stalled on the wide landing and waited for him to join her. Then they walked the rest of the way up together.

"Where did you move from?" he asked.

"Atlanta. New job." Claire didn't want to go into her life story. She was still a little amazed that she'd been so ready to reveal herself to Amy. It wasn't like her. She suddenly remembered the guy with the glittering eyes, just sitting on the grass in Seaside yesterday, and shivered. Maybe she should be more cautious.

"What are you going to be doing?"

"Sales in the area." Claire knew she was being abrupt. Harry Potter seemed friendly, but you never knew.

On the third floor, he showed her a room with six bunks covered in identical nautical print bedspreads. There were also two master suites, complete with sitting room and luxury bath. The fourth floor contained two more master suites and two rooms with double beds. Each bedroom was beautifully decorated in a different color scheme and motif.

The fourth floor also held a sitting area with huge windows looking onto the beach. The room jutted out over part of the great room below. A nautical railing ran along the balcony. Claire noted a heavy white rope attached to the railing and coiled on the floor.

"Look at that," she said, pointing.

Daniel stared at the rope. "Maybe it's a sort of fire escape or a swing for the kids."

Claire looked over the edge. It gave her a sense of vertigo and she quickly stepped back. Maybe a little dangerous for kids, she thought.

They took the elevator down. "Wow, this place is unbelievable. It must sleep thirty people. How often is the family here?" Claire asked.

"Not often."

"So this house is usually empty?"

"Yes, pretty much. It will probably be rented in the summer." His responses didn't invite further discussion. As the elevator opened onto the second floor again, he said, "Ready to see the coach house? Follow me."

They went around behind the elevator, down a short hallway to a painted turquoise door. Daniel punched in a code and opened the door. He turned back to her and said, "Of course you can program this door if you decide to rent the apartment."

They entered into a wonderful, light-filled room. Through the floor-to-ceiling windows, the Gulf and the beach stretched out in the distance. A kitchen alcove to the left contained white cabinets with granite counters. Daniel pulled out a stool and sat down as Claire looked around.

A colorful Italian pitcher and bowl decorated the kitchen counter along with salt and pepper shakers shaped like lemons. Inside the cabinets, Claire found pots and pans and a set of blue and white dishes for four. "Everything looks brand new."

"It is. Nobody has ever lived here. You'll be the first." He was scrolling through his phone.

Claire kept exploring. In the living room, a blue area rug set off a white sofa and a pair of matching armchairs. Yellow and blue pillows were piled in the sofa corners. Seascapes adorned the walls, and a bowl of shells was placed on the rattan and glass coffee table. The bedroom, in soothing shades of apricot and turquoise, held a king-sized bed with a pile of pillows. A chaise lounge draped with a cozy blanket sat in the corner. The attached bathroom was luxurious beyond anything Claire had ever seen, all marble and crystal with a pile of apricot towels. The bedroom shared the living room's view of the beach. Claire pulled open a sliding glass door and stepped out onto a deck that ran along the beachside of the apartment. Except for the encroaching forest to the west, she could see for miles. She closed her eyes and felt the breeze blow back her hair. This place felt like happiness.

Claire stepped back inside. In the kitchen, Daniel was getting a drink of water. He turned around as she entered. "So what do you think?"

Claire couldn't help beaming. "I love it here. It feels perfect. And it looks like the place is furnished with everything I could possibly need." She pulled out the other stool and sat down. "But what about the rent? I have a feeling it might be out of my price range."

"The owner texted me a little while ago. He seems eager to rent it to you." Daniel named a price much lower than Claire had imagined.

"Really? No more than that? I'm amazed."

"Remember, he's also considering you as a caretaker. He feels you'll be providing him a service."

Without thinking twice, Claire said, "Okay, if that's the price, I'll take it." She was acting totally out of character, being this impulsive, but she wanted to live here surrounded by the sand, the sea and the wind.

Daniel put the glass in the sink and leaned against the counter, his hands spread out on the smooth surface. He looked at her seriously through his round Harry Potter lenses. "Listen, I would love to rent this place to you, but I'm wondering if it's a good idea."

"Why?" Claire knew she was still smiling like an idiot.

"There's no one around. You'll be out here by yourself." He looked deep into her eyes. "That could be risky."

Claire's smile vanished as her face burned with

sudden anger. Who was this guy to tell her what she should or shouldn't do? It was like being back with Jeremy. She stared at him without flinching. "Listen, you don't know me. I like the idea of being on my own. Okay?"

Daniel stepped back, holding up his hands. "Okay, okay. Sorry to upset you."

Suddenly, Claire felt foolish. Why was she attacking this guy she barely knew? "I'm sorry, Daniel. I overreacted. But I still want the place." She tried an apologetic smile. "If that's all right?"

Chapter 10

Monday was a day like no other. At six AM, Claire called Randall and told him she quit. He ranted and raved. Then he cajoled. Finally, he hung up on her. She had assured him that her assistant, Curtis, knew everything she did. He would make an excellent marketing manager. In addition, Curtis had a killer desire to succeed. He was Randall's kind of man.

Then Lucca called. They talked for a long time. He sent her forms to e-sign and market research information. In addition, there was a lot to read about leather and the fabrication of leather goods. He said he would send her promotional brochures and boxes of samples. She told him she probably had a place to live and would text the address to him later that day.

Later, she skyped with Gabriella. As they talked, Claire took pages of notes and asked a million questions. Gabriella seemed open to sharing her tried and true methods for selling Letízia merchandise. At the end of the call, Claire put in an order for an exquisite leather backpack to carry her laptop, contracts, and promotional brochures. At Gabriella's suggestion, she also picked out a fabulous purse.

It was one o'clock when Daniel called. Claire was still in her PJs, sitting on the bed reading. She'd been drinking the motel coffee, which tasted like toasted mushrooms. But she'd been too absorbed to care.

"Pack your bags," Daniel said, after a genial greeting. "You've been approved. You can move in as soon as you're ready."

"Wow, that's fabulous. You mean today?"

"Yep. I've got the rental agreement here for you to sign. Then I need a check for two month's rent. One month's fee will be held in escrow until you move out."

"Could I meet you a little later this afternoon? All I need to do is throw my stuff in a bag and I'm ready to go."

"How about we meet for a late lunch? I can give you the entrance codes and you can sign the paperwork."

"Well…" Claire stalled. She wasn't quite sure if lunch was a good idea. She didn't want to encourage him. The last thing she needed was a significant other.

He must have sensed her hesitation. "Come on, we'll celebrate your new home. I've got the perfect spot. It's called The Perfect Pig."

"The Perfect Pig? As in, bacon and pork chops?" Claire realized she was starving. Cold cereal and orange juice from the motel's buffet breakfast felt like a lifetime ago. "I could probably devour an entire ham. Well, okay and thanks."

Daniel gave her the restaurant's address. It was down 30A, on the way to her new home. They would meet at three o'clock.

Before leaving, Claire called Amy, who was back at work. "Guess what, Amy, I've got a place to live."

"Great, Claire! That's fabulous. Where is it?"

"It's in Lemon Cove. I've got a furnished coach house over a three-car garage. It's never been lived in. I just love it."

"Lemon Cove? Wow! Very upscale."

"Do you want to come over and check it out tonight?"

"I'd love to, but I'm buried under with work here. I want to go home and collapse tonight. How about tomorrow?"

"Sure, cool!"

"I'm happy for you, Claire."

#

41

Claire showered and dressed in white jeans and a French blue-and-white striped top. She loaded her bags into the car and took off. Glancing into the rearview mirror, she did a double take. She slowed before entering the road and turned her head enough to clearly see the front of the motel. A sense of unease settled over her. The hitchhiker from the Alabama gas station stood there, waving at her. Waving goodbye.

Chapter 11

Daniel was seated at an outside table under an umbrella. He wore a white linen suit with a pink-striped bow tie and matching pocket square. He stood as she approached and held her chair out. "Are you all right? You look like you've seen a ghost."

"I'm fine. Just a little paranoid." She sat down and reached for the glass of ice water.

"Do you want to explain?"

"No, I'm fine. I just need to calm down."

Daniel sat next to her. "Why don't we get the business part of our luncheon over. Then we can relax."

Relax. That's exactly what she needed to do. Chances were she'd never see the creepy hitchhiker again. She took a deep breath and smiled at Daniel. "Okay, let's get to work."

He pulled the papers from a briefcase at his feet. She signed them and handed him a check. They agreed that in the future she would set up a direct deposit from her bank. He gave her the garage door opener as well as the codes for the fence, the main house and her coach house. She tucked the opener and the slip of paper with the codes into her purse and sat back in her chair.

A waiter arrived with two glasses of bubbly wine. "I took the liberty of ordering champagne," Daniel said. "Here's to your new home. I hope you'll be happy there."

"Thanks, Daniel. I'm sure I will." They clicked glasses.

"And here's to a new friendship. I hope we can get together often." He leaned forward and clicked her glass again. Claire smiled faintly.

They ordered lunch. Daniel chose the pulled pork

sandwich on a brioche bun, while Claire decided on blackened grouper tacos with avocado slaw, black bean salsa and Sriracha aioli.

"So can you tell me more about Letízia? I noticed that's who you work for." Daniel said.

Yesterday she'd felt reticent about sharing her life with Daniel. But today she felt as though she owed him. She told him about Atlanta, her job there, and Jeremy without too much detail. Then she told him about Lucca and Letízia. They continued to talk after the food arrived.

Daniel took a bite of his sandwich and wiped his mouth. He looked puzzled. "Why did you leave the corporate job? It sounds as though you had a real career going."

"It just became too much. I never had time to relax; never had time to read a book or hang out with friends. It was always work, work, work. And my boss called day and night. I was never off duty." She sipped her champagne.

"It seems to me you're going to be busier than ever if you want to make a go of it here. Self-employment doesn't mean less work; it means you change task masters. Now instead of working for your old boss and striving for his approval, you'll need to satisfy yourself. And I'll bet you'll be pretty hard on yourself."

Claire smiled at that. He had her pegged right. "You're spot on. Already I'm feeling the adrenalin. My mind is bursting with marketing plans and I'm itching to get out there and see what I can do." She looked down at her plate. She had devoured every bite of the tacos.

As they were getting ready to leave, Daniel looked flushed. "I hope to see you again, Claire. Would you like to have dinner on Thursday night? It's New Year's Eve. We could eat out at The Bay. They've got a great band playing."

Claire felt cornered. On the one hand, she liked

Daniel, but she wasn't really attracted to him. She didn't want to give him the wrong idea. On the other hand, she needed to get out and meet people. After a quick inner debate, she said, "Thanks, Daniel. That would be nice." As she folded her napkin and placed it on the table, she wondered if she was making the wrong decision. What did she really know about this guy?

Chapter 12

Claire drove down 30A feeling exhilarated. Lunch with
Daniel had been fun. He really was a nice guy. Ten minutes
later she drove by Grayton Beach. Just before turning into
Lemon Cove, she passed four cute little houses, each
painted a different color. She noted a yoga studio, a gift
shop, and a hair and nail salon. Definitely places to come
back to, when she had the time.

#

Claire drove slowly down Lemon Drive, taking her
time to look at the houses she passed. No one was outside.
Daniel had told her the population along the Emerald coast
was greatly reduced during December except for the week
between Christmas and New Year's. Then in January and
February the population dropped again. Snowbirds from up
north preferred southern Florida where they could find
temperatures in the eighties. Here the highs were in the
upper sixties and low seventies during the winter months.

A car honked behind her. She eyed the rearview
mirror and saw a little red sports car. Where had it come
from? Its irate driver was shaking his hands in the air,
yelling at her to get going. She pulled over to let him pass.
He gave her a dirty look as he blew by.

When the road turned along the beach, she noticed
an elderly couple out walking a dog. Further on she saw a
family coming up from the beach. Two little kids were
running and laughing while their parents lugged beach
chairs and plastic buckets. So not all the houses were empty.
The everyday sights of people going happily about their
business pushed the jerk sports car driver from her mind.

She drove around the dunes and saw the house
ahead. It resembled a fortress with its metal fence and

massive façade. She pulled up to the gate, dug out the paper Daniel had given her, and typed in the code on the keypad. The gate swung open. After she drove through, it shut behind her. The clang as it closed gave her a sense of security. No one could wander in here.

Considering that she had her suitcases to lug upstairs, Claire decided to use the elevator. She typed in the front door keypad code from Daniel's list and pushed the door open. The light switched on overhead. She looked up at the sparkling colored-glass chandelier. It was exquisite and must be connected to a sensor. She went back to the car and rolled in the two heavy bags. After shutting the door, she pushed the up button beside the elevator. From the control pad, she could see it had stopped on the fourth floor. As she waited, she looked over at the hooks and cubbies she'd noted the day before. She frowned. Something was missing. The oars, that was it. Idly, she wondered where they'd gotten to. Just then the elevator arrived. She pulled the bags inside and pushed the button for the second floor.

When Claire exited the elevator, the lights came on in the hallway and the great room beyond. The strains of Pachelbel's *Canon* followed her down the hall to the coach house. She opened the door to her new abode and then just stood there, drinking in the view of the afternoon sun pouring into the room. After a moment, she rolled her suitcases across the living room and into the bedroom and then raised the blinds so she could see the expanse of beach below. When she opened the sliding door, a little breeze blew in. She could see the couple with their dog. It was bounding in and out of the waves.

Claire left the bedroom and went over to the kitchenette. There was a large cardboard box on the counter. Inside she found a bottle of red wine, two boxes of crackers, some nuts, a baguette and some Keurig coffee capsules. A folded note tucked in with the foodstuffs read: *Welcome, Claire. Here's a few groceries to get you started. Daniel.*

Typical guy, she thought, leaving her such an eclectic assortment…but his kindness touched her. She opened the refrigerator and found more surprises: a bottle of white wine, a wedge of Brie, a chunk of white cheddar, a salad pack, some grapes, a quart of milk and a piece of chocolate cake. She had to laugh. Daniel had thought of everything. She picked up her phone, located Daniel's number and called him. She got his voicemail and left him a message of thanks.

Next, Claire opened the back door that led to the stairway down to the garages. She had not inspected them yesterday. Daniel had said she could park her car in the garage furthest from the main house. She found the light switch and descended the stairs. The three-car garage was completely empty. The sound of her feet reverberated on the metal steps, giving her a sense of how alone she was in this empty house. It was kind of spooky.

She shook off the feeling, found the garage door opener and pushed the pad. The door slid open. She got into her car and drove it into the garage, then retrieved her other bags, shut the garage door and went back upstairs.

It didn't take long to unpack. There was plenty of room in the walk-in closet to stash her things. Since her packing had been haphazard to say the least, she realized she would need to go shopping soon and buy a couple of pairs of shoes, some socks and a light jacket.

By now the sun was going down and the air coming through the open sliding door had turned chilly. Claire shut the door and went into the kitchen. She opened the bottle of red wine and poured a glass. She took it over to the window and looked out at the beach. She could see light playing on the waves but in the distance the panorama was black.

She sipped her wine, then walked over and set the glass on the kitchen counter. Time to get some work done. She pulled out her computer and took it into the kitchen, set it next to the wine, hooked a stool out with her foot, and sat. After checking email and reviewing her bank account, she began working on her business plan. She was so engrossed that when she next looked at the time, it was 11 o'clock and she was starving. She eyed the salad pack, but then grabbed the piece of chocolate cake and devoured it, licking the frosting off the plate. So much for good nutrition.

Claire fell asleep quickly, listening to the rolling waves. Sometime during the night, she woke and thought she heard a noise. She got up and went to the window. The moon was out and the sand gleamed white as snow. She looked up and down the beach but there was nothing to see. No more noises either, except the murmur of the surf. She checked the lock on the sliding door, then padded back to bed.

Chapter 13

Tuesday morning was glorious. The sun pouring through the windows woke her. Claire put on her pink sweats and made a cup of coffee. She curled up on the sofa while she sipped the brew and gazed out at the beach. The water was an amazing symphony of blues. Sitting there, she came to the conclusion that she was happy. Happier than she'd been in the last ten years. Her new job promised to be challenging and exciting. Her home was warm and inviting and she'd made some new friends.

The truth was, no one knew her here. She could become whoever she wanted. The people she met had no clue about her background and would take her at face value. It was incredibly liberating. She picked up her phone and called her parents. If she was lucky, she'd get her father instead of her mother.

Luck was with her. "Hi, baby girl," her father said. "How are you doing down there?"

"Dad, it's wonderful. I've found a place to live. It's a brand new furnished coach house. I just love it. Right now, I'm looking out at the Gulf of Mexico and the sun is shining."

"How about work?"

She told him about Lucca and Letízia. "I'm officially starting my sales blast next Monday. Lucca told me to wait until the Christmas-New Year's break is over. Then I'm going to travel up and down the coast and pitch the line of purses. They've been giving me a lot of help. I feel good about it all."

"Sounds good. Your voice has a lilt I haven't heard in a while. I'm glad you took the plunge and left Safetynaps and Jeremy. I hated to see how miserable you'd become."

Claire was silent. Had her unhappiness been that obvious? They talked a few more minutes, and she gave him her address on Lemon Drive. Then they hung up.

#

She made herself some scrambled eggs and toasted the French bread. Then she spent several hours working. Gabriella called and they went over some questions Claire had emailed. After she hung up, she put on her running gear and started down the steps to the garage. Before heading to the beach, she walked around the exterior of the house. On the other side of the main building was the swimming pool. A blue-and-white striped, mesh cover was spread over the water. Chairs and chaise lounges were arranged around the pool. Behind the house was a full outdoor kitchen, with a grill, refrigerator and work space. A wide green lawn spread to the fence. Planters filled with yellow and purple pansies were placed here and there. Daniel had told her that gardeners, as well as pool maintenance men, came periodically and had the code to the gate.

The ten-foot fence continued across the back of the house, where another gate opened onto the National Forest. A narrow footpath led into the dark woods. Why would anyone want to wander around in there? Amy had said they'd seen bears in the woods.

Claire continued walking around the house. On the other side of the building, pebbles covered the distance between the coach house and the fence. She glanced up at her balcony. It looked to be some twenty feet from the fence and its sharp metal pickets.

Claire jogged out the front gate and turned towards the beach. In the distance, she saw people walking and clusters of beach umbrellas. The temperature had climbed and it was seventy-two degrees; perfect for running but too cold for a swim.

She ran and walked as she had the day before but she felt like she had a little more stamina. On the way back, she heard somebody coming up behind her. She turned as a man wearing a grey tee-shirt and running shorts overtook her. As he flew by, he turned and yelled over his shoulder, "You don't run much faster than you drive."

Belatedly, she recognized the jerk who'd honked at her yesterday. "Asshole," she muttered. Some of her pleasure in the day had gone, but she shook it off as best she could and finished her run.

When she got back to the house, she halted in surprise. Next to the gate was a set of oars, just like those she recalled seeing in the entrance hall to the main house. Probably the same ones, she thought, with their dull red shafts and handles. Sand was clumped on one worn blade. Who had been using them? Probably the owner of the house. She opened the gate, picked up the oars and carried them into the house, where she let herself in and placed the oars back among the beach paraphernalia. Then she ran up the stairs to the second floor of the mansion and glanced in at the living room. It seemed eerily quiet. She turned and hurried down the hall to the coach house door. Once inside her new home, she slammed the door shut.

Chapter 14

Amy called at six o'clock to say she was out front. Claire ran down to open the gate. Amy drove in and parked. When she got out of the car, she looked up at the main house. "Wow, this place is enormous. You'll have to give me a tour."

"We can do that after dinner if you want. I'm supposed to check things out every week."

Amy extracted several bags from the car and handed a couple to Claire. The word *Goatfeathers* was printed across the sides.

"What in the world did you bring?" Claire asked.

"Dinner and some house-warming gifts."

"Oh, Amy, you didn't need to do that."

"I know. But giving surprise gifts is fun. You take these two, I'll get the rest."

Inside, they put the bags on the kitchen counter. Then Amy wanted to look around, so Claire obliged. "I love this place. What a find." Amy smiled at Claire. "You know you owe it all to me."

"You're so right, I do." Claire reached out and touched her arm. "Seriously, Amy, meeting you at Starbuck's was serendipity."

Amy went into the bedroom and poked her head in the closet. Then she opened the door out to the deck and they went outside. The sun was setting, the sky a brilliant display of pink and orange. Amy looked down the coastline towards Grayton Beach. "You know, it would almost be faster to walk home along the beach. I'm nearly next door."

Claire laughed. "Right. I can run over and borrow a cup of sugar when I need it."

They looked the other way, west towards Destin.

Next to Citrus Haven, the forest came right down to the beach. "See where the Gulf seems to push into the land? You can't see from here, but that's Lemon Cove. It's an inlet surrounded by woods. There's a running path around it," Amy said.

"I'll have to jog down there someday and check it out."

Back inside, Amy opened the two *Goatfeathers* bags. "Shall we eat? I'm starving."

"Me too." Claire brought out two plates and silverware. She opened the bottle of white wine Daniel had left and poured them each a glass.

It turned out Goatfeathers was a seafood restaurant on 30A not far from Lemon Cove. Amy had brought spicy steamed shrimp as well as fried green tomatoes and an order of hush puppies: a fabulous, southern Gulf dinner. While they ate, Claire told Amy about her plans for the business and the help she had received from Gabriella and Lucca. "I think I'll be able to make a go of this."

"It sounds good to me. On Monday, you'll have to come to the store and I'll introduce you to Alexa. That might just be your first sale. She's arriving back in the States on Saturday and said she would be in my store on Monday afternoon."

"I'll be there." Claire peeled a large shrimp. "I haven't told you everything. New Year's Eve I'm going out for dinner with Daniel Rutherford."

"Daniel Rutherford?" Amy frowned as she dipped a bite of green tomato in the accompanying sauce. "Who's that?"

"Maybe you've seen him around. He looks like Harry Potter…really, he does…with black hair and round glasses. No scar, though."

"Is he twelve years old?"

"Ha. No. He's the realtor I dealt with when I rented this place." Claire sipped her wine.

Amy grinned. "Was it love at first sight?"

"No, actually I'm not really attracted to him. But he's nice, and what else would I do on New Year's Eve?"

Amy took a sip of wine and looked around the room. "Who owns this place, anyway?"

"I don't know. Daniel talked like it's an individual. But on the contract, there's just the name of a holding company. I think it's Bartholomew, Inc. Daniel told me the main house is usually empty."

"Why doesn't the owner just sell the place? It's got to cost a fortune to maintain." Amy pushed her plate away and sat back.

"No clue!" Claire said with a frown.

After dinner, Claire opened her presents. There was a cream colored, soft throw to cuddle up in; a lush house plant in a cute mosaic pot; a "tubshroom" to keep hair from going down the drain, and a framed map of 30A. Claire gave Amy a hug, tears in her eyes. She hadn't had a good friend like this for a long, long time. Friends were so precious.

Chapter 15

Claire worked for a while on Wednesday morning, then
decided to walk up Lemon Drive to 30A and check out the
shops and the yoga studio. After days of sunshine and
warmth, the weather had turned cloudy. She wore her pink
sweatshirt over her jeans and long-sleeved shirt. The gate
clanged shut behind her, a reassuring sound. She walked
along the road and around the dune that hid the house from
the rest of the small community. Apparently, the owner of
Citrus Haven really didn't want any close neighbors. From
what Daniel had said, the surrounding land was also owned
by Bartholomew Inc. Was the owner Mr. Bartholomew?
When she had the time, she would google the name.

Claire was so deep in thought that she nearly
bumped into a man standing by the roadside. He wore
running clothes, and sunglasses hid his eyes. "So you walk
like you drive," he snapped, fists on his hips and a frown on
his face. "Completely unaware of your surroundings."

"I... I didn't see you. I was thinking." Claire felt
irritated. Who was this guy that kept popping up, acting like
such an ass?

"Thinking? Nothing wrong with thinking, but you
better watch where you're going." He was smiling now. He
pulled off his sunglasses and offered his hand. "Daxton
Simmons. People call me Dax." He had a rugged face,
strong nose and very white teeth. His dark eyes drilled into
hers.

His sudden switch in mood rattled her. "I'm Claire."
She said as she tried to pull her hand away.

His grip was strong. "Do you live around here?"

She didn't feel like telling him exactly where she
lived. "Yes." She gestured to the houses ahead along the

beach. "Listen, I've got to get going. Nice to meet you, Dax." She gave a little wave and walked away with determination. She could feel his eyes on her back. How odd that she kept running into this guy. Was he some weird kind of stalker, or was her imagination working overtime? She glanced over her shoulder and saw that he was still watching her. He must also live "around here," but she wasn't about to ask him where.

The yoga studio was called Sunshine Yoga. Bells trilled softly as Claire opened the door. Several women were exiting the studio, and Claire guessed a class had just ended. They were chatting and laughing. As they passed her, several women said hi. She nodded back, then waited by the counter and studied a brochure describing the classes offered and the schedule. There was a Rise and Shine Power Vinyasa class, Quick Fix, and something called Rock Your Core. It all seemed somewhat daunting.

When the last person had left the building, Claire poked her head around a screen and looked into the spacious studio. Opaque windows lined one wall, mirrors lined the other. In the middle of the room, a statuesque blond in a black leotard was studying her phone. She had a perfect body, perfect posture and long legs. When she became aware of Claire, she looked up and smiled. She had one of those dynamic smiles that lit up her face. "Hi, y'all," she said. Her southern drawl had a singing lilt. Claire liked her right away.

"Hi, I'm Claire Hall. I'm here to inquire about yoga classes." Claire held up the brochure. "I've never tried yoga, so I need a beginner's class."

"Well, it's never too late to start." The woman came forward, seeming to glide across the floor. "I'm the owner of Sunshine Yoga. My name is Rhea Bell."

They went back out front, and Rhea went through

57

the selection of classes with Claire. "The least strenuous class I have is at 10:15 in the morning. I've got a bunch of serious seniors."

"I'm probably going to have to come before eight. I need to be on the road by nine AM. Or I could come in the early evening. I see you've got Power Yoga at six-thirty."

"Hmmm! Power Yoga might be intense. I'm thinking you should come to the seven AM class to start. You'll really like the girls. It's a diverse group at different ability levels. I could adapt certain poses for you." Rhea pointed to the morning class.

"Wow, seven AM, that's serious yoga." Claire laughed. "I need special clothes, right?"

"I've got some yoga gear in the back, if you want to check it out. There's a sale on right now. I'm trying to get rid of last year's stock."

Twenty minutes later, Claire left the yoga studio with black tights, a black tank top and a purple long-sleeved tee. Rhea had been super nice and Claire felt like she'd made another new friend. She headed back home, humming to herself and swinging her bag.

As she walked, she studied the houses. Only a few looked occupied, and according to Daniel most of them would be empty after the holidays. At the turn along the beach, she picked up her pace. The sky had turned a menacing grey, dark storm clouds were rolling in from the Gulf. As she rounded the dunes it began to rain. She started to run. Up ahead Citrus Haven loomed against the roiling sky. As she approached the house she realized the gate was open. She'd closed it, hadn't she? Was someone there? The brick driveway was empty. She ran through the gate, just ahead of a crack of thunder and the sizzle of lightning.

Chapter 16

Up in her apartment, Claire dropped her sopping wet clothes on the bathroom floor. Then she took a quick, hot shower and put on sweats and warm socks. Back in the kitchen, she was still shivering but not because of the cold rain. Had she or had she not shut the gate? Was there someone in the house? The thought of someone hiding out in all those rooms with their nooks and crannies made her nervous. On the other hand, maybe the owner was there? Why did she feel so unnerved? There was no logical reason. Nonetheless, she opened the bottom kitchen drawer and took out the purchase guides for the lock keypads. Ten minutes later, she had changed the codes for the door from the main house into her apartment as well as the kitchen door that led to the garage. She used the birthdate of her best friend in elementary school: 1126, November twenty-sixth.

Taking action made her feel better, and she realized she was hungry. Standing in the kitchen, she devoured some cheese and crackers with a bunch of grapes. It was still pouring outside. She picked up her copy of *The Woman in Cabin Ten* and the cream-colored throw Amy had given her. In the bedroom, she curled up on the chaise lounge. Outside, the storm raged. The waves crashed up on the beach and the leaden sky exploded with lightning bolts, a thrilling spectacle. But five minutes later Claire was fast asleep.

When she awoke, it was late afternoon and the storm had subsided. The ocean was still pounding the beach. In the distance, the horizon blurred between the grey sky and grey water. She pulled out her phone and scrolled through her messages. She was still receiving emails from business contacts at Safetynaps. Jeremy had also sent emails and texts asking, no, pleading with her to respond. Was she being a total bitch not to answer him? She would call him next week. She owed him that.

Claire dialed Amy's number. When she answered, Claire told her about the visit to the yoga studio. "I'm wondering if you want to go with me. There's a special price for the first month. It's that place right before you turn into Lemon Drive."

"I don't know. I feel like a big klutz when it comes to sports."

"This isn't a sport. You're just stretching and building your muscles. You're not competing or anything," Claire said.

"I don't know. What time would we go?"

"The instructor told me to start with the seven AM class."

"Seven AM?" Amy's voice rose several octaves.

"Yes. Come on, try it with me. You told me you get up early."

Eventually Amy capitulated and agreed to try it out the following week.

Claire rang off and went back to her texts. She saw one from Daniel: *Will pick you up New Year's Eve 7:30. Dress casual.* She texted back, *Thanks, see you then.* Dress casual. What did that mean around here? She got up and opened the closet doors and surveyed her clothes. Most of them were things Jeremy would approve of. She felt a rush of irritation. Tomorrow she'd go shopping, maybe at the Mercantile in Seaside. Or she'd go back to Pier Park in Panama City Beach. There were a lot of shops there.

Claire gathered her clothes from the hamper and added the wet clothes on the bathroom floor. Daniel had told her she could use the washer and dryer in the main house. She loaded everything into a couple of plastic bags. The unreasonable fear she'd felt earlier had faded. There was no one in the house, waiting to grab her.

When she opened the door to the main house, the hallway seemed especially dark, but she could see light filtering in from the great room. She stood for a moment, listening. If someone *was* there, she would skip doing laundry. She heard nothing, so she walked down the hall. Overhead the recessed lights sprang on. Before heading downstairs, she stepped into the great room. The second she crossed the threshold, the overhead lights came on, illuminating the room like a stage set. Classical music poured from the loudspeakers. She froze, her gaze ricocheting around the room. No one was there, yet she felt like a captive in a fishbowl. She took a few steps into the room. On the back wall, the security TV screen slowly rolled through images of the entryway, pool, back yard and garages. No one was visible anywhere. Feeling foolish, she called out, "Hello, hello, is someone here?" No response, but the music would have drowned out any answering voices.

Shaking herself, she stepped back into the hallway. The music stopped and the lights faded. Motion sensors had picked up her entrance into the space. There was nothing to fear.

As she started down the stairs to the laundry room, lights came on to illuminate her way. Motion sensors again. Nothing to be afraid of. Inadvertently, her gaze fell on the cubbies and hooks full of beach items at the bottom of the stairs. The oars were missing.

She froze near the bottom step, breathing fast and shallow. There were marks on the floor, leading to the locked storage closets. Slowly, she moved closer, and saw they were sandy tracks. She tried to reason with herself. The owner or whoever came by, got his oars, tracked some sand in the process. There was nothing creepy going on.

#

Claire filled the washer with her clothes, then realized she didn't have any detergent. She opened the cupboard overhead and luckily found a bottle of Tide. Once the washer started, she went back to the entryway and opened the door to the three garages by the pool. She saw no car, although the air held some sweet, chemical smell she didn't recognize. Then she went down the corridor to the garages under her coach house. The enormous space was empty. Spooked, she raced across the cement floor and up the stairs to her apartment. A quick tap-tap, 1126, and she was safe inside. She pressed her back against the door and began to laugh. She was being so ridiculous. Wasn't she?

Chapter 17

The next morning, the sky appeared washed clean by yesterday's storm. The violence of the waves had subsided and the ocean was a smooth sheet of translucent blue. Claire drank a quick cup of coffee and left for the yoga studio in her new outfit. She arrived at the same time as two other young women. They introduced themselves and Claire felt instantly welcome. Rhea unrolled a mat for her near the front of the studio, so she could give Claire pointers during the class. There were ten women and two men, spaced around the room by the time class began. Rhea put on some Asian music that could have been Indian or Japanese. Claire kept her eyes on Rhea and tried to mimic her actions. She felt as though she was always several steps behind the rest of the students and Rhea corrected her posture several times.

About fifteen minutes in, another student arrived. Claire looked up and then away. Daxton Simmons had just strolled into the room. He unrolled his mat behind Claire and glided smoothly from a downward dog to a plank, followed by several push-ups. He was one big muscle. Then they moved into a child's pose. She was uncomfortably aware of him crouched behind her, but he never made eye contact or acknowledged her presence. Near the end of the class he left without speaking to her, or anyone.

Rhea addressed the rest of them as they prepared to leave. "Hey y'all, there'll be no class tomorrow, Friday, or over the weekend. I'm going up to Birmingham to see my parents. I'll see you Monday, bright eyed and bushy-tailed. Enjoy the holiday weekend." She walked over and joined Claire, helping her roll up her mat. "What did you think?" Rhea asked.

Claire groaned. "I felt totally inept. Hopefully, it'll

get easier."

"You've got a naturally limber body. I think with a little practice you'll be a star."

"A star, right." Claire laughed. "Oh, by the way, I have a friend who will be joining us on Monday. She's never done yoga either."

"Great, the more the merrier," Rhea drawled.

Despite her awkward start, Claire left feeling awesome. It was good to be with people and her body was tingling from the exercise. She'd used muscles she didn't know existed, and probably would be feeling some pain tomorrow.

At home, she took a shower and got dressed in shorts and a tee. The weather had turned warm again. She drove down Lemon Drive, half expecting to see Dax along the way, but he wasn't lurking around. Fifteen minutes later she parked in Seaside. At a little coffee shop called Amavida, she got a latte and a croissant and took them outside to sit in the sun. It was the best coffee she'd ever had and the croissant was tender and flaky. Dax's odd behavior, yesterday's storm and the weirdness with the oars vanished from her mind. Life was good.

Afterward, she wandered around the shops but didn't see any outfits that seemed right. Finally, at Mercantile, she found a billowy white tunic and a fabulous black beaded necklace. With her black slacks and black stiletto sandals she'd look informal but very chic.

Next, Claire hit the grocery store. She'd been existing on Daniel's box of supplies, which was emptying fast. She bought the basics like flour, sugar, bread, and peanut butter as well as some frozen dinners and a quart of ice cream. Champagne was on sale, so she bought a bottle along with a couple of bottles of red and white.

Back home at Citrus Haven, she opened the door

into the main house so she could use the elevator to carry up the groceries. Today, she didn't fear any ghosts lurking in the hallways. She noticed the oars were back, but it didn't faze her.

After putting everything away, she went for a walk along the beach, turning west this time. The dense forest was on her right. The tree line ran right along the beach. In ten minutes, she arrived at the inlet called Lemon Cove. A sandy footpath skirted the inlet. She turned right and followed the trail. The Lemon Cove council had spent plenty of money on this path. Wooden bridges spanned the swampy areas around the cove, and every so often attractive pavilions provided shade and wooden benches. She passed a middle-aged couple walking a chocolate lab. They stopped to chat for a moment and she told them she had just moved to the area.

"Now, you be careful," the woman said. "They say there are alligators in the cove."

"Come on, Lenore, don't frighten the lady," her husband said. He shook his head and laughed. "We have never seen an alligator around here."

"Anyway, I always keep Cocoa on a leash." The woman bent down to pat the dog.

"Thanks for telling me. I'll be on the lookout!" Claire said.

The man chuckled. "You do that, honey. Maybe you'll see an elephant, too."

Claire continued on the path, which shifted between sandy trail and wooden crossway. She met no other people, and after twenty minutes turned to go back the way she came. Coming around a bend, she noticed an old rowboat, upside down and chained to a tree. It would be fun to go boating, she thought. Years ago, her family had rented a house in the Poconos and they'd canoed and water-skied on a lake up there. It had been a good time.

At home, Claire took a bath, sprayed herself with her favorite perfume, and got dressed. She was ready at exactly seven o'clock. From the kitchen window, she could look out at the driveway. She figured Daniel would arrive right on time. He was that sort of person.

Seven-fifteen went by, then seven-thirty. She took off her high heels and paced the apartment. By eight o'clock, she decided to call him. The phone rang and rang but he never picked up, and it didn't go to voice mail. What was going on? Some emergency, or had he stood her up? Claire paced some more, drawn again and again to the kitchen window, but no headlights flashed around the dunes. At nine o'clock she tried calling again. Nothing. Anger bubbled up. Why had she accepted this invitation from someone she barely knew.

At nine-thirty, she took off her clothes, pulled on her old flannel PJs and opened the bottle of champagne. She made herself a peanut butter and honey sandwich, and watched New Year's Eve festivities in Sydney and Paris on TV. By the time the ball descended in Times Square, she had finished most of the champagne. So much for New Year's Eve.

Chapter 18

Claire woke to the ringing of her cell phone. She sat up and groaned. Her head was spinning and she felt slightly nauseated. Oh God, why had she drunk all that champagne?

She got up in search of the phone. It was somewhere in the living room. As she hunted for it, the ringing stopped and then started up again. Her head throbbed and her mouth felt as dry as the Sahara Desert. Finally, she found the phone between the sofa pillows. She pushed the green button. It was Amy.

"Hi, I couldn't find my phone. Oh, my God, I feel terrible." Claire fell back against the sofa cushions, her eyes closed.

"What's wrong?"

"I spent New Year's Eve alone and drank most of a bottle of champagne. I have a major hangover."

"What happened? I thought you were going out with that realtor guy...Harry Potter."

"He never showed. I waited and waited and finally, I gave up."

"That's weird."

"Yeah, especially since he texted me yesterday afternoon to make sure of the time." She paused, rubbing her forehead with her fingers. "Ultimately, it doesn't matter. I didn't really even know the guy."

"Yeah, but still...well, drink lots of coffee. You'll feel better."

"What did you do last night?"

"I went out with a guy I met the other day."

"What guy?"

Amy didn't answer.

"So, what guy?" Claire said again.

Instead, Amy said, "Listen, I'm calling to invite you to a barbeque this afternoon at our place. Irma is having some neighbors and friends over."

"That would be great. I'd love to. I'll bring my famous brownies."

"Yum! Three o'clock. See you then." Amy hung up.

Claire frowned at the screen. She wondered why Amy didn't want to tell her about her big date. Maybe Claire was being too nosy. After all, they barely knew each other.

#

After a couple of aspirin, three cups of coffee and a run on the beach, Claire felt a lot better. At three o'clock she was climbing the steps up to Irma's front porch, brownies in hand. Several people sat on the porch, drinking beer and talking. She recognized Françoise and said hello. The woman blew her a kiss and held up a glass of red wine.

Inside, she found Irma in the kitchen, on the verge of taking a platter of fish kebobs and shrimp outside. On the kitchen table were bowls of salad, biscuits, and desserts, and another platter with steaks and chicken.

Claire set down the brownies. "Hi, Irma. Can I help you?"

"You sure can, girl. Bring out the meat and chicken, if you wouldn't mind. I want to get cooking."

Outside, there were two grills going. Amy was spreading cloths over long tables as she chatted with a tall, broad-shouldered man. As she looked up and waved at Claire, the man turned around. His eyes opened wide and he smiled. "Who is this, Amy?"

"My new best friend, Claire. She just moved down here."

Claire smiled back and walked over. Amy drew a breath to make introductions, but the man stopped her.

"Claire and I already know each other." Today he was dressed in shorts and a short-sleeved blue shirt that matched his eyes. They crinkled as he smiled.

"How's that? Was she caught speeding down 30A?" Amy asked.

Claire laughed. "No, this man stepped in and helped me out when a hitchhiker was pestering me at a gas station up north."

Amy looked back and forth between the two of them. "Claire, this is Leo Martin. He's our local sheriff."

"Sheriff? Were you on duty in Birmingham?" Claire asked.

"No, I was visiting friends for Christmas. I was on my way south that night." He took a sip from a can of Coke. "You made it down here safely, I see."

"Yes, no problems. But I've got to tell you, I've seen that guy around here a couple of times. He still gives me the creeps."

Leo frowned. "What do you mean? Where did you see him? Did he bother you?"

"No, he didn't do anything. He just stared at me. I saw him in Seaside last Friday. Then again outside my motel in Panama City Beach last weekend." Claire shivered, despite the warm afternoon air. "I felt like he wasn't there by accident. There's something menacing about him."

Leo reached into his back pocket and extracted a card from his wallet. "If you see him again…if you think he's stalking you, give me a call. We can track him down."

Claire took the card and put it in her pocket. "Thanks. Hopefully, I'll never see him again."

"Did you relocate down here?" Leo asked.

"Yes, I've found a place to live and I'm starting a job marketing some beautiful Brazilian purses. I'm on a new career path." She told him more than he needed to know about Lucca and the Letízia line.

He started to laugh. "I can tell you'll be successful. You're all charged up."

Claire blushed. "The truth is, I've never done anything like this before; cold-calling and retail. But I'm going to make it work."

Leo nodded, just as his cell phone rang. He pulled it out of a back pocket. "Excuse me, I've got to take this call." He stepped away, phone to his ear, and listened. Then he lowered the phone and strode over to Irma. "Emergency, Irma. I've got to go. Sorry." He turned to Claire. "Nice to meet you. We'll talk again soon." He went around the house and out of sight.

Amy had moved off during their conversation and was helping Irma with the grilling. Claire took a Diet Coke out of a cooler and joined her.

"Hey Amy, this morning I looked up Daniel Rutherford online. I couldn't find his name anywhere. Wouldn't you think that as a realtor, he would be easy to find?"

"That's odd." Amy turned a chicken leg with tongs and then slathered on some barbeque sauce.

"I was wondering if you could ask your friend Randy how he found Daniel and the rental."

"Sure, I'll text him right now." She handed Claire the tongs and dug out her phone. Her thumbs flew over the screen. "He'll get back to me in a minute. He's always working."

Ten minutes later, he called. Amy listened for several minutes, nodded her head, and then hung up.

"What did he say?"

"He found the information about your rental online but he can't find the site anymore. It's been removed. But get this, he also went to a listing of local realtors on the

Emerald Coast. Then he looked up a listing of Florida realtors. He couldn't find Daniel Rutherford anywhere."

Chapter 19

Friday morning, Claire heard a truck pull up outside. A glance out the window revealed a FedEx guy unloading several boxes from the back of his truck. Purses and bags from Letizia, she guessed. She ran down the garage stairs and out to open the gate. "Hi, can I sign for those?"

"Sure. I rang the bell a couple of times. I thought no one was home." The FedEx guy was wiry with sandy hair and a lopsided grin.

"Sorry, I live in the coach house and there's no doorbell."

"You live out here by yourself?" He gazed up at the house.

She decided to lie. "No, there's other people in the house." Claire signed the form and handed the clipboard back to the man. He took it and hurried back to the cab of his truck before she could ask him to carry the boxes into the garage.

She was still standing there, hands on her hips, trying to decide where she wanted to store the purses and bags, when Daxton Simmons came up from the beach along the path around the house. His grey tee-shirt was plastered to his body and sweat poured down his face.

"Looks like you've bought out Amazon," he said. His teeth flashed white in his tanned face. "What did you buy?"

Claire felt irritated. It was none of his business what she bought. Deliberately not looking at him, she said, "It's merchandise for my business."

"Do you want help dragging those inside?"

Against her better judgement, Claire acquiesced. "Actually, I would. I want to line them up in the garage." She gestured behind her.

Dax picked up a couple of boxes and headed for the open garage door. She followed him with two of the smaller boxes. They weren't all that heavy. In the garage, she asked if he could please put them under the stairs.

"Are you sure you don't want to stash them upstairs?"

"No, there's really no room up there. I've got to go through them and decide what I'm going to load in my car as samples." She definitely didn't want Daxton up in her apartment.

"What's inside? They're not heavy, just unwieldy."

He went out and brought in two more, and Claire followed him with a smaller box. "Leather purses, backpacks and computer bags…they're Brazilian," she said.

Together they made two more trips. Lucca had sent enough bags so she could actually sell some items. When they had stashed all the boxes, Dax started down the driveway. He turned to wave and Claire called out to him. "Dax…Thank you."

"The pleasure was all mine."

He'd been nicer than she expected, and he *had* been a help with the boxes. Claire made an impulsive decision. "Would you like a glass of lemonade? I was going to make one for myself."

He considered her for a moment, using his arm to wipe his forehead. "I'm pretty sweaty. But that'd be nice."

"Sit down by the pool and I'll get the lemonade."

She'd made the simple syrup and squeezed the lemons yesterday. Upstairs, she filled two glasses with ice and lemonade, set them on a tray, grabbed a hand towel, and brought everything back downstairs. Dax was nowhere in sight. She walked over to the pool, placing the tray on a glass-topped table. She looked up as he came around from behind the house. "This is one hell of a place. It looks like

73

there are fabulous views of the beach and the Gulf." He gestured up to the windows of the kitchen and the great room.

"Yes, from up there you can see for miles." Claire sat down on a padded patio chair. "So now you know where I live."

"I always knew where you lived. I saw you drive by last week." Dax wiped his face and neck.

"Where do you live? In one of the houses on stilts?"

"Yes, a matter of fact I do." He hung the towel around his neck and picked up the nearest glass.

"Aren't you afraid a big storm will come along and wash you out to sea?"

"I don't worry about things I can't do anything about." He took a long drink of lemonade and wiped his mouth. "Man, that's good. A beautiful girl that can make awesome lemonade. Who would think?"

Claire blushed and looked down at her hands. No one had ever called her beautiful. And she knew she wasn't but the compliment made her feel good inside. She tilted her head and looked up at him. "You're a real sweet-talker, aren't you?" In the next second she was ashamed of herself because she was flirting with him like Scarlett O'Hara.

"No, I'm not. I'm normally a straight talker." His gaze didn't waver.

Claire recrossed her legs. "So what do you do?"

"I sell insurance."

"Are you married?"

"No, I'm divorced." He gave her a wry smile. "Any more personal questions?"

"Are you from around here?"

"No, from Jacksonville. Okay, now what about you? Let's play twenty questions." He took another drink and turned the glass in his large hands. "Why did you move in here?"

"I loved the coach house. It has a great feel."

"Couldn't you find an apartment up on Highway 98? Why here?"

"I didn't know about any apartments on Highway 98. This place just fell in my lap, so here I am." Maybe Dax could supply her with some information if he lived nearby. She cleared her throat. "So, if you saw me drive by, maybe you've seen the owner of the main house—Citrus Haven? Maybe you've met him?"

"No, I haven't. I've seen some landscapers headed this way, and a pool guy. That's it." He changed the subject. "What kind of rental agreement did you sign? Could you get out of it?"

Why had he asked her that? "It's for a year. And I'm planning on staying here, not moving into some dark little apartment."

"I think you ought to move. Next week, Lemon Cove will be empty. No one will be around in January and February."

Claire stood up. "I've got work to do." She picked up Dax's empty glass and her own.

He stood too and followed her to the entranceway. "I'm just making a suggestion. You'd be safer, and happier." He fished a card from a pocket and tucked it between her fingers. "Here's my card. Call me if you need anything."

Claire thought to herself: *Safer...and happier? What a weird thing to say. He barely knows me. What business is it of his?*

As he walked down the road, she yelled at his receding back, "I love it here and I'm not moving."

He shook his head and yelled back, "Thanks for the lemonade."

Chapter 20

The first box Claire opened contained the backpack and purse she had ordered for herself. She ran upstairs to inspect them closely. This was the first time she'd actually seen the merchandise, though she trusted Lucca's eye for quality. In the bright sunlight of the living room she studied the buttery-soft leather, the stitching, the zippers and the lining of each item. The bags were beautiful and as well made as Lucca had promised. That was a relief. She grabbed some color markers and her laptop, and headed downstairs.

Back in the garage, she opened each box and inspected the contents. Then she wrote a brief description on the outside. On her computer, she accessed the spreadsheet she'd prepared earlier in the week and recorded the purses by type, color and size. Finally, she went back and pulled out a selection of bags to show Amy's boss, Alexa Cosmos, on Monday afternoon. She organized them in the trunk of her car.

By the time she'd finished, it was late afternoon and she was famished. She cleaned up and put on jeans, a blue tailored shirt and a dark blue sweater, then headed out. Instead of turning right on 30A towards Seaside, she turned left towards Blue Mountain Beach. She pulled into a restaurant on the water called Vue on 30a. Since it was early for dinner, there were only a few patrons in the restaurant. She ordered a glass of wine and the pistachio crusted grouper. When the wine arrived, she took a long sip and felt herself relax. Through the window she watched the rolling waves and the seagulls dancing through the purple sky. Her work that day had been invigorating and positive. It was a step forward in her new business.

An elderly man was just finishing up at another

table. He and the waitress were laughing together. When he got up, Claire noticed he'd left a newspaper on his table. He saw her looking at it and smiled at her.

"Here honey, want my paper? I've got to tell you, this is pretty much local news. It's not the *New York Times*." He chuckled as he handed her the paper with a shaking hand.

"Thanks so much. I've just moved here, and it would be good to check out the local news."

"Oh, yeah? Where did you move from?" He walked slowly over to her table, leaning on a cane.

"Chicago, by way of Atlanta."

"You did the right thing. It's real nice here. Let me introduce myself. George Ralston." He stuck out a gnarled hand.

She shook it. "Claire Hall."

"I've lived here since the eighties. I came down here with my wife for a little vacation and we stayed..." He went on and on, and Claire couldn't help but smile. He was obviously lonely, and thrilled to have someone to talk to.

When the waitress brought Claire's fish, she tapped George's shoulder. "George, you've got to let this young lady eat."

"Right, okay, Julie. I'm off like a herd of turtles." He waved to Claire as he hobbled away. "Bye, honey. See you soon, I hope."

Julie filled her water glass. "You were very patient. George could talk your ear off. I hope he didn't bother you."

"No problem. He seems like a nice old guy."

"Can I get you anything else?"

"No, thanks. Everything looks great!"

When Julie moved away, Claire took a bite of grouper. It was cooked to perfection. She ate half of her meal before turning to the newspaper. It was folded to a

77

page with real estate ads. She remembered what Dax had said about apartments available on Highway 98. In spite of herself, she checked out the rentals. There was nothing on 98, but there were a couple of other apartments in places she'd never heard of before: Crestview and Chipley. Well, she wasn't planning on moving anyway.

She took another bite of fish, and a forkful of risotto. Then she turned to the front page and went still. She stared at the picture beneath the headline for a long time. It was Harry Potter—Daniel—but it wasn't. He wasn't wearing round glasses or a bow tie. His eyes stared out at her but it wasn't the regard she recognized. It was a mug shot, and he looked sneaky and arrogant. Her gaze switched to the headline. *Boone Williams, Found Murdered off Highway 98.* What followed were the gruesome details of a vicious, gang-style assassination.

Claire pushed away her plate and stood, suddenly feeling sick. Five minutes later she was in her car, barreling home down 30A.

Chapter 21

It was nearly dark, when Claire drove around the dunes and approached the house. Frantically, she punched in the gate code, drove in and heard it slam shut behind her. The empty expanse of the garage seemed frightening. Once parked, she shut the garage door and ran up the stairs as though being chased. She tapped in the door code—1126—and she was in her apartment.

Inside, Claire went around the room and turned on all the lamps. She shut the blinds and curtains. Then she collapsed on the sofa. What had she gotten herself into? Who had Daniel—no, Boone—worked for? Why had he rented her the coach house? Who owned Citrus Haven? There were so many questions and very few answers.

She called Amy, but got voicemail. Either Amy was still working or out on a date with her mysterious boyfriend. Who else could she contact? Dax? Definitely not. She didn't trust him. What about Leo Martin, the sheriff? She didn't really know him. But he would probably want to talk to her. She had talked to Daniel just days before his murder and he had texted her hours before his death. She pulled out the card the sheriff had given her and called him. The phone rang and rang, then went to voicemail. She left a message: "Hello, Sheriff Martin? This is Claire Hall. I have some information about"—she stumbled over the name—"Boone Williams. Please call me at your convenience. Thank you."

That night Claire slept fitfully. In her dreams, Harry Potter surfed through the waves chased by evil men in speedboats. In the morning, Claire opened the blinds but the sun was barely visible through a heavy fog. She made some toast and drank a couple of cups of coffee. Even then she didn't feel whole.

She pushed away her dishes and pulled out her laptop, then typed *Boone Williams* into the search engine. His murder was a minor event in the Florida papers. She clicked on an article at random and read it. Williams was known to authorities as a small-time criminal and con man who'd been in and out of jail several times, mainly for drug trafficking, and it was alleged he had ties to the cartels. He'd been beaten before being executed and thrown in the woods off Highway 98, not far from Lemon Cove.

All of this didn't jive with the feelings Claire had when she'd met him. He'd seemed too polished to be some petty criminal. His conversation at lunch had been interesting and well-informed. He was a con man, though, and clearly he'd successfully pulled the wool over her eyes. It made her wonder who she could trust.

Trembling, she got up and went to the window. Outside, the fog was lifting and rays of sun warmed her body, but still she shivered. As she stood there gazing out at the waves, her phone rang. It was Sheriff Martin, returning her call. "What can I do for you, Ms. Hall?"

She swallowed hard. "I called because I have some information about Boone Williams, the man who was found murdered in the woods. Do you want me to come in to the police station?"

There was a long pause.

"Hello?" Claire said.

"I've got a better idea. Why don't we meet tomorrow afternoon at The Wine Bar in Watercolor? We can have a glass of wine and some cheese, and you can tell me what you know about Williams."

Wine and cheese…like a social call? Claire felt confused. "But don't I need to come into the station to make a statement?"

"No, at this point, I'll just get your story. Is five

o'clock okay?"

Maybe they did things differently in Florida. "Sure, thanks. See you tomorrow."

Chapter 22

Sunday morning, Claire awoke to a ringing phone. Was it Amy calling her back? Without looking, she pressed the green button.

It wasn't Amy. It was Jeremy, spitting fire. "Why haven't you answered the phone? Why haven't you responded to my texts? You owe me answers, Claire!"

She *did* owe him answers. "I'm sorry, Jeremy. I've needed time to think about our relationship." What a wimpy answer, she thought, and how placating she sounded…just like she always had.

"And what have you decided?" His voice vibrated with anger.

Claire braced herself and whispered, "That it's truly over. I'm not coming back."

Jeremy was silent for a long time. When he spoke again, she heard tears in his voice. "I had everything planned for our future together. All you had to do was follow my lead."

He didn't get it. "Jeremy, I don't want or need someone to organize my life. I want to decide my own future."

"You'll mess up."

"I probably will. But I'll get up and keep on going."

More silence. Then: "So it's over?"

"Yes. Goodbye, Jeremy." This time, the words came out clear and strong. After a few seconds of silence, she hung up. There were tears in her eyes, but she also felt an overwhelming relief.

Claire spent much of the day cuddled up on the chaise, buried in *Mothering Sunday*, the novel Kate from the bookstore had lent her. The book club would take place that

Thursday. It was a pleasurable and easy read, a romantic tragedy based around one pivotal moment. *Like my life, only without the tragedy*, she thought, then laughed at herself for being melodramatic.

#

When Claire arrived at The Wine Bar, Leo Martin was already seated on the outside terrace. He was dressed casually in shorts, a charcoal Henley and flip-flops. A party of four sat at the far end of the terrace and an older couple in Adirondack chairs were sharing a carafe of wine in the waning light. The sun was making its descent and the evening air was soft and mellow.

Claire waved and made her way to Leo's table. A carafe of red wine and a glass were in front of him. He stood up and pulled out a chair for her to sit down. They greeted each other and then he summoned a waiter.

"I took the liberty of ordering wine for myself and a cheese tray to share. Choose a wine you'd like and we can order a carafe for you."

"Sounds wonderful." She scanned the menu and spotted Miraval rosé. Produced at the Jolie and Pitt winery in France, it was light and crisp. "I'll have the Miraval rosé, please."

They made small talk until her wine and the cheese arrived. The platter contained three different cheeses, with walnuts, grapes and sliced French bread. "This looks fabulous, a perfect Sunday supper," Claire said.

After they had helped themselves, Leo got down to business. He leaned forward so his voice didn't travel far. "How did you know Boone Williams, Ms. Hall?"

Claire put down her wine glass and leaned forward as well. "Please, call me Claire. I knew the man as Daniel Rutherford. And I have to tell you, he looked nothing like his mug shot in the paper."

Leo raised his eyebrows. "What did he look like?"

"Like an older Harry Potter. He had his hair combed forward covering his forehead and he wore big, round glasses. He also wore a suit and a bow tie. He was quite, what shall I say, debonair. Nothing like the scummy looking picture of Boone Williams. But I'm sure it's the same guy." Claire picked up her wine glass and took a sip.

Leo nodded, then spread some brie on a slice of bread and took a bite, chewing slowly. "Where did you meet this Harry Potter look-alike?"

Claire frowned, annoyed. "You don't believe me, do you? You think I made this up?"

"No, no I don't. I'm just wondering if it *is* the same guy." He took a couple of grapes and ate them.

Claire felt like getting up and leaving. "Listen, I'm sure this Williams guy is the realtor who rented me my current apartment. I even had lunch with him. And he was supposed to take me out on New Year's Eve." She must have raised her voice; the older couple in the Adirondack chairs was looking their way.

Leo reached over and covered her hand with his. "Calm down. I don't believe you're lying or fantasizing. You seem sure of what you saw. But your experience with Williams just doesn't sound like his MO."

Claire tugged her hand away and busied herself spreading goat cheese on bread. "I am positive this is the same guy."

Leo pulled a notebook out of his back pocket and flipped it open. "Okay. What did Williams say his name was, again? Tell me how you met him and what transpired."

Claire took a gulp of wine and told the whole story. Leo took notes and asked several questions to clarify, ending with, "So what happened New Year's Eve?"

"He texted me that he'd arrive at seven, but he never

showed."

"And you never heard from him again?"

"No, but he was probably dead by then, or being held prisoner or something…" Claire's voice trailed off. She put down the slice of bread and goat cheese.

Leo slapped his notebook on the edge of the table. "I wouldn't feel too sorry for the guy. He's not worth crying over."

"What I don't get is how he came to play the realtor role for the place where I live?"

"You're out in Lemon Cove, right, the big house at the end of the road? Did you sign a contract?"

Claire nodded. "Yes. As a matter of fact, I brought it with me." She pulled the contract out of her bag and handed it over. "Maybe we should contact the owner of the house, tell him his realtor is dead." She shook her head. "Him…or them. It's some outfit called the Bartholomew Group.

Leo took out his phone and snapped pictures of the pages of the rental contract. "The police will handle all that. We'll do the research. You needn't be involved."

Claire sat back, feeling relieved. She held her glass in both hands. "He seemed like such a nice guy. I guess I'm a really bad judge of character…"

"Or Williams was a superb con man. But I know, no one wants to be duped." Leo motioned to the waiter to bring the check.

"Let me pay my share, this was a police matter," Claire said.

"No way. I invited you here, and I've enjoyed our time together, even if it wasn't in the best of circumstances. Let's get together again soon. Would you like that?" He stood up.

Claire smiled up at him. "Yes, I would."

Leo accompanied her to her car. "Are you thinking

of moving out of the coach house?"

"No, I'm not. Should I?"

"It seems pretty lonely out there. In January and February, you won't have many neighbors." He gestured to the street. "Can you tell the difference tonight? There's no traffic. Everyone clears out after New Year's weekend."

She looked up and down 30A. The road was empty in either direction. She opened her door and got in her car. Leo pushed the door closed, then leaned in the half-open window. "I'm sure you're safe, but keep the doors locked. By the way, have you seen that hitchhiker anytime recently?"

"No, not since last week."

"Good. He's probably moved on." Leo straightened and waved goodbye, and Claire drove off.

Chapter 23

When Claire arrived at yoga Monday morning, Amy was already there, wearing a pink tee-shirt and flowered tights. She stood at the back of the room, looking uncomfortable.

Claire beckoned to her. "Come on up front so you can see Rhea."

Amy gestured for Claire to come closer. "I don't want to be in the front. I'm going to hide out here," she whispered. Then she sat down on her mat.

"Okay. I'm going up front. Talk later."

#

Rhea put them through their paces. It had been several days since Claire's last session so it felt like she was starting all over again, although she did remember some of the poses. When she glanced back, she saw Amy looking panicked and sweating profusely.

After class, they left together for breakfast at Another Broken Egg Cafe in Grayton Beach. Once they were seated, the waitress came over with menus. Amy ordered Bananas Foster French Toast with sausage and eggs. Claire chose the granola, fruit and quinoa bowl.

Amy didn't say much as they waited for the food. She definitely didn't look her usual cheerful self. After she'd stirred sugar and cream into her coffee, she looked up, and Claire saw tears in her eyes. "I feel just terrible, Claire. When I looked at myself in the mirror and compared myself to the other women, I felt like a…like a…" She wiped her eyes with the corner of a napkin. "Like a big lump. I mean, you have a great figure and Rhea has a fabulous body with her long legs." She sighed and shuddered. "I'm tired of the way I look."

Claire reached over and took Amy's hand. "Don't

cry, Amy. You carry a little extra weight but you always look nice."

"No, I don't. Don't lie to me Claire. I look dumpy." Just then the waitress arrived with their breakfast selections. She put two plates piled high with food in front of Amy and the Quinoa bowl in front of Claire. Amy looked at Claire's healthy breakfast and then at her own selection. Then she started giggling. "This is the problem, right? I should be eating your breakfast."

Claire laughed, too. Amy pushed away the pancakes covered with bananas and whipped cream and started on her eggs. As they ate, Claire told her about her discovery that Daniel Rutherford was actually the man who'd been murdered and thrown in the woods. Then she told Amy about her wine and cheese meeting with Leo Martin the night before.

"So Harry Potter was actually this con man, Boone Williams? Unbelievable. But I still don't get what he was doing masquerading as a realtor." Amy carefully cut a sausage patty in small pieces.

"Me, too. I'm wondering if my rental agreement is legit."

"Maybe you should find another place to live. Have you contacted the owner?"

"The owner is a corporation, the Bartholomew Group. Leo said the police will look into it. I'm glad to leave it in his hands. Right now, I really don't want to move."

"Yeah, your place is really great." Amy eyed the pancakes and then pushed them farther away.

"What did you do last night?" Claire asked.

"I was out on a date. We went to Panama City Beach, walked around and went to a bar."

"So are you going to tell me about this guy?"

Amy smiled nervously. "He's nothing special but he's nice."

"Where did you meet him?"

"In Seaside." Amy stood up. "Listen, I better get going. I've got to get to the shop. Alexa will be coming in this morning."

"Okay, I'll see you later." Claire stood up too. "Hey, I forgot to tell you—a selection of purses arrived Friday. I'll be able to show you and Alexa the summer line. Two o'clock, right?"

"Yep, I'll see you then."

Chapter 24

Claire dressed in her favorite black power suit and a white silk shirt, then put on pearl earrings and polished black pumps. She was ready for battle. Yesterday, she'd moved her wallet, keys and other paraphernalia from her old purse to the lovely, new, soft one. Her backpack was filled with her computer, brochures and order forms. In the car, she had organized the merchandise to show customers.

It was cool and sunny when she pulled out of the driveway. She didn't see anyone on Lemon Drive as she made her way to 30A. She turned left and headed towards Blue Mountain Beach. Ten minutes later she pulled up outside a gift shop she had researched the previous week. The shutters were drawn and a large sign announced that the shop was closed for the season and would reopen in March. Claire made a quick notation in a notebook. She would enter the information on her laptop when she got back to the coach house.

Five minutes later, she pulled up outside the second store she'd planned to pitch that morning. From the car, the place didn't look all that prosperous. The walls could do with a paint job and the windows needed a wash. There were no other cars in the parking area. She looked at herself in the rearview mirror, smoothed back her hair, and then got out with her bags.

When Claire pushed open the shop door, a bell tingled in the back. A minute later, a stubby woman with a helmet of short, grey hair and sharp, black eyes came out from behind a curtain. She crossed the room with the ferocity of a bulldog. "Whatever it is, I don't want any."

Claire swallowed and tried to smile. "Hi, I represent Letízia, a Brazilian purse company. May I show you—"

"I told you I don't want any. Get it?"

"But you haven't even taken a look." Claire took a step into the shop.

The woman put her hands on her hips. "I don't need any more purses. Get out of here."

"Could I come back in a month?"

She looked Claire up and down. "No. I do not want any fancy purses."

Claire nodded. "Okay. I'll leave my card in case you change your mind." She pulled one out of her pocket.

The woman scowled. "Oh, my god, girl, don't you get it? I said no, and I said to leave!"

Claire placed a card on a dusty shelf by the door as she backed out, mumbling, "Sorry, thanks, bye."

Back in the car, Claire rested her forehead on the steering wheel and closed her eyes. She felt as though she'd been physically attacked. That woman had been so angry. Why? What had Claire ever done to her, except ask to show her a couple of cute bags? She sighed, sat back up and started the car. It was time to move on. As she pulled away, she glanced over at the shop's open door. The woman stood there, glaring.

Claire drove past Gulf Place and stopped at a small gift shop in an upscale strip mall, where she lugged her two bags and a box up on the stoop. The shop door was pulled open by a slim woman in jeans and a floral top. She was heavily made-up and wore her hair in a skinny ponytail. She looked Claire up and down, with a brittle smile. "Don't bother coming in. I'm not buying new merchandise at this time." Then she shut the door.

Strike three. Claire hauled everything back to the car, feeling frustrated and incompetent. She checked her GPS and turned back the way she'd come, towards Grayton Beach. Ten minutes later, she pulled up outside a curious building. It was painted a deep red and resembled a Japanese pagoda with a curved roof. Over the door was the word *Kōfuku* and some Japanese characters. She got out of the car, grabbed her bags and started up the stairs.

The door opened and a sprightly girl greeted her with a ten-watt smile. She had curly red hair pulled back in a messy ponytail. Big brown eyes and an upturned nose sprinkled with freckles were settled in a softly round face. She wore white jeans and a smooth, draped top. "Hi, welcome," the girl said, and stepped back so Claire could enter the store.

Claire smiled. Talk about a hundred and eighty-degree switch from the last shop. She introduced herself, plopped her bags on the counter and pulled out a brochure. Then she looked around the boutique. The interior was all natural wood, with a cream-colored wooden floor. Hanging on racks were white, cream and beige garments of diaphanous, floaty material. Claire stepped closer. The styles looked vaguely Japanese, sort of a kimono. Her gaze zeroed in on a rack where beige string bags hung next to floppy straw hats. "Wow, this stuff is amazing. The dresses and tops are so unusual."

"Yeah, that's what everybody says. Maura designs everything herself. She's the owner. It's all manufactured upstairs. I mean, they sew the dresses upstairs. There's a studio."

"Is Maura here right now? I'd love to talk to her," Claire said.

"No, she's gone for the first two weeks of January. Things are like, really dead around here. At first, we weren't going to open up at all. Then she changed her mind. I'm glad 'cause I still get a paycheck. I'm Mandy, by the way." The redhead gave a little wave with her fingers. Intricate henna designs decorated the back of her hand. "You can show me what you're selling. I can probably tell you if Maura would like it."

"Considering the color scheme of everything in your store, I think I have a limited number of items that might fit in." Claire flipped through the brochure, looking for white and beige bags.

"This one is cute." Mandy pointed to a cross-body bag with a gold chain. Then she flipped back to the front of the brochure. "Just let me look through this, okay? You can look around the store."

Claire ambled around the shop, taking everything in. At the back there were glass sliding doors that looked out on a Japanese sand garden, bounded by a wall. A small path led to a koi pond, complete with a pretty little bridge over the water. "What's out here?" she asked.

Mandy looked up. "It's a mini-replica of a famous Japanese garden. Right now, it doesn't look like much, but in the summer it's gorgeous. There's like, all these flowers."

"Can I go out there?"

"Sure. I think the Zen meditation class is over."

"Zen meditation?"

"Yeah, the Buddhist priest is here a couple of times a week. He's back under the gazebo thing."

Claire slid the door open and stepped outside. In the far corner of the garden three people sat under a small gazebo, talking quietly. At the sound of the door opening, they turned to look at Claire. She felt as though she was disturbing them and stepped back inside.

"What happens during Zen meditation?" Claire asked.

"They look down at the floor and try to empty their minds. It's supposed to be a good thing to do if you're stressed out." Mandy was poring over the brochure. "I love this yellow cross-body bag."

Claire noticed the people getting up to leave. A young woman with long, blond hair and a guy with a limp walked down a narrow path towards a side exit. The third person, a tall Asian man, stared over at Claire. He wore black pants, a black shirt and a dark green padded vest. He stood motionless and his eyes bored into hers. She felt as though he was looking into her soul. She stood frozen, returning his gaze. Slowly, he turned and followed the others out. Claire stepped back into the shop, feeling as though she had experienced some sort of mystical encounter.

Chapter 25

Claire drove home before heading back out for her meeting with Alexa Cosmos at Beach Mania. Before reaching the dunes on Lemon Drive, she passed the landscaper's truck. It looked as though there were two Hispanic guys inside the truck's cab. She'd seen them before when she was returning home. This time of year, it didn't seem there'd be that much gardening to do. Then again, she didn't know anything about plants or their care.

At home, she was too nervous to eat. She grabbed a Diet Coke out of the fridge. While she drank it, she reviewed the catalogue for the umpteenth time. She needed to be totally on top of the merchandise. The morning had been a disappointment, except for her last stop. She'd left her card with Mandy. She'd go back to Kōfuku in two weeks, when the owner was there. Perhaps she'd make a sale then. But she hadn't sold anything yet. Maybe she wouldn't. Maybe nobody would ever want to buy any purses. Maybe she was totally incompetent. On the other hand, it was her first morning on the job. What did she expect? Nobody had said this would be easy. She finished her Coke and threw the empty can in the trash. In the bathroom, she brushed her teeth, reapplied lipstick and then it was time to go.

In Seaside there was an abundance of parking places. The holiday crowds had definitely left town. Claire pulled out the large box of samples from the trunk of the car. It was heavier than she'd thought. She balanced her backpack on top and walked across the horseshoe drive to Beach Mania, nearly tripping at the curb. Luckily, the front door was open. She walked in and plonked the box on the counter at the back of the store.

Amy came out and gave her a hug and then held her at arms-length. "Look at you. That suit must have cost a fortune. You look like a Wall Street financier."

"Do I? Is that good or bad?" Claire was feeling unsure of herself.

"Well, let's just say it's pretty fancy for Panama City Beach." Amy laughed. "Let me get Alexa, she's working in back."

A moment later, a formidable woman appeared at the door. She was classically beautiful in an off-putting way, with thick dark hair swept back from a strong face. Dressed neatly in a sleek sheath and heels, she came forward, holding out her hand. Claire felt momentarily daunted, but when Alexa's face broke into a smile, Claire responded in kind.

"Hello, Claire. Amy has told me a lot about you." Alexa's voice was low and rich.

"Thanks so much for meeting with me today. I know you just got back from Greece."

"No problem. Amy kept things going here while I was away. I'm blessed to have her."

Amy beamed.

"I thought you and I could go around the corner to Heavenly's. They have marvelous gelato. I've missed it while I was gone."

This was an unexpected turn of events. "Sure, okay. Shall I bring a brochure?"

"No need. We're just going to talk and get to know each other," Alexa said. She led the way out of the store and around the corner.

It turned out that Heavenly's Shortcakes sold cookies and cupcakes as well as ice cream. Claire realized she was actually hungry, since she'd skipped lunch. Alexa ordered two scoops of strawberry gelato and Claire chose salted caramel.

"Put it on my account," Alexa said to the young man who served them. Then she led the way outside. They sat in the shade at the far end of the terrace. Alexa took a taste of gelato. "Delicious." She took another mouthful and swallowed. Then she turned to Claire. "Tell me about yourself."

Claire ended up opening her soul to Alexa like she had to Amy. Between bites of ice cream, she talked about Safetynaps, Randall Cunningham, Jeremy, Lucca Silva and her move down to the Emerald coast area. Alexa listened closely, nodding now and then.

"So I'm on this mission to sell these purses that are really well-made, fashionable, attractive and the latest style, but…" Unexpectedly, Claire felt on the verge of tears. Here she was with a potential client and she was losing it.

Alexa's intelligent gaze seemed to be assessing Claire. "So what happened this morning?"

"I was a flop, to say the least. I didn't sell anything to anybody." Claire studied the pool of melted ice cream in her dish. "I left a card at a place called Kōfuku with a girl named Mandy."

"I know Mandy. I tried to hire her away from Kōfuku. She has a nice way about her. People automatically like her and trust her." Alexa continued to study Claire. "Would you like a couple of tips on cold-calling, from my point of view?"

Claire nodded. "Yes, for sure."

"Okay. Number one, before selling anything, you've got to get to know the person you're dealing with. You need to show empathy and interest in that person. Remember, it's all about them."

Claire nodded. "Make them feel comfortable…"

"Don't wear that lovely black suit and those pearls

that probably cost a fortune. You're a formidable lady dressed in your power suit. Wear something neat and attractive, but don't alienate your customers."

Claire fingered the soft Italian wool of her suit jacket. She'd never thought of herself as formidable before.

"When you enter the store for the first time, don't carry any boxes or backpacks. Just walk in and look around. Talk to the shop girl or the owner about the merchandise, about the weather, about the music on the stereo, about their children. When they're softened up, then go in for the kill." Alexa grinned and opened her eyes wide.

All of this made perfect sense to Claire. That angry, older woman who had yelled at her this morning might have liked to talk about her woes. Although Claire didn't think she would ever buy anything. But the skinny woman at the second shop might have. "You're right. Everything you've said makes perfect sense."

Alexa scraped the last bite from her gelato dish. "Now, about Beach Mania."

Claire laughed. "How am I going to make a pitch to you? You're going to know all my secrets."

"Guess what? I've already chosen the bags I would like. Since Amy told me about you, I've been studying your website."

Claire couldn't believe her ears. "Really? Thanks so much."

"However, before closing the deal, I would like to inspect the purses you've brought in that great big box. Amy said the workmanship was exceptional, but I need to see for myself."

"Of course. I think you'll be pleased with the details."

Alexa folded her hands on the table. "I have another proposal. I was intrigued by the purses and matching scarves. I'm wondering if your manufacturer would consider producing a child-size version for my Baby Beach Bunny shops. I think the grandmothers visiting my stores would buy those for their grandkids."

"I'll talk to Lucca about it and get back to you." Claire felt elated. This was turning out to be a spectacular afternoon.

As they got up to leave, Claire looked across the street and froze. The hitchhiker was seated at a table, with a beer in one hand and a cell phone in the other. His hair was styled instead of scraggly, and she noticed he wore preppy shorts and a polo shirt. He looked up and smirked at her. A chill ran down her spine.

Chapter 26

After leaving Beach Mania, Claire practically skipped to her car. Alexa had ordered several styles of bags. Claire called Lucca from the car and told him about the sale.

"On your first day? I'm impressed," he said. "I knew you'd do well." They discussed logistics, and he assured her Letízia would FedEx the merchandise to the Beach Mania warehouse. Claire told him about Alexa's request for child-sized purses and matching scarves, and Lucca approved of the idea. "I'll talk to my cousin and get back to you."

Claire rang off and let her mind percolate all the way home. It wasn't until she pulled into the garage that she remembered the hitchhiker. Seeing him had shocked her, but she hadn't shown her fear in front of Alexa. Once upstairs in her apartment, she texted Leo Martin even though it was probably too late for him to do anything. By now the guy must have disappeared. Minutes later, Leo called her back. "We'll do a drive-by in the area, see if he's still lurking around. Is this guy harassing you?"

"No, he just stares at me. And smiles in a nasty way."

"Did he follow you to Beach Mania?"

"I don't know. I don't think so."

"You understand, Claire, this man isn't doing anything illegal. We can't pick him up and send him off to Australia."

"Right. I understand. I thought you wanted me to contact you if I saw him."

"If he harasses you in any way, then contact me. Meanwhile, we'll be on the lookout."

She hung up, feeling dissatisfied, but Leo was right. The hitchhiker had never said anything to her, or intimidated her. He just stared at her.

#

The week went by quickly. Claire ventured further afield. Following Alexa's suggestions, she concentrated on developing a rapport with store owners and salesgirls, and made a few insignificant sales. Nothing as big as Alexa's order, but still, it was something.

On Wednesday, Claire arrived at her yoga class and saw Amy in the small front lobby, deep in conversation with Rhea. Claire didn't interrupt. She went into the studio, found a spot on the floor and rolled out her mat. When Amy came in, she was beaming. Something good must have happened. Rhea started the class and it seemed more rigorous than the last time. Claire could feel her muscles complaining but in a good way. Like last time, Dax arrived a bit late and placed himself behind Claire. When she looked into the mirror, their eyes met but he showed no sign of recognition. Had she offended him? He could have at least smiled.

After class, Amy came over. She was sweating profusely.

"So, what are you so happy about?" Claire asked.

"Rhea told me about this great program for losing weight, getting in shape and having more energy. It's called Reelife. I'm so excited."

"Tell me about it."

"There's shakes and snacks and vitamins. Every week you pick a day to be your cleansing day when you drink a special shake that removes the impurities from your system. It really works. I mean, I saw pictures and everything."

"Wow, it sounds pretty strenuous. Do you still eat regular food?"

"Yeah, for dinner."

101

"Good, because I want to have dinner with you on Sunday."

"It's a deal."

Chapter 27

It was already dark at 6:30 on Thursday evening, when Claire left the house. She wasn't sure where the book club took place. In Seaside she parked in the horseshoe drive and walked quickly up the steps to the Sundog Bookstore. It was closed, but a note on the window said the book club was upstairs in the Community Center Assembly Hall. Claire had no clue where the Assembly Hall was.

She walked past The Great Southern Café where she'd had lunch with Amy a couple of weeks earlier. It looked inviting: soft lights, lively conversation and the tinkle of dishes and silverware. She went up the short flight of steps. When the hostess greeted her, Claire asked for directions to the community center. "I'm going to the book club there. Sorry to bother you."

"No bother. It's on Smollian Circle. This is what you do." The hostess came down the stairs and pointed her in the right direction.

Claire thanked her and started out. She crossed a street and walked past Beach Mania. It was closed. She turned right and ducked into the covered passageway that led towards Smollian Circle. As she walked, she had the feeling someone was following her. She turned around, but there was no one behind her, just the moving shadows of the waving palm trees. She picked up her pace. Up ahead she was glad to see several cars pulling into parking spots. Walking around alone in the dark gave her the creeps.

She followed two women up the outside staircase to the loft above the community center. As she opened the door, she was struck by the bright lights and loud laughter. Several people were seated around a large, round table. Claire recognized Kate, the book store employee, so she walked over and said hello. Then she searched for a seat around the table. To her surprise, Aunt Irma was there as well. Claire sat down beside her.

"Hi! You didn't tell me you were a reader," Aunt Irma said.

"I haven't had the time to read these last few years. I met Kate at the bookstore, and she told me about the book club, so here I am." Claire pulled out her copy of *Mothering Sunday* and placed it on the table. "Where's Amy tonight?"

"I don't know. She's been going out a lot with a fellow she met here in Seaside."

"Have you met him?"

"No, she's pretty secretive about him. I don't know why."

Thinking of Jeremy, Claire said, "Maybe in case it doesn't work out."

Irma nodded as she flipped through the pages of the book.

There were twelve people around the table, a mixed group age-wise. Claire was surprised to see the Buddhist guru from the Zen meditation group. He was studying her, and she lowered her eyes. She didn't want to be drawn into his intensity. She found it unnerving.

Kate tapped her hand on the table, and conversation stopped. "Let's get started. We've got a new member in our little group." She indicated Claire, who introduced herself and said she had recently moved to the area. After that they went around the table and everyone introduced themselves. Claire learned that the Zen meditation teacher went by a single name, Seijun. After they had all introduced themselves, Kate leaned forward. "What did ya'll think of the book?"

"It was intense," Irma said. "And sensual."

Quiet laughter went around the room. Kate led the

discussion, asking questions and providing background on the author. Claire said little but observed everyone. A husky man with strong features and an arrogant demeanor, whose name she didn't recall, took over much of the conversation. About halfway through the discussion, Claire leaned over and asked Irma who he was.

"That's Reginald Brim. He wrote the *Glory Days Trilogy*. It won the Pulitzer Prize. But he hasn't published anything in the last five years," Irma whispered back.

Claire looked at him with new appreciation. No wonder everyone kowtowed to him. When they'd finished discussing *Mothering Sunday*, someone asked Reginald what he was working on these days.

"I'm writing a book dealing with the aftermath of the war in Iraq." He smiled and then showed a little humility. "You all know that, well, things were difficult for me for a while. Every day when I sat down to write, the words just didn't come. But now, it's flowing. I'm writing up to two thousand words a day."

"What changed?" Kate asked.

"My creativity has returned. My mind is bursting with ideas." He looked around the table and then at his hands, his fingers drumming a tattoo on the table. "It's like magic," he said.

"That's great, Reggie. When it comes out, the book club will read it. We'd love to have you lead the discussion," Kate said.

They all nodded in agreement except for the Zen meditation teacher, who'd given his name as Seijun. With narrowed eyes, he was carefully studying Reginald Brim.

Chapter 28

Claire walked back to her car with another young woman, named Beth. Beth had dark hair in a bob, dark-rimmed glasses and a slight figure. Claire felt grateful for the company. The streets had quieted down and there wasn't anyone around. They chatted as they walked. Beth worked as a mortgage loan officer at a bank in Rosemary Beach. She was from New Jersey and had jumped at the chance to work in Florida. When they got to their cars, they exchanged phone numbers and planned to have dinner some night soon.

Heading home along 30A, Claire passed only one car. As she turned and drove down Lemon Drive, there were no lights to be seen. It was cloudy overhead and she could hear the moaning of the ocean as she approached the house. She opened the gate, drove into the garage and parked the car. As she raced up the steps to the coach house, she noticed a faint odor. She'd smelled it before. It had a sweet chemical tinge that she couldn't identify.

In her apartment, Claire double-locked the door, switched on the lights and threw her bags on the kitchen island. She was tired and hungry. She pulled out a frozen artichoke and basil pizza from the freezer and poured a glass of wine. While the pizza was cooking she got into her PJs and fluffy slippers. Tonight, it felt a little like winter. There was a strong wind off the Gulf and it was supposed to get down to the low fifties. She pulled the curtains closed and grabbed the wool throw Amy had given her.

As she ate her pizza and drank the wine, she scrolled through her texts. Amy had agreed to come over for dinner on Sunday. A client Claire had pitched yesterday asked her to return and talk further. Claire had followed Alexa's advice and chatted up this woman, and after an hour of gabbing, the client had become Claire's dearest friend. The shop, a relatively large one, sold outdoor apparel, leather jackets and fishing gear. The owner was interested in the buttery-soft brown and black bags.

Claire went to bed smiling. It had been a good day.

#

A loud bang woke her at two AM. She sat up abruptly, and thought she heard muffled voices. Nerves jangling, she got out of bed, went to the window and pulled back the curtains. Outside it was pitch black. She couldn't make out any movement. She walked to the living room, where the window gave a longer view of the coastline, but still saw nothing. From the kitchen window over the garage doors, she could make out the gate. It was shut and no cars were parked in the driveway. She was about to turn away when she noticed a light flickering in the entryway to the main house. It looked like someone was in there with a flashlight.

Had the owner arrived and parked in one of the garages? She unlatched the kitchen door to the garage and stepped out onto the landing. In the semi-darkness, she saw only her own vehicle. She shut the door and bolted it, then walked over to the door that led into the main house and pressed her ear to the wood. The low rumble of voices reached her. Claire carefully unlocked the bolt, undid the chain lock and pulled open the door. The voices were louder. It sounded like two or three men, arguing downstairs in the entryway.

Staying close to the wall, Claire took a few steps down the hallway. She was careful not to go too far, knowing the sensors would pick up her movement. Then the lights would go on and the music would start blasting. As soon as she could hear more clearly, she halted and listened.

"You shouldn't have brought him on. I don't trust him."

Someone mumbled in response. Frustrated, Claire strained to hear better.

"This is your second mistake…" Another indistinct reply.

"You'll regret it…"

"He's got two fish on the line—"

Claire heard a door opening. Cold air swept up the stairs, followed by a bang as the door to Claire's apartment blew shut.

"What was that?" a sharp voice said from downstairs. Silence fell, as if the intruders were listening. Claire crept soundlessly along the wall, back to her apartment. She entered the code, then slipped inside and quietly shut the door behind her. She pushed the bolt and slid the chain across. Then she leaned against the door, trembling, waiting for them to come.

Chapter 29

Claire didn't sleep much that night. For a long time, she sat and watched the door. Would someone creep up and stealthily turn the knob? Would they break the door down? Did they suspect she'd been listening to their conversation? Eventually, she got up and went to the kitchen for a drink of water. She peered out the window that gave a view of the brick drive, and this time didn't see any light in the entryway to the main house. Then her eyes caught a glimmer in the dunes. She squinted through the darkness, blinking, and thought she saw a man walking with a pin flashlight. His silhouette appeared and disappeared as he loped over the dunes. Arms wrapped around her chest, she watched the figure disappear into the night.

Later, lying in bed, she ran an internal battle with herself. Should she find another place to live? Was this coach house too dangerous? And yet, for all the odd occurrences, nobody had bothered her. Those men, whoever they were, hadn't come storming up the stairs. She should get ahold of herself.

She rolled onto her back and stared up at the ceiling. Should she call Leo? But what would she tell him? That she'd heard two men, maybe three, arguing in the house? She couldn't say who they were, or what they looked like. He would think she was nuts. She turned on her side.

And yet, what were they doing downstairs? And what were they arguing about? She tried to remember what little she'd heard...something about a guy they didn't trust...or that one of them didn't trust. What had the other man said? "He's got two fish on the line…" What could that mean? Her mind went around and around until she finally fell asleep at five AM. At six-fifteen the alarm went off. It was time to get up and get ready for yoga.

#

When Claire arrived at Sunshine Yoga, Amy was already there. She was stretching on her mat, trying to reach her toes. She beamed up at Claire. "Guess what? I've lost five pounds already!"

"Wow, that's great. Maybe I should try this Reelife stuff."

"Come on, Claire, you've got the perfect body. But you might think about taking the vitamins. I've got so much energy because of those. I feel fabulous." Then she took a good look at Claire and frowned. "You look strung out. Are you all right?"

"I'm fine. I probably just need one of your power drinks." Claire didn't feel like talking about her interrupted night. She rolled out her mat and lay down, stretching her full length. "So we're on for Sunday, right?"

"Yeah, but no carbs, okay?"

"Right, no carbs."

Rhea turned on the music, signaling the start of class. After a series of stretches and a Downward Dog, Claire stood up and glanced into the mirror. She saw Dax in the last row, studying her.

After class, Amy left quickly. They were taking inventory at Beach Mania that day, and she had to get to work early. Claire wiped her sweating face with a towel, then draped it around her shoulders. As she was rolling up her mat, Dax came over. "How are you? I haven't seen you around."

She kept her head down. "I've been very busy."

"How are sales going?"

"Pretty good. It's slow, particularly this time of year. A lot of places are closed." She stood up, tucking her mat

110

under her arm.

"You look tired," he said. "Something keep you awake last night?"

Why had he asked her that? "No, I just didn't sleep well."

"Are you feeling lonely out there? Have you thought about moving?"

Claire looked him in the eye. Was he smirking? "Is that some pick-up line? 'Are you feeling lonely'…no, I'm not lonely and I'm not moving. I'm perfectly happy right where I am." What business was it of his where she lived?

Looking irritated, he turned to leave. "Fine. Take care of yourself."

Claire followed him outside. He got into his car and peeled out onto 30A like some teenager pumped up on testosterone. What a jerk!

Chapter 30

At home Claire took a long shower and applied make-up, gently patting concealer under her eyes. To cheer herself up, she threw on jeans and a fabulous, new blue-green sweater she'd bought on-line that made her eyes look sea-green. As she put on a slim gold necklace her sister-in-law had given her, she thought about Timothy and Beth Ann and their brood. Maybe next summer they could come down for a week. What if she snuck them into the big house? Who would ever know? There was certainly plenty of room. On second thought, that would be an impossibly bad idea.

At the kitchen island, she opened her laptop and checked her schedule. She planned to zero in on several shops in and around Panama City Beach, working her way further east each day. By the time she left it was nearly ten o'clock. On her way, she drove past Kōfuku, and on impulse she pulled into a parking space. As she approached the shop, she saw Mandy dragging a mannequin wearing a long diaphanous dress out onto the porch. Mandy steadied the mannequin and looked up. "Hey, Claire. Good to see you." She arranged the skirt around the mannequin's feet. "Maura isn't back yet."

"I know. I just stopped by to say hi." Claire ascended the steps.

Mandy pushed back a handful of ginger curls. "How are things going?"

Claire shrugged. "Good days and bad days." She turned as another car pulled up. The driver's door opened and Seijun got out.

Claire felt riveted in her spot as he came toward the shop. He reached the porch and nodded a greeting. "Are you going to join us today?" he asked.

"Join you? No, I'm on my way to Panama City Beach."

"Come out back for a minute. We can talk." Seijun strode up the steps and held the door for her. He wore a sort of robe that made him seem even taller than he was. She followed him inside, through the shop and out the sliding glass doors at the back. Outside, he opened a cupboard near the wall of the shop and pulled out a box. "We need to feed the koi." He gestured toward the back of the garden. Dumbly, Claire followed him down the stone path through the carefully raked sand garden to the little bridge that spanned the koi pond.

"This pond is a miniature of the famous Kyoyochi pond that was built in the twelfth century in Japan," Seijun said. "There are beautiful gardens there and a temple."

"I know nothing about Japan," Claire said. "I'm sure it's beautiful."

At the summit of the bridge, Seijun opened the box and sprinkled a handful of nuggets into the water. Together they watched the fish swarm and gobble the food.

"These little guys are relatively new. This garden is protected by trees and a wall, but last spring a heron found our little pond and gorged itself on the helpless fish." He paused. "We are all helpless when the herons of life swoop down."

Claire didn't know what to say to this. She nodded, then asked, "What does your name mean in Japanese?"

"It means 'pure life.' The name was given to me when I was ordained."

"Pure life…that's something to strive for," Claire murmured.

"But difficult to attain."

They stood together in silence. To Claire's surprise, it felt companionable.

"You should attend my meditation sessions, Claire," Seijun said. "It would be good for you. I can see you are stressed."

Claire swallowed. "How…how do you know that?"

He turned to look at her. "You hide it well, but both times I've met you, you've radiated anxiety. Centering yourself and controlling your thoughts will bring you some relief."

Meeting his gaze gave her the same feeling she'd had before, as though he could see into her soul. It was frightening and comforting. She blinked and turned away. "I…I'll look into it."

"Good. I'll plan on seeing you next Monday." He tucked the box of fish food into a pocket of his robe, then went down the bridge and over to the gazebo. He sat on a bench and folded his hands, waiting for his followers.

Claire felt light, insubstantial. She floated down the path towards the shop door.

Chapter 31

The rest of the morning flew by. Claire made a small sale in the last shop she visited. The other three store managers had asked her to come back; which was a victory in itself. She felt she'd established a friendly relationship with each of them.

As she drove back down 30A, the conversation with Seijun flooded her mind. Seijun—pure life. He definitely had charisma. She felt drawn to the garden, and to the hope of mental peace. She'd read about the benefits of meditation and practicing mindfulness. Maybe it would help her manage her anxiety about her job, the strange voices at the house, and the gnawing memory of Daniel Rutherford's gruesome murder. She couldn't think of him as Boone Williams, somehow—only as Daniel.

It was two o'clock and she was starving when she arrived in Rosemary Beach. The Wild Olives Bistro on the corner of Barrett Square looked inviting. She could sit outside in the sun and relax. A cement truck and several construction vehicles were parked along the street across from the restaurant, but she found a space between two vans.

As she got out of the car, she noticed The Hidden Lantern bookstore under the portico. Claire decided to go in and get the next book for the book club. She could read it while she ate lunch. A friendly woman with granny glasses and rosy cheeks greeted her as she entered. "Can I help you?" She had a neat cap of dark brown hair and wore a button-down shirt and a khaki skirt.

"Yes, I'm looking for *Commonwealth* by Ann Patchett."

"Oh, yes. She's a great writer. Let me get it for you.

Have you read *Bel Canto*?

"No, I haven't," Claire said.

"You might consider it after you've finished this book." The woman walked to a table near the door and picked up a copy of *Commonwealth*. Claire noticed copies of Reginald Brim's *Glory Days Trilogy* on the table as well.

"I met Reginald Brim recently," Claire blurted out.

The woman grinned. "He's our local claim to fame. You know, he's finally writing a new book."

"Yes, that's what I heard." Claire handed the woman her credit card.

The woman swiped it and handed it back. "Reginald's wife is a friend of mine. She's glad he's conquered his writer's block. He's been a bear to be around." She rolled her eyes as she handed Claire her book.

They ended up chatting for a while longer. As they talked, Claire surveyed the store. She wondered if the owner would be interested in carrying Letízia tote bags or the backpacks. They could be marketed as a kind of book bag. She decided to come back another day and pitch the idea.

After leaving the bookstore, Claire found a table at Wild Olives and sat down. As she perused the menu, a familiar voice said, "Hello, Claire. May I join you?"

She looked up. Leo stood there in a suit and tie that reminded her of something her old boss, Randall Cunningham, would wear: well-cut and very expensive; though he filled it out much better than Randall ever had.

"Yes, sure. I'm having a late lunch." She smiled as he sat down. "You look nice today."

"I spent the morning in court. I was on my way back to the station when I spotted your car."

She handed him the menu, and they chatted until the waiter arrived. Claire chose a prosciutto, mushroom and goat cheese flatbread and iced tea. Leo ordered a hamburger and a beer. "How are you doing?" he said as the waiter hurried off. He loosened his tie. "Any more hitchhiker sightings?"

"No. The guy's probably left town." Claire laughed nervously. Should she mention the men in the house last night? She fingered her fork, turning it over and over.

As if he'd read her mind, Leo leaned forward in his chair. "I wanted to tell you that we haven't come up with any new information on the Bartholomew Group, but we're still working on it. The company represents a variety of investments and businesses, and has multiple off-shore accounts. The team is unraveling the mess." He patted her arm. "All this could take a while."

"I don't really care who owns it, but if I had an issue, I'm wondering who I could contact."

"Are you still convinced you want to keep living there? Have you looked into other arrangements?"

"No, but you're the second person to suggest that to me today. Maybe I *should* look into it." She sighed. "What about Daniel, I mean Boone Williams? How is the investigation going?"

"Nothing new to report. We don't have much to go on."

"Did he have any family? Maybe they could help."

"None that we've found." Leo shook his head. "I'd hate to add an unsolved crime to my record. We'll keep digging."

Claire was about to tell him about the men in the house the previous night when the waiter arrived with their drinks.

"Let's talk about something else," Leo said. "I'd like to forget about work for a while."

"I know how you feel." Claire sipped her iced tea.

As they ate, they discussed books, movies and the

117

Artist Festival that was weeks away. Claire was impressed by Leo's knowledge of the authors, artists and poets who would be attending. There was a lot more to this man than crime-solving.

It was nearly four o'clock when Claire said goodbye to Leo and started back to her car. As she drove back towards Lemon Cove, something that Leo said niggled at her mind. But for the life of her, she couldn't figure out what it was.

Chapter 32

The long weekend stretched out in front of Claire. Amy wouldn't be coming over until Sunday afternoon. In the past, she'd been grateful for a day or two at home. But today she felt as though she needed to fill the hours. While she drank a mug of coffee, she called her parents and had a nice, long talk. She kept her voice upbeat and told them about the successes of the week. She didn't mention the uncertainties of her living arrangement. Before she hung up, her dad asked her to send some pictures of the house and the area. She agreed to do so.

After the call, she dressed in running clothes and set off, jogging east along the shoreline. With most people gone, the beach was empty except for a few fishermen. They sat on stools, their rods bowed, the lines stretching into the surf. She used her phone to take a couple of pictures of the house and the beach.

There was a slight breeze and the morning light danced off the water. Despite everything, Claire felt glad to be in Florida. After twenty minutes, she headed back, passed her house, and kept going all the way to Lemon Cove, where she turned right and jogged down the sandy path that went along the inlet. Her running stride was smooth and she felt as though she was getting her rhythm back.

She ran along, feeling in the zone, when she heard footsteps pounding behind her. It hit her suddenly how alone she was. This early in the morning, the landscape was deserted. What if it was one of the men from the house, following her? Without turning around, she sped up, sprinting over a wooden bridge. Ahead, the trees bent over the pathway, casting deep shadows. She saw a bend and then another open stretch. She tried to pick up her speed but she was tiring. At the next wooden bridge, over a section of grassy marsh, a voice called out, "Hey, Claire. Slow down! It's Dax."

With a mix of relief and annoyance, she turned around. Dax was coming up behind her, panting and dripping sweat.

"You scared me," she gasped. "I thought someone was chasing me."

"I was, but you sped up. You've gained some momentum of late." Huffing and puffing, he drew up beside her and they slowed to a walk. "So what did you want?" she asked, not caring that she sounded rude.

Dax took a deep breath. "I'd like to invite you out to dinner tonight."

Claire stopped walking and stared at him, sweat dripping down her face. "Are you sure?"

He smiled "Yeah, I'm sure. Why would I invite you if I wasn't sure?

Part of her was thrilled, especially since she was dreading being alone for almost two whole days. The rest of her felt she should avoid this man. Her doubts must have shown in her face, because he said, "I know you spend a lot of time alone. I thought you'd enjoy some company."

Those words brought tears to her eyes. Yes, she was feeling alone. Without looking up, she nodded, afraid to speak in case her voice betrayed her. She wiped her eyes on her forearm. Dax stayed silent. She was touched by his kindness. Perhaps she had misjudged him.

They started running again and passed the spot where the rowboat was chained up. Further on, they approached a miniature latticed pavilion. Without speaking, they went in and sat down on the wooden bench. The water lapped against the pylons. Insects buzzed among the sea oats and a bird swooped down skimming the water.

Finally, she took a breath and said, "Yes, I would like to have dinner tonight. Thank you."

When she looked over at him, he was smiling. "I'll pick you up at seven."

Chapter 33

Just before seven, Dax called and asked if she wouldn't mind meeting him outside the gate. When Claire saw the lights of his car come around the dunes, she skimmed down the stairs, through the garage and out the gate, closing it behind her.

Dax reached across and pushed open the door. He was driving a black SUV with dark tinted windows. She slipped into the seat and pulled the door closed, then attached her seat belt. "Wow, where did you get this car? It's nothing like that snazzy red one you were driving before."

"I use this for business. It's great for transporting stuff."

She laughed. "Do you need to transport a lot of stuff as an insurance salesman?"

He grinned. "Okay, maybe I just like it. It's big and roomy."

Along Lemon Drive, all the houses were dark. "Where are we going?" Claire asked.

"The Bay. It's out on 331, on the water. It's a great spot for music and sushi."

Daniel had planned to take her to The Bay on New Year's Eve. Claire shivered, bringing her hand to her throat.

Dax glanced at her. "You don't like sushi?"

"No, that's not it. I love sushi." Her voice sounded weak. *Come on, Claire. Get ahold of yourself.*

"You've been to The Bay? You don't want to go back?"

She took a deep breath. "I was supposed to go there on New Year's Eve, but my date never showed."

"He stood you up? What a jerk."

122

Claire didn't want to talk about Daniel, or rather Boone, tonight. It would jinx their evening together. "Let's talk about something else." In the dark, she sensed Dax looking at her. She turned toward him and smiled. "Okay?"

"Okay."

#

It was a perfect night. When they arrived, they decided to sit outside and enjoy the music. They claimed two of the comfortable chairs set in the sand around a fire pit. Behind them, the water lapped softly. Claire had a glass of sauvignon blanc and Dax ordered a craft beer. The live band played a mix of blues, reggae and rock. Claire wrapped her pashmina around her, leaned back and relaxed, while Dax entertained her with stories about his childhood. He was one of six kids who'd gotten into all sorts of trouble growing up. Now they were spread out across the country from California to D.C. His parents had retired to Sarasota, and he spent time with them whenever he could. It sounded like a happy, healthy relationship.

Claire found she liked people who opened up about their families. In her experience, acquaintances who refused to talk about their childhoods and didn't get along with their parents were often unhappy adults. That made her think about Jeremy, who had basically disowned his parents. He'd never told her why but she'd always felt he must have had a miserable childhood.

After a while, they went inside and got a table. Claire let Dax order. He seemed to know the waitstaff and the bartender. This must be one of his favorite hangouts. They shared the Billy Roll, a delectable sushi dish, followed by delicious grilled snapper. Claire had another glass of wine and forgot about Daniel Rutherford.

"How is your business coming?" Dax asked.

"Mostly, it's going great." Claire told him about

Alexa's suggestions for cold-calling and about the successes and disappointments she'd had that week. "As they say, no one said this would be easy, but I'm feeling pretty good so far." She pushed her plate away and pulled her wine closer. "Thanks for a wonderful dinner." She looked into his eyes. He had nice eyes, warm and kind. She felt a bit nervous, so she prattled on. "I also attended a book club Thursday night. Have you read *Glory Days* by Reginald Brim?"

"No, I'm not much of a reader, but I do know Brim lives around here."

"Apparently, he hasn't written anything for five years. But in the last few weeks, he got back on track. He'll probably write another blockbuster."

"Interesting." Dax was studying his glass. "What sort of person is he?"

"Off the record, I found him overbearing. Like he knows everything about writing." She sipped more wine. "I guess he knows a lot, but still. He kind of took over the book club."

Dax kept his eyes on his beer glass. "Did he explain what turned him back on?"

"He said it was magic. Maybe that means his muse." She finished the last drop of wine in her glass. "Actually, he's married."

Dax looked up. She couldn't decipher his expression. Claire babbled on. "Of course, that doesn't mean he doesn't have a muse on the side. Like maybe a gorgeous blonde in a bikini." She giggled.

Dax wasn't smiling. "Claire, have you thought about moving?"

"Yes and no. I just love my place but sometimes I do feel...alone." She paused. Could she tell him about the night visitors? About Daniel? About the mysterious Bartholomew Group?

Dax covered her hand with his large, warm one. When Jeremy held her hand, it always felt unnatural. She looked at their hands and then up into Dax's eyes. They held worry and concern. "Please think about moving to an apartment somewhere else," he said. "It would be safer."

She pulled her hand away. Once again, a man was telling her what she should do and where she should live. He'd done it before, she belatedly recalled. "The house is surrounded by a high metal fence and there's a security system."

"Still, think about it."

Claire sighed. "I'll think about it." *But I won't do it.*

When they got back to Citrus Haven, they sat for a minute in the car. Dax turned towards her. "Thanks for a wonderful evening."

"That's my line." Claire paused. "I guess we can be friends now, right?"

"Yes. Good friends, I hope." He leaned over, took her hand and kissed her gently. His lips were soft and warm. She responded with a deep yearning. They kissed for a long time, their fingers intertwined. Then Claire pulled away. "I better go inside," she whispered. She opened the door and got out. "Thanks again."

"I'll watch while you go in. Wave to me once you're inside." He gestured up at the kitchen window. "I want to know you're safe."

Chapter 34

Sunshine poured through the window Sunday morning. Claire lay in bed for a while, thinking about her date last night. She'd misjudged Dax. He had turned out to be thoughtful, kind and interesting. She didn't want to dwell on his kisses, yet there had been something magical about them. His lips were soft, yet demanding. It was a long time since she'd kissed anyone except Jeremy. If she was honest with herself, she'd never enjoyed Jeremy's love-making. It had always been something to get through. Why, oh why had she stuck with him all those years?

She got up, ate breakfast, went for a run and did some shopping. In the late afternoon, Amy came over from Grayton Beach. She was breathing hard when Claire went downstairs to open the gate. Claire looked around and realized Amy's car wasn't there. "You ran over? Wow, you really are into this fitness kick. Good for you!"

Amy beamed while she caught her breath. Claire led the way upstairs. When they were in the kitchen Amy said, "I've lost two more pounds. My pants are loose around the waist. This Reelife is magic."

"It sure sounds like it. Would you like a glass of water?"

"Yes, please. A big one."

While Amy downed her water, Claire pulled a package of grouper filets out of the fridge. She put it on a tray with a platter of sliced red and yellow peppers, eggplant and zucchini. There was also a bowl of fresh fruit. "I planned a healthy dinner for us. I'm going to grill the fish downstairs. We can sit outside and chill."

That morning Claire had checked out the backyard grill. It worked well and was hooked up to the main house gas lines. Daniel had told her she could use it. Of course, Daniel's words were of little value at this point. She handed Amy a bottle of Pinot Grigio. Then they went through the door into the main house.

Before they headed downstairs, Amy walked into the great room to look around. She was caught off guard when the music blasted and the lights came on. She started to laugh. "Claire, this place is amazing." She walked across the room and over to the large kitchen windows. "I can't imagine living here. It's awesome." She wandered over to the windows that flanked the fireplace. From there, the treetops of the National Forest spread out below. She stood there looking down at the patio and outdoor kitchen. "Hey, look. There's a path that leads from the backyard into the woods."

Claire came over and looked down. "I remember seeing the gate. We'll have to check it out." She wondered who used this path. It looked well-trodden through the grass before disappearing into the woods.

As they started downstairs to the ground floor, Claire felt a momentary sense of trepidation. At the landing, she stopped and turned to Amy. "I haven't told you, but there were some men in here a couple of nights ago. I heard their voices. I don't know what they were up to."

Amy stopped on the bottom step and looked at Claire. Her pretty face reflected concern. "Hey, you're white as a sheet. If you're frightened living out here, find someplace else to live."

"I did. Today. I was going to tell you about it. I visited some apartments up on 98. But they were so dark, with no views. In one of them, there was this putrid smell." She shivered. "I didn't want to live there."

"Hmm…" Amy sniffed the air and held up a finger. "There's a smell here, too. What is it? Kind of sweet and pungent at the same time."

"I don't know. I've noticed it, too. It comes and goes." Claire led the way down the short hall. "Come on, let's go outside."

Amy lingered on the bottom step. "What's that noise? It's coming from down there." She pointed at the hallway to the storage rooms.

"I don't know. A refrigerator or a generator? Let's

get out of here."

Reluctantly, Amy followed her out the back door. Claire put down her tray on the granite counter top and got busy preparing the grill. Amy poured them each a glass of wine. They chatted while Claire grilled the vegetables and fish. Then they sat down at the patio table and ate dinner. It was getting cooler and the light was fading. They both pulled on sweatshirts.

Claire poured herself more wine. Amy covered the rim of her glass with her hand. "I don't need those extra empty calories."

"Neither do I, but the wine calms me down."

"Claire, if you're nervous about living here, you've got to find a new place."

"Let's not talk about it, okay?" Claire took a sip of wine. "So, tell me about the man in your life."

"He's really nice to me." Amy looked down at her clasped hands in her lap. "He doesn't have much money, so sometimes I have to pay if we go out." She sounded apologetic, as if she was making excuses for this mystery man.

"What does he do?"

"I don't really know…some kind of sales. But he meets with his business associates a lot."

Claire had her suspicions about this guy. She wondered if this was another con man.

Amy was chattering on. "He likes to meet new people. I've been introducing him to friends and acquaintances, you know, people who frequent Beach Mania. Last night, he came over to meet Françoise. They hit it off. Afterwards he went over to her house to look at her paintings. I guess he's into art. I didn't go because I had to work this morning."

"Right." Claire wondered why she wasn't one of the

chosen few to meet Mister Wonderful. As Amy talked on and on about this guy who seemed to be taking advantage of her, Claire studied the back wall of the house, mentally measuring the distance from the laundry room windows to the far edge of the wall. It struck her that the storage rooms were enormous, at least as large as the expanse of the living room and kitchen on the first floor. What could be stored in there?

Chapter 35

In the early morning, Claire heard voices emanating from the main house. She lay still, sheets clutched to her chest. Were they coming closer? Were they outside her door? She strained to listen. Gradually, the voices faded. She didn't fall asleep right away, but lay awake evaluating her options.

Should she contact Leo? Would he think she was nuts? Whoever was in the house had the codes and thus the right to come in. Could these unknown intruders have anything to do with Boone Wilson's murder? Boone, as Daniel, had rented her this place. If the police started watching the house, they might come closer to solving the crime.

Then, she thought about Dax. Could she ask his advice? But she knew what he would say. He'd tell her to get the hell out of there and move to a dark, depressing apartment somewhere else. Her stubbornness took hold, and she let out a sharp sigh. She didn't *want* to leave this place. Doing so felt like surrender, and she was tired of surrendering. *Nothing's actually happened, no one's hurt me or anything. It's just…weird. I can handle weird. Can't I?*

Eventually, she fell back asleep.

#

Claire woke up at eight o'clock, too late for yoga. She texted Amy and told her she'd slept in. Then she went into the kitchen to brew coffee. An unpleasant odor of cooked fish rose from the unwashed dishes in the sink. She rinsed them and put them in the dishwasher. She drank a cup of coffee and poured a bowl of cereal, but pushed it away after a couple of bites. She felt too wound up to eat. Maybe she should try Zen meditation to settle her down.

She looked at the clock. She didn't have much time if she wanted to make it.

Claire ran into the bedroom. She pulled on jeans and a sweatshirt, threw water on her face and combed her hair into a ponytail. Then she was out the door.

As she drove, she considered her day. She had an appointment at eleven at a store in Gulf Place. Then at two she was supposed to meet Alexa and discuss the child-size purses. Lucca had given her the go-ahead. Today she and Alexa would talk pricing and quantities. She could fit in Seijun's class this morning.

Claire arrived at Kōfuku a little after nine. She pulled into a parking spot on the side of the building and made her way around back. As she entered the garden, she looked over at the little gazebo and saw three people sitting on the stone benches. It was a peaceful scene. She pulled out her phone and took a couple of pictures of the garden and the gazebo. Her dad had been stationed in Japan for a while. He would be interested in the garden.

Seijun saw her and beckoned. She hurried down the twisting path through the sand garden and ascended the steps of the gazebo. Seijun stood and took her hand. "Welcome, Claire. We are glad to have you." His voice was warm with sincerity. "Let me introduce you to William and Celestina."

Claire nodded at the other two students. William was a heavyset man with a bushy black beard and a remarkable ski-jump nose. One blue eye looked directly at her, while the other seemed to be examining the ground. *Strabismus*, Claire thought. The man's stubby, red-knuckled hands rested on his knees. Across from him, Celestina smiled and said hello. She wore a tie-dyed tee-shirt over a multi-tiered full skirt. Her lovely face was a perfect oval. Her long straight hair was parted in the middle and covered her shoulders. Silver hoops dangled from her ears. She looked like a flower child from the 1960s.

Seijun handed Claire a round black pillow and gestured for her to sit down across from him. She placed the pillow on the cement bench and settled herself.

"This is Claire's first time at meditation. Let me take a minute to explain our ritual to her." Seijun shifted his gaze to her face. "It's important to practice meditation every day—say, five minutes or so at first. The right state of mind emerges naturally from deep concentration on your posture and breathing. Now fix your eyes on a spot on the ground."

Claire tried to get comfortable on the pillow, her back straight, her eyes focused on a spot on the stone floor.

"It's hard at first, but practice makes perfect," Celestina said, and giggled. Her feet peeked out from under the voluminous skirt, and Claire noticed several silver rings on her blue-nailed toes.

Seijun smiled. "Shall we begin?" He tapped his phone, and there was the sound of a tinkling bell. "At the first bell, we take several deep breaths. At the second bell, we meditate.

At the second bell, Claire began to count her breaths. *One, two, three, four...*she heard a bird chattering in a tree overhead. She started again. *One, two, three, four...* an airplane rumbled in the distance. *One, two, three, four, five...*she wondered if Alexa would put in a big order today for the child-sized purses. Claire sighed and looked over at Seijun, whose eyes were deep pools staring in front of him. She glanced at William. He seemed to have entered a trance. Claire closed her eyes a minute and then took another deep breath and glanced at Celestina. The other woman's pretty face was serene. Claire decided to envision each number in her mind. She visualized the number one, then the number two. She did this up to ten and then started again. For a brief time she lost herself in the process, until the bell tinkled on Seijun's phone. Another quiet moment passed.

Then Celestina piped up. "How did you do?"

Claire rolled her eyes. "Not well at all. My mind kept wandering. This has got to be the hardest thing I've ever tried."

"You'll get better. Keep at it," Celestina said.

Chapter 36

Claire rushed home after the meditation session. She had promised Seijun she would practice, and he'd said he would send her a text with the Insight Timer app he'd used. She would have her own little tinkling bell to time her sessions.

At home she showered and changed into pink jeans and a breezy, striped tunic. If she hurried, she would just make her eleven o'clock appointment. She ran back down the stairs, hopped in the car and tore down Lemon Drive towards 30A. In the rearview mirror, she checked that the garage door and gate were closed. She was five minutes down the road when she realized she had left behind the box of purses she'd planned to show the new client. Furious with herself, she turned around in a gas station parking lot and headed back home. She was going to be late for the appointment now. Hopefully she could salvage it.

As she raced around the dunes, she spotted a birdwatcher crouched by a hillock of sand and scrub grass. She'd seen them around before, in the woods and on the beach. Funny, though, this guy seemed to be zeroing in on Citrus Haven.

She looked ahead to the house. The gate was open and a dark blue van was parked near the front door. The garage door nearest the entrance was open and a man was coming out, carrying a box. As she got closer, she could read the signage on the van. *Pool Service and Repair.*

She drove up beside the van and got out of her car. "Hi," she said, trying to keep her voice friendly. "What are you doing?"

The man, Hispanic and on the short side, flashed a big smile. "Check water pipe." He nodded towards the open garage door and placed the box in the back of the van. Then another man came out with another box. His face went blank when he saw Claire. The first guy said, "No problems. All set." He smiled again. Then he reached into the truck and began to reel in some tubing. Claire took a couple of steps around the van and saw that the tubing stretched towards the pool.

The second man shut the garage door using the keypad. Finished with the tubing, the first man slammed the van's double doors. With more smiles, both men got in the truck and took off. Everything had happened so fast, Claire had said nothing and done nothing. On the other hand, she was just a tenant in the coach house. She didn't have the right to question these men. As they drove away, she wondered what was in those boxes they'd hoisted into the van.

Frustrated and perplexed, she raced up to her apartment to grab the box of purses she'd prepared. Then she was back in the car and on her way. She glanced over at the dunes and saw they were empty now. It was too bad because she could see a hawk careen through the sky in a dizzying spiral. But, the bird watcher had disappeared.

Chapter 37

The week flew by. Every morning when Claire got up, she tried to meditate for five minutes before heading out to yoga class. Sales did not go well and she got turned down again and again. When she got home in the late afternoon, she pulled on her running gear and pink sweatshirt and went for a run on the beach as the sun set.

She spoke briefly to Amy, who was in a state of euphoria. She'd lost three more pounds and was bouncing with joy, actually hopping up and down on her toes as they talked. They agreed that Amy would come over for dinner again that Sunday.

Dax didn't show up at yoga all week. Claire knew he covered the northern part of Florida and was often traveling. He must be out of town. After their date, she'd hoped he would call to talk, or at least say hi. She was more disappointed than she wanted to admit. Maybe the attraction she'd felt that night was one-sided. Maybe she wouldn't hear from him again. Why didn't he call?

Then there was Citrus Haven. She couldn't help remembering the pool van. It seemed a little too convenient that the workmen had shown up right after she left. They had obviously been surprised to see her. She remembered the man in the dunes with the binoculars. Had he been spying on her comings and goings? The feeling that she was being watched was nerve-wracking.

#

In the late afternoon on Wednesday Claire met Beth in Rosemary Beach. Beth had texted her that morning to ask her if she wanted to go for a walk on the beach after work. It had taken her a minute to remember she'd met Beth at the book club. They agreed to meet in Barrett Square near the town hall.

"I really needed to get out of that bank and get some fresh air." Beth said as they headed down the wooden walkway to the beach. She took a deep breath and looked up and down the coast. The water made gentle ruffles on the shore and small clouds scooted through the sky. "I didn't get a break all day."

"I know what you mean. I used to have a corporate job and some days I didn't even know what the weather was like outside."

"What did you do?" Beth led the way down towards the shore where the sand was packed and easier to walk on.

Claire gave a short recital of her former life as well as a rundown on what she was currently doing in Florida.

Beth giggled. "I'm kind of like you. I left my family and friends to come down here and try something new. In New Jersey, I felt like I was stuck in my job. But I didn't have a boyfriend or anything."

"Are you glad you made the move?" Claire asked.

"Yes, I've made new friends, I got a raise this year and I think I've got a chance to move up in the bank. They're building branches up and down the Panhandle."

"That sounds promising." Claire zipped up her windbreaker.

"Oh, listen. Before I forget. On Friday, I usually meet a couple of girls for a drink. I think you'd like them and I know they'd like you."

"Sounds good. Were they at the book club?"

"No, I met them in Panama City Beach at a fundraiser for breast cancer. We walked together." She turned to Claire. "My aunt had breast cancer. I wanted to do something."

Claire nodded. "I understand. It seems as though every family is touched by cancer these days."

They trudged along without speaking. The sky had taken on tones of red and orange and the breeze had picked up. They turned around and headed back the way they'd come.

"Anyway, let me tell you about the girls. Louise is knock-down gorgeous. She even modeled for a while. She works at the front desk of an upscale resort, though I think she has some family money and doesn't really need a job. She's super-nice. Then there's Olivia. She's kind of feisty, but really nice, too. She's on the road a lot as an inspector for McDonald's. Every few months, the inspectors make a surprise visit and check each restaurant's cleanliness and food preparation. But Olivia's in town this week."

It was getting chilly and they picked up their pace. "We're meeting at The Wine Bar in Watercolor on Friday, about six-thirty, if you want to join us," Beth said.

"I'd like that." They had arrived back at the stairs that led up to the street. Above them, a couple was walking down. The man had round glasses like those Daniel Rutherford had worn. The sight of them gave Claire a start. Once they'd passed the couple and were up on Water Street, Claire turned to Beth.

"This might sound weird but did you ever see a guy around Rosemary Beach who looks like Harry Potter? You know, the glasses and the hair; maybe wearing a white suit?"

Beth turned to face her, eyes wide. "Yes, I did. It was *so* weird. He was standing outside the bank, talking to someone...someone I'd seen before." She frowned, as if trying to remember. "Why? Who is he?"

Claire's heart beat faster. "Oh, just a guy I met. You're sure you don't remember who he was with?"

138

Beth shook her head. "No, just somebody I've seen around."

#

Wednesday night, Claire awoke to the sound of a door banging shut and muffled voices. She got up and went to the kitchen window, but saw nothing. Then she spent a few minutes listening at the door to the main house, it was quiet. Amazingly, she was able to get back to sleep.

Chapter 38

On Friday when Claire came home, she had the weird sensation that someone had been in her apartment. She stood on the threshold of the kitchen, looking around. A cupboard door under the sink was partly open. But she could have done that herself and forgotten about it. Feeling foolish, she called out, "Hello?" Of course there was no answer. She went through the kitchen, living room and bedroom. Everything was in its place. Nothing seemed to be missing. And yet she felt sure someone had been there. Was she going crazy?

That evening at six o'clock, she drove over to The Wine Bar. Cooler weather had swept down from the north, so Beth and her friends had chosen to sit inside. Claire found them at a high table with stools in the corner. The place was busy, with a friendly vibe.

Beth greeted Claire and introduced her friends. Louise was a willowy blond with a marked Southern drawl, who welcomed Claire with a slow smile. Beside her sat Olivia, fast-talking and intense, her pretty heart-shaped face surrounded by a mass of dark curls.

After Claire had ordered a carafe of wine, they all quizzed her about her move to the Emerald Coast and her business. Olivia and Louise had plenty of suggestions about possible customers for her merchandise. Then the conversation turned to the artist festival coming up. "I'm dreading the traffic on 30A," Louise said. "All those tourists. The festival brings in tons of 'em."

"You might not be thrilled, Louise, but the restaurants and shop owners are elated. Think of all that money rolling in." Olivia rubbed her thumb and forefinger together.

"What I love about the week is the music. The Hungry Tigers will be performing on Friday night in Seaside after the poetry reading," Beth said.

"Oh please. The Hungry Tigers! They're like a bunch of mewling tomcats," Olivia scoffed. "I'm going down to The Hub in Waterside. They've got a jazz trio performing Friday night." Her dark eyes flashed with excitement.

Claire poured the last of her wine into her glass. She took a sip and looked across the room. To her surprise, she saw Celestina sitting with Françoise at a table in a far corner. No longer a flower child, Celestina wore a black pencil skirt and a silk blouse of iridescent blue, with dangly earrings and an exquisite matching necklace. Beside her, Françoise was dressed in black. The two women were deep in an animated conversation.

"Excuse me a minute. I see some friends over there." Claire smiled at her companions, got up and walked over to the corner table. As she approached, the two women stopped talking and Celestina blushed.

Claire felt embarrassed. Clearly, she'd intruded on a private conversation. "I just came over to say hi. Sorry if I interrupted you," she said.

"No, no," Celestina said. "Sit down. Do you know Françoise Lambert?"

"Yes, I do." Claire smiled at Françoise, who had recovered her poise and was smiling broadly. She looked jubilant, in fact. "How are you, Françoise?"

"I am doing, what you say, awesome. Yes, I am awesome. Sit down and have a glass of champagne." She gestured to the bottle of Veuve Clicquot on the table.

"I've got a glass of wine over there. I don't want to disturb you, I…"

"We are celebrating, Celestina and I. We are

celebrating my new painting. I have finished it this week and I have a buyer. He is a man from New York. A very important man who loves my work."

"Congratulations. That sounds great." Claire turned to Celestina. "What about you, are you a painter too?"

"No, I design jewelry."

"Did you design that necklace and earrings? They're lovely." The shade of blue in the blue-and-silver design matched Celestina's blouse.

Celestina smiled. "As a matter of fact, I did."

"I can see both of you are terrifically talented. I've never been artistic myself but I admire gifted artisans."

The two women looked at each other and laughed. Claire felt as though she was missing something, as though they were sharing an inside joke.

Chapter 39

Claire slept late Saturday morning. She lay in bed for a while after she awoke, thinking about Dax. A week had gone by since they'd had dinner together. She wondered where he was this weekend.

While she ate a bagel and cream cheese, Lucca called and they tied up some loose ends. Gabriella's region was going strong, Lucca said. February was Miami's high season. Along with Canadian and New England snowbirds, there were a hefty number of European and South American tourists. Claire felt a little jealous. Next week, she would need to make a killing.

When she got off the phone, she decided to drive down to Seaside to the farmers' market. The girls last night had said they shopped there every week. The produce was organic and locally grown.

There was a party atmosphere in Seaside. Everyone was there, young families with children, seniors and millennials. Under a row of canopies, local farmers and purveyors of a variety of products peddled their wares. Claire noticed fresh greens, organic honey and artisanal cheeses. She took a picture of a little girl holding a baby lamb in her arms. Under one canopy, two men were selling Sri Lankan fast food. The aroma was deliciously spicy. Claire bought the makings for a tossed salad and a box of fragrant strawberries. She also bought a wedge of brie.

As she headed for her car, she ran into Kate from the bookstore. Kate looked drawn and pale, like she might be coming down with something. "Hi, are you in a hurry?" Kate asked.

"No, I'm just putting this stuff in the car."

"I'm on break. I was going to get coffee at Amavida.

Could you join me?"

"Sure." Claire put her purchases in the trunk, then followed Kate across the street. Once they got their coffee, they sat outside at a small table.

"Thanks so much for inviting me to the book club. I really enjoyed it," Claire said.

"I'm glad you came." Kate smiled wanly and took a sip of her cappuccino.

Claire noticed her hand was shaking. "Are you all right?"

Kate looked out across the street towards the bustling market. Tears welled up in her eyes. "No, I'm not. Something terrible has happened."

Claire leaned forward, her eyes filled with concern. "Tell me about it."

"Do you remember Reginald Brim, the author who had lots to say at book club?"

"Sure, he's the one who wrote *Glory Days*."

"Right." Kate's lips trembled. "Well, he died Thursday night. They say it was a heart attack."

Claire sat back, shocked. "Oh my gosh, he looked healthy a week ago. I remember he seemed thrilled to be writing again."

"Yes, his wife said he'd been obsessed with this latest book and was working long hours. Wednesday evening, he told her to go to bed; he wanted to stay up because he was on a roll. Apparently, he was writing more than two thousand words a day. Early in the morning, she got up and was worried because he hadn't come to bed. She found him slumped over his computer. He was dead."

"Were you close to him?" Claire asked.

"Not really, but when things weren't going well, he hung out in the bookstore. He could talk for hours." Kate smiled briefly. "We hadn't seen much of him lately. I was surprised when he came to book club...and that he'd read the book."

"He wasn't that old, was he? Maybe in his fifties?"

"Yes." Kate sighed and dabbed her eyes with a napkin. "I'll miss him. He was a fixture in our community. He'd lived here for years."

They fell silent for a few minutes, sipping coffee and contemplating the busy market. Kate sighed again. "Life just goes on, doesn't it?" She gave a raw laugh. "Here today, gone tomorrow."

"Yes. Sudden death puts life in a new perspective," Claire said. "Carpe diem and all that."

A shadow fell over the table. She looked up. A man stood there, silhouetted by the bright sunshine behind him. After a moment she recognized Seijun. He was holding a cup of coffee in one hand and a newspaper in the other.

"By the looks on your faces, I see you've heard about Reginald," he said.

"Yes. It was a real shock." Kate sighed again and then looked at her watch. "Sorry to rush off. I've got to get back to the bookstore." She gestured to Seijun. "Here, take my chair."

He sat down as Kate rushed away. He crossed his legs and held the coffee cup to his lips. As so often in his presence, Claire felt simultaneously drawn to him and discomfited. This man had some kind of power over her. She felt as though he could divine her every thought.

"I suppose you barely knew the man," Seijun said, continuing the conversation about Reginald Brim.

"Yes, I met him just the once."

"He came to meditation sessions for a while last fall, looking for a way to break his writer's block. He had been drinking a lot and he wanted to handle his problem differently. Apparently, meditation was not the answer.

145

After several weeks, he just stopped coming."

Claire nodded. They sipped coffee and gazed across the street. After a minute or so, Claire searched for something to break the silence. "So where do you come from? Were you born around here?"

Seijun turned to her, looking surprised at the change in subject. "I'm from California originally. I've been here about eight years."

"How did you become a Buddhist priest?"

He took his time answering. "I was experiencing some difficulties in my life and a friend suggested Zen meditation. One thing led to another. I worked with some profoundly spiritual priests that turned my life around. I spent time in a monastery, studied the teachings, and eventually I was ordained."

Claire thought about this. "This might be an impertinent question, but how do you support yourself? Do people pay you for meditation instruction?" Suddenly she realized he hadn't charged her for the session she'd attended. "I didn't pay you anything the other day."

He chuckled. "No one pays me. I do the meditation sessions to help people, to share my knowledge, to lead them into a more meaningful life." His eyes narrowed as he studied Claire. "I'm a part-time art dealer. I handle Asian antiquities; statues, scrolls, jade, things like that."

"I have to admit, I know nothing about Asian art."

"Not many Americans do. As you might have guessed, I'm a mixed-breed." Seijun raised his eyebrows and smiled at Claire. "My mother was Japanese and my father was an American serviceman. They met in Japan when he was stationed there. Anyway, I have relatives that work with me who live in Japan. They supply me with Japanese, Chinese and Korean treasures."

"Do you have a shop around here?"

146

"No, we sell solely online. I work with my brother, who still lives in California."

"How do you transport the statues and scrolls? They must be valuable."

"Yes, they are. Items are often vacuum-packed. Sometimes temperature is an issue, or humidity. It's like coddling a baby." He chuckled.

Claire realized she was feeling more comfortable with Seijun. They talked for about twenty minutes more. Then he had to leave, to do his shopping before the market closed. "I hope to see you Monday, Claire. Have a good weekend."

"You, too. See you Monday."

Chapter 40

At home Claire stashed her groceries and then looked around the apartment. With the sun shining in, she could see dust motes floating in the air. It had been nearly a month since she'd moved in and she'd never properly cleaned the place. She remembered that Daniel had told her she could use the vacuum cleaner and supplies on the ground floor. While she was down there, she would put in a load of wash.

In the bedroom, she gathered up her laundry and stuffed it into a couple of plastic bags, then carried them out and opened the door into the main house. For fun, she decided to see if she could trick the sensors. Staying close to the wall, she crept down the hallway. When she got near the great room, she crouched low and scooted around the corner to the staircase. No lights came on and no music boomed. She felt a thrill of triumph at successfully outwitting the system.

In the laundry room, Claire started her wash and then wandered over to the window. Across the yard on the other side of the fence lay the opening into the woods that she and Amy had noticed last Sunday. Where did it lead? She went down the short hallway and opened the door that led to the outdoor kitchen.

The day was warm and sunny with little puffs of clouds skittering through the sky. Claire walked over to the fence, where she found the keypad to the back gate under a metal cover. Taking a chance, she tapped in the code for the front gate. The back gate clicked open. Moving quickly, she followed the sun-dappled trail straight through the sea oats that surrounded the property and into the woods. The path was well-trodden, the sandy soil compact. She heard the buzzing of insects and twittering of birds. After fifteen minutes, the lapping of water reached her ears. She must be nearing Lemon Cove. Then the path opened up and she nearly fell flat on her face. There, right in front of her was the wooden upside-down rowboat. That gave her a jolt. The path led directly to it. Why? Who used it? Where did they go? More to the point, what was going on at Citrus Haven? Clearly, someone was using the boat. Someone was using the path. Someone—several someones—had come skulking around late at night. And some fake pool maintenance guys had taken boxes from the house. Something illegal must be going on. She would have to tell Leo.

As she walked back to the house, clouds moved in and obscured the sun. Suddenly the woods seemed dark and sinister. She kept looking behind her, to the right and the left. Was someone following her? Her spine tingled and beads of sweat gathered on her forehead.

Finally she reached the fence, tapped in the code and pushed open the gate. She let it clang shut behind her and ran across the yard and into the house, where she collapsed onto the entryway steps, breathing heavily. What was the matter with her? She had to get ahold of herself.

As she sat there, she became aware of the low hum Amy had noticed. It sounded like the rumble of a motor. She sat still, listening. What could it be? Maybe some sort of refrigeration. She stood up and shook herself. She had come down here to get the vacuum so she could clean the apartment. It was time to get to work.

Claire walked down the hallway to the utility closet and pulled open the door. She found the light switch on the wall. The vacuum cleaner was on the floor next to a bucket and mop. On the shelves were rags and various bottles of cleaning products. In this little room, the motor-hum was much louder. It seemed to emanate from the storage room next door. Under the reverberation, she thought she heard a voice, muffled as though wrapped in cotton. She looked around the little room, inspecting the walls, but saw nothing unusual. Then she looked up and saw a grate along the juncture of wall and ceiling. The sounds must be coming through it from the storage rooms.

Claire grabbed the vacuum, some rags and a bottle of all-purpose cleaner. After quietly closing the utility-room door, she wheeled the vacuum over to the elevator and pushed the button. Over her shoulder, she looked back down the hall, expecting someone to charge out of the storage room and down the hallway. The elevator took forever to arrive. Upstairs, she walked quickly down the short hall pushing the vacuum before her. Once in her apartment, she pulled out her phone.

Chapter 41

Leo returned Claire's call late in the afternoon. He apologized but said he had been extremely busy with important matters. From the sound of his voice, she guessed he didn't think her call was that significant. She explained about the night-time visitors, the path to the cove, the boat, the storage room and the pool maintenance guys.

He listened without interrupting her. When she'd finished, there was a long silence. He was obviously thinking through what she'd said.

"Leo, something is going on here."

"You're probably right. But I don't think the sheriff's department is in a position to do much about it. We can't come charging in there without a warrant and no judge is going to issue one on the information you just gave me."

"Even though Daniel, I mean Boone Williams, was killed? Something illegal must be going on."

"You don't know that. This could be a business venture. Maybe they store pool cleaning supplies in those storage rooms."

"Who, and why do they come here at night?"

"Maybe it's the owners of that house. They have a right to come and go as they please."

Claire felt frustrated. "Couldn't you assign some officers to watch the house and see what's going on?"

"Claire, we're stretched thin as it is. I don't have the manpower to monitor Lemon Drive day and night. That's nuts."

Claire sighed. Maybe she was being unreasonable.

"Listen, Claire. I appreciate you keeping me abreast of the situation. I feel bad to let you down. I really do." He sounded sincere. "You're obviously upset." He took a breath. "I think you should move out of there."

"I've looked at apartments. Nothing is as nice as this."

"What about Destin or Panama City?"

"I like it here. I like the friends I've made in the area. I just don't want to move."

"I've got to get back to work," he said bluntly.

"Okay. Thanks for returning my call. Oh, by the way, what about the Bartholomew Group? Any news?"

"The money trail is murky. We still don't have a full understanding of the company." She could sense his irritation. "I've got to go." He hung up.

Claire sat on the sofa, staring at the phone. Was she being foolish? She lay back against the pillows. Her gaze took in the stunning living room, the sleek, kitchen, the cozy bedroom. Then she looked out at the white sand and the aquamarine water. Seagulls were sailing through the sky. It was picture-perfect. She loved it here.

She closed her eyes and tried to analyze her feelings. When she dipped down into her psyche, she knew that part of the reason she didn't want to move was because she felt uncertain about the future. In her heart of hearts, she wasn't convinced that her job with Letízia was sustainable. The way things were going, she couldn't survive on the commission. By summer she might have to go back home, so why move to another place? Maybe her decision to relocate down to the Emerald coast had been solely based on a desire to escape Jeremy, Safetynaps and Randall Cunningham. Maybe she didn't have it in her to start over. Maybe she would fail.

Chapter 42

Amy arrived Sunday in the late afternoon. Again, she had

jogged over from Grayton Beach. As she came up the stairs, she giggled at Claire. Her upbeat mood was infectious. She was good company, Claire thought.

Claire had decided they'd have dinner in the apartment. She'd set the table in the dining area with blue and white placemats. and placed in the center a small vase of pansies from the garden. She'd prepared a big salad with the greens she'd bought at the Farmer's Market. On the counter, she had the makings of a simple lemon chicken dish, plus a bottle of sauvignon blanc and two wine glasses.

"Would you like some wine?" Claire asked after Amy sat down on a stool at the counter.

"Sure, but only one glass. I've been drinking Perrier at the bars."

"So you've been hanging out at bars," Claire said as she poured the wine.

"Just a couple of times a week. I go with this friend of mine. He likes to try different places. You know, to meet different people."

"Is this the secret boyfriend you don't want me to meet?"

Amy blushed, looking down in confusion. "Well, I can't explain it. He doesn't seem to…uh…want to meet you."

Claire felt annoyed. "That's crazy. He doesn't even know me to dislike me. Who is this guy, anyway?"

Amy picked at a hangnail. "I don't know. He's weird, I guess." She looked up at Claire. "Can we talk about something else?"

"Sure. I'm sorry. I didn't mean to beat up on you." Claire reached over and patted her arm. "So, how's business?"

"Slow, but we're filling the shelves and back room with merchandise. Only ten days until the Art Festival.

Usually we do really good that weekend and several days before and after. Alexa hired a designer to help dress the windows."

"Sounds like you're busy."

"Yes, but tomorrow's my day off, so I can chill." Amy took a small sip of wine. "How's the purse business going?"

"I have good days and bad days. I've started to worry whether I'll be able to pull this off. I've got savings but at some point I need to be making more money."

"Come on, Claire. It's been less than a month. Give yourself some slack. You know this is the slow season. Business owners are nervous about stocking too much merchandise. When things are flowing, they'll be more likely to invest in inventory. Remember, March is a big month and it's a little over a month away. Families come down for Spring Break. Everyone will need a new handbag." She smiled at Claire.

"I hope you're right." Claire got up, went around the island counter and opened the refrigerator.

"Can I help you?"

"Sure, you can toss the salad while I whip up the chicken."

Ten minutes later they sat down at the table. Amy admired the table setting. "This looks so pretty. Next week, I'll invite you out to dinner. I'm just not into cooking."

"Fine by me." Claire cut a piece of chicken and topped it with a slice of mushroom.

"We could go to Stinky's. Have you been there?"

"No." Claire giggled. "Is that really the name?"

"Yes, and the food is fabulous."

They continued to talk about the latest fashions. Amy regularly spent time on the internet looking at clothes, accessories and jewelry. She watched the award ceremonies on TV and knew what every movie star wore on the red carpet. "It's fun, but it's also good for business. Beach Mania has to know where fashion is moving."

"I'll bet you're a big help to Alexa."

"Yes, we spend a lot of time discussing trends. When she goes to Europe or New York she takes pictures of shop windows and people in the street. We try to stock the merchandise that's hot."

They finished the meal with a bowl of strawberries, so sweet and delicious they didn't need sugar. After dinner they relocated to the sofa. Claire had more wine and Amy drank a cup of coffee. Claire decided not to talk about Citrus Haven and the fears she was experiencing. She wanted to have an upbeat evening.

"I saw Françoise Friday night. She seemed in much better spirits," Claire said.

"Yes, she's flying high. Apparently, her mojo is back. I think Aunt Irma misses her, though. Françoise used to come over every day, sit on the porch and mope. Now she's too busy."

"Speaking of talented people, did you hear about Reginald Brim?" Claire asked.

"Yeah, it's a shock to our little community. He was our resident writer."

They were quiet for a minute. Then Amy yawned and rubbed her eyes. "I'm sorry but I need to head home."

"Do you want me to drive you?"

"No, I'll jog. I've got a flashlight."

"If you're sure…"

"I'd love to borrow a sweatshirt, though. It's gotten chilly out there. I forgot to bring one."

"No problem." Claire went into the bedroom and grabbed the pink hoodie she always wore. She'd washed it yesterday.

Amy pulled it over her head and down over her chest and hips. She grinned at Claire. "I don't think I could have fit into this a few weeks ago."

Claire grinned back.

As Amy raced down the stairs, she yelled up at Claire, "See you tomorrow at yoga."

Chapter 43

Monday morning, Claire felt energized. Dinner with Amy had been fun. She got to yoga early and chatted with Rhea while she waited for class to begin. As they discussed Rhea's latest decorating project, Claire kept a lookout for Amy or Dax, but neither one of them showed up. Class began and it was brutal. At the end, Claire felt as though she'd stretched every muscle in her body. On the way home, she texted Amy, but got no response right away. As for Dax, *get real and forget him*, Claire chided herself. She might never see or hear from him again.

Zen meditation was a quiet affair. Celestina didn't show up. It was just Claire, Seijun and William. The two men were in deep conversation when she arrived but broke it off as she approached. Seijun started the session with the tinkle of the little bell on his phone, and for twenty minutes, Claire battled her uncontrollable psyche. Her brain wanted to ponder the happenings at Citrus Haven or her relationship with Dax or her schedule for the day. After about fifteen minutes, she finally managed to let go of her worries and calm down.

Back in the car, she plugged in the address of the Grand Boulevard shopping mall. It was an upscale complex on the way to Destin. She spent most of the day there, laying the groundwork for future visits and making contacts. Since there were fewer customers in January, the managers of several stores took the time to chat with her. Although she made no sales, she snagged one firm appointment with the owner of an independent shoe store for the following week. Before starting the car for the drive back to Lemon Cove, Claire checked her phone. Still no text from Amy. That was odd. She always responded quickly.

157

On her way home, it began to pour. The sky was a molten grey and shafts of lightning zigzagged to earth. The road was slick and visibility was poor. Claire was relieved when she finally pulled into the garage. Upstairs, she shucked off her clothes and wrapped up in her French terry robe, then poured herself a glass of wine. She was still charged up, so she opened her laptop and got to work. She liked to make notes while the day's visits were fresh in her mind. Periodically, she checked her phone. No texts. She remembered Amy had said this was her day off. Maybe she'd spent the day vegging out and had turned off her phone.

It was after eight when Claire finished evaluating Monday and scheduling Tuesday. By now, she was starving. She finished up yesterday's leftover chicken and ended up eating the rest of the strawberries with a scoop of vanilla ice cream.

Wrapped up in the throw Amy had given her, Claire picked up her copy of *Commonwealth*. Outside the wind whistled and the waves crashed on the shore. Several times she glanced at her phone. She couldn't concentrate on the book. The darkness of the rainstorm seemed to penetrate her cozy coach house, bringing with it a sense of impending doom. *Stop it*, she told herself. *It's just a storm.*

Chapter 44

Tuesday morning, the weather was still grey and gloomy. As Claire fixed coffee, she debated whether or not to go for a run down the beach. She decided to wait until she got home. Hopefully by then the weather would clear up.

She was on the road by nine-fifteen and arrived in the outskirts of Destin for her first appointment. Between stores she glanced at her phone, but there were still no texts from Amy. The number of a contact from yesterday, a Mrs. Robbins, turned up. She called the number, and Mrs. Robbins asked if Claire could come by with samples on Thursday. As the woman specified the reference numbers from the catalogue, Claire couldn't help smiling. This looked like a deal.

It was two o'clock when the call came. Claire had stopped in a Starbuck's for an iced green tea latte. She didn't recognize the number, and debated whether to respond. Then she went ahead and pushed the green button on her phone.

"Claire," a vaguely familiar voice said.

"Yes. Who is this?"

"Oh, Claire. Something terrible has happened." The caller choked back a sob.

Suddenly Claire remembered the last time she'd heard those words--when Kate told her Reginald Brim had died. "Who is this?" she asked again.

Another sob. "It's Alexa, Alexa Cosmos. Did...did you hear?"

"Hear what?" For Alexa to call, this must be about Amy. She must have had an accident, on the way home from the coach house, or—

"It's Amy. She...she killed herself." Alexa broke

159

into tears.

Claire froze, cold with shock. This couldn't be. Amy, a suicide? But she was so happy. Claire remembered her face before she'd left on Sunday night. It had radiated joy and hope.

"Claire, are you there?"

"Yes. But I don't believe it. She was at my house Sunday night. We talked for ages. She was just so happy about life."

"I know. I thought so too. But she must have been hiding her real feelings."

"How did you find out?"

"The...the...police, they were here. Someone found her body on the beach near Lemon Cove." Alexa began to sob again. "I have to go, Claire. We'll talk." Then she rang off.

Claire left the Starbuck's and got into her car. Blindly, she drove home. No tears came, just an empty feeling. How could this be? Sunday night, Amy was exuberant. Suicide? It was impossible. She remembered her premonition last night and shivered. She'd known instinctively something was wrong. But this...?

She was just turning off of 98 towards 30A when her cell phone rang. In her nervousness, she fumbled the phone and it fell to the floor. Reaching down, she felt around under her seat. The phone stopped ringing as her fingers grasped it. She looked at the screen. It was Leo.

The phone rang again. She pressed the green button. "Leo? It's about Amy, right?"

"Miss Hall. This is Sheriff Martin."

"I know. What can you tell me? What happened?" The words tumbled out of her mouth."

"We'd like to talk to you about a police matter."

"I want to talk to you, too. Something is really

160

wrong. Amy couldn't—"

"Miss Hall, could we meet you at your house? We have some questions about an ongoing inquiry."

His unusual formality rattled her even more. "Leo, what's this 'Miss Hall' business? It's me, Claire."

His tone was pure business. "When would you be available?"

"I'll be home in fifteen minutes."

"We'll meet you there. Thank you." He hung up.

Claire felt light-headed. Her world was spinning out of control. She drove home mechanically, braking, accelerating and finally turning on to Lemon Drive. When she came around the dunes, she saw a patrol car pulled up in front of the iron fence. She punched in the code and the gate swung open. The police car followed her into the expanse of the driveway. She opened the garage door and drove in. As she got out of her car, she looked back. Leo and another officer exited the police vehicle. The officer was a young rookie, slim with a crew cut.

Leo and the young man approached her. "I'm Officer Martin and this is Officer Rawlings," Leo said, as if they'd never met. What was going on? "We have several questions to ask you."

Claire looked from one man to the other. "Okay, come upstairs." They followed her into the garage and up the metal staircase that led to her apartment. The stairs vibrated as they all trudged upstairs. Inside the apartment, she threw her bags on the counter and turned to face the two men. At that moment, realization hit, and she felt the tears coming. This was where she'd last seen Amy. Sunday night came flooding back. She covered her face with her hands and sank into an armchair, sobbing.

The policemen were quiet for several minutes. Then Leo said, "I'm sorry, Miss Hall. I know this is difficult but we need to ask you some questions about Sunday night."

Claire knew she needed to pull herself together. She looked up and wiped her eyes with the heels of her hands. Leo and Officer Rawlings stood uncertainly in the middle of the room. Claire got up and went over to the counter to grab some tissues, then gestured to the sofa. "Please sit down." Leo sat on the sofa and the young officer took a stool by the kitchen island counter. He pulled out a notebook. Apparently, he was the designated note-taker.

Claire sat back down. She dabbed at her eyes and blew her nose.

"Can you tell me about Sunday night? Irma Müller told us Amy came here in the late afternoon."

"Right. We had dinner and talked. It was a quiet evening."

"Did Miss Sullivan seem unusually depressed, nervous, distracted?"

"No, that's the thing. She was happy…joyful. Things are…were going really well in her life."

"Often a depressed person hides their feelings. They put on a good face to mask their suffering."

"No, this wasn't like that. Amy had a job she loved, a new boyfriend, and she was getting in shape. It was real."

Officer Rawlings was scribbling down notes. Leo leaned forward, his elbows on his knees. He looked at Claire with sympathy. "How long have you known Amy?"

"About a month."

"So you really didn't know her well?"

"No, but…"

"Did you know her boyfriend?"

"No, I didn't, but…"

"What time did Amy leave your house?" Leo asked.

His questions were so rapid, Claire felt frustrated. "I don't know…maybe about eight. We were talking and then she yawned and said she wanted to go home."

"Why did she run home along the beach?"

"Like I said, she was into this fitness thing. She'd already lost weight and she wanted to keep it up. I offered to drive her, but she said no."

Leo rested his hands on his knees, looking at her intently. "You said she had a boyfriend. What did she tell you about him?"

"Well…not much. I never met him, but…"

"But what?" Leo's eyes zeroed in on hers.

Claire got up and walked to the window. She needed to calm down. She looked out at the beach, which held a rosy glow in the dusk. She sighed and then came back and sat down. "She told me he didn't want to meet me. Not why, though. It was all a big mystery."

Leo sat back, as if considering that.

"Can you tell me how she died," Claire asked quietly.

"She over-dosed. Heroin," Leo said bluntly.

Claire shook her head. "I can't believe it. I would have noticed if she was high or into drugs. I used to have a friend who was a cocaine addict. I'd recognize the signs."

"You told me you only met Amy a month ago. You didn't know her past." His expression was one of pity and disbelief.

"What about her past?" Claire retorted.

"She had a history. At sixteen she was arrested for possession. At seventeen she was picked up with a bunch of kids, all of them high on cocaine. At nineteen, she passed out in a bar, high on lord knows what."

"So what? She was a teenager. She told me she did stupid stuff as a kid. But she'd become a responsible adult. Talk to Alexa Cosmos. Amy was her trusted assistant. Talk to Irma, for God's sake."

Leo shook his head. "We found a syringe in her hand. We'll check for fingerprints. But I'm sure they'll be Amy's."

"So you think she came her for dinner, made plans with me for next week. Told me she was happier than she'd ever been. And then she went out and killed herself." Claire's voice rose an octave. "That is *crazy*," she spat at Leo. "What about the boyfriend? I think he was taking advantage of Amy. Maybe he killed her?"

Claire glanced over at the rookie. He looked flustered as he scribbled down her every word.

"We haven't found him yet. Irma said his name was Ronny. She didn't know his last name."

"You've got to find him. I bet he was involved," Claire said, but she felt Leo wasn't listening to her.

Chapter 45

After Leo and Officer Rawlings left, Claire stood in the middle of the living room, her arms at her sides, her hands clenched. Tension made her want to scream. She was positive Amy hadn't committed suicide. Maybe they had only been friends for a month, but Claire felt she knew Amy better than Leo did. Somehow she had to prove she was right. Amy deserved that much.

In the bathroom, she splashed cold water on her face. Her hair was a mess. She brushed it and pulled it into a ponytail. Then she picked up her purse and headed for the door.

#

When Claire arrived at Aunt Irma's house the porch light was on but no one was sitting outside. She walked up the steps and looked in through the screen door. It was dark in the living room, but she could see light emanating from the kitchen. She heard the sound of quiet voices and cutlery on plates.

"Hello, it's Claire Hall," she called out. "Can I come in?"

"Sure," someone yelled. "We're back here."

Claire walked down the hall and into the dimly lit kitchen. Irma was seated at the kitchen table with Françoise and two other neighborhood ladies. They all had cups of tea. On the table were plates of chocolate chip cookies and slices of banana bread. The four women looked up as Claire entered the kitchen. Irma stood up and reached out her arms. Claire walked over and they hugged.

"I'm so sorry, Aunt Irma. Amy loved you like a mother." Claire felt tears in her eyes.

Irma held Claire tight. "I know she did and I loved

165

her like my own daughter." They eased apart and Irma patted Claire's shoulder. She grabbed a tissue from a box on the table and blew her nose, then gestured to an empty chair. "Here, sit down. My dear friends are keeping me company." Irma gave a wobbly smile to the women around the table.

"Would you like some tea?" a neighbor lady asked Claire.

"No, thank you." Claire clasped her hands tightly.

"Did Leo Martin talk to you?" Irma asked.

"Yes, he did." Claire didn't know whether she should voice her suspicions here. Maybe the pain was still too fresh.

Then Françoise blurted out, "Did he tell you it was suicide?"

Claire glanced at Aunt Irma, who looked pale and exhausted. Was this the time or place for this discussion?

Françoise continued. "It is, what you say, bullshit? Amy did not kill herself. She was too content in life."

Claire nodded. "I agree, it wasn't suicide. But Sheriff Martin seems to think so."

"He must have proof," Irma said.

They fell silent, each caught up in their own thoughts.

"Claire, how was Amy Sunday night? Was she upset about something?" Irma asked.

"No, she was on cloud nine; happy about her diet, her job and her boyfriend. The mystery guy."

"Ah, yes, I didn't like that young man. There was something off about him," Irma said.

"You did not understand him, Irma," Françoise said. "He was an aesthetic. I found him agreeable."

Irma rolled her eyes. "An aesthetic? Now *that* is BS."

"What was his name? I'd like to talk to him," Claire

said.

"Ronny," Irma said with disgust. She looked over at Françoise. "Do you know his last name?" The Frenchwoman shook her head, drumming her paint-spattered fingers on the table.

Claire had a thought. "Could I go upstairs and look through Amy's desk? Maybe she has his name and number written down."

"Sure, but hurry up. The police are coming back to go through her rooms. They'll probably be off limits then."

"Thanks." Claire grabbed a cookie and headed upstairs.

Amy's apartment was made up of two rooms and a bathroom. The living/dining/kitchen area had previously been the master bedroom. A sofa and chair faced a TV on one side of the room. A corner had been made into a postage-stamp kitchen with a fridge, microwave and hotplate. Under a window was a small table piled with magazines.

A wide doorway led into the bedroom, which looked like something out of an L.L. Bean catalog. A pretty quilt covered the queen-sized bed, and a rag rug lay on the floor. A blue glass lamp with a flowery shade stood on the white bedside table. She could imagine Amy here, sitting up in bed, reading before she went to sleep. A lump rose in Claire's throat. She swallowed hard and turned away.

She went into the bathroom and opened the medicine chest. On the shelves were aspirin, Advil, a box of Band-Aids, toothpaste and a toothbrush. She felt uncomfortable going through Amy's belongings. Her friend had been dead only forty-eight hours and here Claire was, pawing through her stuff. It struck her that she should probably be wearing latex gloves like the detectives on TV shows.

Under the sink were boxes of tampons and cleaning

products. The shower held bottles of shampoo, conditioner and body wash. Amy's make-up was organized on a little table beside the sink. Claire saw nothing out of the ordinary.

Back in the bedroom, she opened the closet and shuffled the hangers across the rod. She noticed two outfits that still had tags. They were size six. Amy had probably planned on fitting into those dresses by summer. On the floor were sandals and flip-flops but no running shoes. Of course—they'd been on Amy's feet. Claire shivered and continued her search.

The bedside table drawers held some tissues, cough drops and a couple of packages of condoms. Probably the mysterious boyfriend slept over now and then. Claire slammed the drawer shut. She went through the dresser and found a small photo album at the back of the sock drawer. She paged through it and recognized a young Amy, maybe ten or twelve, standing beside a blond woman. There were pictures of Amy as a little girl at the beach and on a slide in a park. Claire bit her lip. What about Amy's mother? Where was she? Someone would need to contact her.

Claire shoved the pictures back under the socks and then stood still in the middle of the room. What was she looking for? Something that would give her a clue as to what had happened to Amy. Maybe there wasn't anything to find.

Back in the main room, she walked over to the mini-kitchen and looked in the cupboards. Two shelves were filled with Reellife products: shakes, bars and vitamins. The refrigerator was full of them, too. Amy must have bought a carload of the diet supplements. The freezer contained several Lean Cuisine meals and a tray of ice. Claire felt incredibly sad. All of Amy's hopes and dreams had been shattered by death. Tears sprang to Claire's eyes, and this time she didn't try to hold them back. She hadn't admitted the truth until now—but Amy had been murdered, and Claire needed to find her killer.

She looked around the living area one more time. The small dining table, piled with magazines, caught her eye. She walked over and leafed through the fashion magazines and copies of *People*. Peeking out between two copies of *Vogue* was a yellow legal pad. Claire pulled it out. On the top sheet was a list of names. Claire flipped the page and saw that the list continued on the following sheet. The names appeared to have been written down at different times, some in pencil, some in blue ink and some in black.

The crunch of tires outside made Claire glance out the window. A police cruiser had pulled up and a tall man got out. It was difficult to see in the dark, but she thought it was Leo, probably back to go through Amy's possessions. Claire glanced quickly at the names. The third one down was Reginald Brim. What could this list be about? She needed to study it and find out who the people were. But Leo would be up here any minute. He probably would tell her she was obstructing justice and tampering with evidence. Claire pulled out her phone and took pictures of the names on the two yellow pages. Then she slipped the pad back among the magazines.

She heard Leo talking to Aunt Irma. He would be coming up the front stairs any minute. Claire tiptoed into the hall, shutting Amy's door behind her. She slipped into the second bathroom and shut that door, flushed the toilet, and then ran the water in the sink. As she came out of the bathroom, she caught sight of Leo. He'd gone into Amy's apartment and was standing in the middle of the living room, looking around. He eyed Claire with suspicion.

"Hi," she said. "You're not going to find anything here. Amy didn't commit suicide. It was murder."

Chapter 46

Claire tossed and turned all night, her mind churning as she slept. She dreamed that Amy was alone on the beach and a black shadow came up behind her bearing a giant syringe. Claire woke up drenched in sweat. Later, she fell into a fitful sleep.

#

At six-thirty, the alarm went off. She only had a few minutes to get ready for yoga. A headache throbbed behind her eyes, and it was tempting to stay in bed, but she got up and pulled on her yoga outfit. Twenty minutes later she was out the door.

The class had just started when she entered the studio. Rhea nodded to her and Claire nodded back. She didn't know if Amy's death was public knowledge but she didn't want to be the one to inform the group. She took a spot in the back and tried to concentrate on the poses, but could only make a half-hearted effort. When the session was over, she picked up her mat and was ready to fly out of class when Rhea caught her arm.

"Claire, I'm so sorry about Amy. I heard about it last night. I can't believe she took her own life."

Without thinking, Claire blurted out, "She didn't, and I'm going to prove it,"

Rhea frowned. "What do you mean?"

"Amy was very happy. Everything was going well in her life. I think someone killed her and made it look like suicide."

Rhea stepped back, a shocked expression on her face. She probably thought Claire was losing it.

At home, Claire poured some cereal into a bowl but was only able to eat a few bites. She pushed the bowl away and sat for a few moments gazing out at the water, her mind blank. Then she sighed and shook herself. She had to get ready for the day. That morning she would be in Destin, where she had several stores on her radar. She needed to concentrate on her job and set Amy's death aside. In the evening, she would spend time studying Amy's list of names. After that, she planned on going into Seaside and asking around.

The morning was uneventful. Claire made stops in three stores. The manager at the first one was snippy and Claire couldn't develop a rapport. In the second, the shop assistant spent a long time discussing the weather and telling Claire about her aches and pains, but she didn't seem interested in talking about purses. In the third, Claire hit pay dirt. The Sweet Sands Shop belonged to a lively middle-aged couple, Tom and Ann Bergner. They were both grey-haired and wore sky-blue polo shirts and khaki shorts, and were so in sync that they finished each other's sentences. Claire figured this must happen when you spent all day and all night together.

While Tom manned the shop, Ann went through the Letízia catalogue and asked to see some samples. Claire ended up bringing in several boxes. She spent a few hours chatting with Ann and filling out order forms. The Bergners wanted a nice variety of summer bags. They knew their market well and assured her they would be buying more purses in the future.

After the business was complete, the Bergners invited Claire out for dinner that evening, but she begged off. Tom helped her carry her box of samples to the car. "Keep in touch, let's have a rain check for that dinner." He placed the last box in the trunk.

"Will do, and thanks so much for the order. It's been great doing business with you." They shook hands, and Tom headed back toward the gift shop.

As Claire swung her laptop into the back seat of the car, her phone rang. "Claire? Are you inside your car?" It was Dax.

"No. Why?" She drew a deep breath, ready to ask him why he hadn't called until now, but he cut her off.

"Say 'Hello Mother.' Then step away from your car. Don't say anything until you're fifty feet away."

"I..."

"Say 'Hello mother' and start talking to her. Get away from your car."

Irritated, and mystified, she did as he asked and headed down the sidewalk in front of the strip mall. She waved and smiled at Tom Bergner, who was watching her from the gift shop window. He must be wondering what in the world she was doing. When she was forty or fifty feet down the sidewalk, in front of a Japanese restaurant, she said, "Okay, I'm at least fifty feet away. What's going on?"

"Thank you. You're still in Destin?"

"Yes, and I just made a great, big, fat sale."

"That's great, Claire." He sounded as though he could have cared less. His next words changed her annoyance to alarm. "Listen, you're in danger. There's a tracker on your car. There might also be a listening device. That's why I asked you to get away from your vehicle."

"What?" Claire was incredulous.

"You need to follow my instructions. Get in your car and drive to the Publix Grocery Store down the street. Do a little shopping. Then drive to O'Shea's Irish Pub. It's west of the strip mall where you are. Go in and sit at the bar. I'll meet you there. You probably won't recognize me."

"How do you know I'm at a strip mall?"

"I'm tracking your car, just like they are."

"Who's *they*?"

"I can't tell you now."

"What's with all this cloak and dagger stuff?"

"I'll explain at O'Shea's. See you there." He hung up.

Chapter 47

Claire walked back to her car. Once inside, she felt strange. The BMW no longer seemed like the safe haven it had been. How long had people been tracking her? How long had they been listening to her conversations? Sitting in her own car, she felt like she was in alien territory. It was alarming.

She found the Publix easily. As it turned out, she needed some groceries. Still feeling strange, she wandered up and down the aisles, putting canned soup, milk, cereal, cheese and fresh produce in her cart.

Back in her car, the groceries loaded in the trunk, she typed *O'Shea's Pub* into her GPS. As she drove, she imagined someone watching her every move and listening to her phone calls. Had they heard her bragging to Lucca or complaining to her mother? What had she said to Amy?

Fifteen minutes later, she parked outside O'Shea's. It was four in the afternoon, not the lunch or dinner hour, so there weren't many cars in the lot. The interior of the restaurant was dark after the bright sunshine outside. It took a moment for her eyes to adjust. She made her way to the bar and sat down in the middle. A skinny old guy on the far left was nursing a beer and talking to the bartender. After a minute, the bartender came over. He was handsome, almost pretty, and wore a sparkling diamond in his ear. "What can I get for you, miss?"

Claire realized she was hungry since she'd skipped lunch. "I'd like a Diet Coke and a Reuben, if it's on the menu."

He grinned. "It certainly is. We've got the best corned beef in the state of Florida, the creamiest cheese and the longest-aged sauerkraut. You'll love it, lass." He spoke the last sentence with a fake Irish brogue.

Claire had to laugh. This guy was a charmer. "Aged sauerkraut? That's new to me."

He brought her the Diet Coke right away. She took a long drink. Then she turned on her stool to look around the restaurant. Some couples were enjoying a late lunch. Were any of them there to spy on her? Nervously, she drummed her fingers on the sleek wooden counter.

On the wall above the bar were three TV's. Two of them displayed sporting events. The third one was tuned to the news but the sound was off. From the captions, the current story was about a renowned sculptor. The screen showed images of two pieces of art: a lion springing on a gazelle and a black marble elephant nudging a baby elephant with its trunk. Each piece was packed with emotion; the lion exuded fearful power, the elephants radiated tenderness. Then the picture switched to the exterior of a row house. It reminded Claire of someplace in New York or maybe Baltimore.

The bartender brought her an enormous sandwich with a mountain of French fries. She took a bite of the Reuben and wiped her mouth. As she picked up a fry, she became aware of a man approaching the bar. She glanced over. He was large and overweight with a considerable paunch. Under a blue baseball cap, he had bushy white eyebrows and a full white beard. He wore an old plaid shirt over a grey tee-shirt and cargo shorts. The guy pulled himself up on a stool next to her.

"Hi there," he said loudly.

She didn't respond.

"Hey honey, how about a beer?" His arm brushed hers and she pulled away. He called out to the bartender, "Bring me a Bud, my man. I'm parched."

How was she going to extricate herself from this pushy guy? Where was Dax? Perspiration beaded on her forehead. She took another bite of her sandwich but the corned beef stuck in her throat. She gulped Coke to wash it down.

"What's your name, honey?" Bud Man was breathing heavily.

Claire did not feel like getting into a conversation with this guy. "Marina," she said. Where had that name come from?

"Marina, that's real pretty." The bartender brought Bud Man his beer. He guzzled half of it. "Hey, could you turn the sound up on that song? I love that song." It was Bruce Springsteen singing "Born in the USA". The bartender looked around the nearly empty restaurant, then reached under the bar. Springsteen filled the room. The bartender went into the back, and Bud Man leaned over and said, "Claire, it's me."

She turned to look at him. She recognized the voice, but not the body. "Dax?"

"Look annoyed," Dax said.

She pulled away from him and shot him her best angry stare.

"In a minute, I'm going to put my arm around you. I'll be dropping several items into your purse."

Claire looked down at her purse, which sat open on her lap.

Dax chugged some more beer and clapped his hands. " 'Born in the U S A,' " he sang. Then he lowered his voice and hunched over his beer. "There'll be two burner phones. My number is programmed into both of them. This afternoon, go running east on the beach. It's safe. There'll be fishermen. Call me then. Do *not* use the phone in your car or the coach house. I'm sure your apartment is bugged…maybe a camera there, too." He sang some more, then lowered his voice again. "After I accost you, move to the end of the bar."

A minute later, his arm went around her shoulders and he belted another verse in her ear. She put on a show of shaking off his arm. "Leave me alone," she hissed. Then she took her plate and glass to the far end of the bar.

The bartender came back and looked from Claire to Dax, scowling. "Did you bother this lassie? For shame."

Claire glowered. Her eyes sent poison darts at Dax.

He laughed. "That girl is colder than a rat's ass in January."

Chapter 48

When Claire got back in the car, she placed the doggy bag containing her sandwich on the seat beside her. After she'd escaped Dax's clutches, she couldn't bring herself to eat. She sat for a moment, staring blindly out the window. What was happening to her life? Her precarious living arrangement, the deaths of Daniel and Amy, her uncertain job, and now this cops-and-robbers game with Dax. She raked her fingers through her hair. What had she gotten herself into?

Before starting the car, she opened her purse. Dax had dropped in two cans of wasp spray, two burner phones and printed instructions that repeated what he'd said at O'Shea's. He'd added the admonition: *Don't talk to anyone before you talk to me.*

Claire drove home in a haze. She knew she was overreacting, but she felt as though she wasn't alone in the car. The thought of being tracked and spied upon unnerved her. Who was it? Who cared where she went and what she said? She felt like she was being sucked down into a quagmire. She opened the window and let the cool air flood the car, taking deep breaths.

At home Claire, made two trips to carry up the groceries, her computer bag and purse. After she'd stowed everything away, she went into the bedroom to change. Dax had said there might be a hidden camera. She took her running clothes into the bathroom to undress. Before leaving the bedroom, she pulled a fanny-pack from the closet and attached it around her waist. In the kitchen, she rummaged in her purse and pulled out one of the slim cell phones and a canister of wasp spray. She put them in her fanny-pack and headed out.

The breeze felt brisk and the sun hung low in the sky. When Claire hit the sand, she began to run as though chased by demons. Ahead, she noticed three fishermen spaced along the shore. Dax had said they would be there. Who were they? The police? The FBI? Some secret organization?

After she passed the first fisherman, who had two lines stretched into the surf, she slowed down. On her left was an area cordoned off with yellow police tape that fluttered in the breeze. This must be the spot where Amy had been found. The surrounding sand bore the prints of heavy boots and the tracks of numerous vehicles. Claire studied the dunes beyond. She envisioned Amy's murderer hiding behind a sandy hillock, syringe in hand. *He wore a mask and came up behind her. With the wind, she couldn't hear his approach. And then she whirled around and he plunged the needle into her arm...*

Claire stood there, seeing it all in her mind. Tears pooled in her eyes and ran down her cheeks. It was unbearable to think she and Amy had been laughing together just a few days ago. She turned away, wiping her eyes with the sleeve of her shirt. Then she took out the unfamiliar phone, turned it on, found the contact list and punched in Dax's number.

He picked up immediately. "Claire, are you all right?"

She felt a sob in her throat. "No, I just walked past the place where my friend Amy was killed."

"Killed? I heard it was a suicide."

"No, I'm sure someone killed her. I just have to prove it." She drew in a deep breath. "So no, I'm not all right. I feel like I've been drawn into some mysterious criminal plot."

He sighed. "In a way, you have. I'm sorry, Claire."

"What's going on?"

"I have a lot to explain. Unfortunately, I can't get together with you so we'll have to communicate by phone."

She felt anger and angst percolating. "Okay. Explain."

"Let me start from the beginning. In the last year, several artists, writers, and musicians have succumbed to heart attacks. The culprit is a drug known on the street as RBBs, right-brain bombs. Components of it are produced in South America, then brought to this country and combined into a capsule. The chemical combination is unstable and the capsules must be ingested within a month. An overdose can trigger cardiac arrest."

"Right-brain bombs? Why would anyone take them?"

"Apparently, the drug increases the ability to think creatively and enhances the imagination. Musicians can feel the music more intimately and perform with clarity. Writers find images and stories flooding their brains. Artists can better visualize the essence of a drawing or painting. Trouble is, they're highly addictive. Artists are initially delighted with the free flow of creativity but then they run riot and overindulge, or they keep the capsules too long and poison themselves."

Claire walked slowly past another fisherman. He glanced at her and then back at his lines. "Is that what happened to Reginald Brim?"

"Yes. And Aart De Vries, the Dutch sculptor who died two days ago in New York."

Claire remembered the TV coverage she'd seen at the bar. "I saw something about him this afternoon."

"Here's the deal. We think a cell of RBB producers is here on 30A. Specifically, they're manufacturing the capsules at Citrus Haven."

Claire walked more quickly. She couldn't think of a thing to say.

"Did you hear me, Claire? They're producing these drugs underneath your coach house."

"I heard you." She felt her heart beating faster.

"These are very dangerous individuals. We think your rental agent was part of the gang, but got taken out for some reason. Are you listening?"

"Yes, I'm listening.

"The drugs are expensive. But artists are willing to sell their souls to feel regenerated."

Claire remembered Brim's excitement when he'd told the book club about his new book. "Don't they realize the dangers?"

"Apparently, when they experience the effects and start producing high quality art, they don't want to stop taking the stuff. Our sources think this crime syndicate might be based right here. If we bring down the local big gun, we can destroy the organization."

Claire thought of the Bartholomew Group, her landlords. Hadn't Leo Martin said their financials were hard to trace? They must be intricately hidden in off-shore banks and blind trusts. Were they the syndicate? If so, the criminal gang owned Citrus Haven.

She passed another fisherman, a short and pudgy guy sitting on a folding stool. She noticed a bulge in his back pocket. It hit her that he was probably armed and there to protect her. Instead of reassuring her, the idea increased her nervousness. She looked up and down the beach and at the dunes. Anyone could be hiding there. She realized she'd arrived parallel to Grayton Beach, and turned around and headed back. "So why don't you just raid the place and close them down?

"Because we want to get to the kingpin. And we

don't know who he is. The network is tightly knit. They sell by word of mouth. We haven't been able to crack the web of distributors."

"Are you working with the local police?"

"No, this is an FBI investigation. Currently, we're keeping it under the radar."

"Is this why you've been hanging out in Lemon Cove?"

"Yes."

"Have you been spying on the house? I thought I saw someone in the dunes the other day."

"That was the day you left and came back ten minutes later. They thought you'd be gone for the afternoon. Those so-called pool men had to hustle when you surprised them."

She knew she should keep her mouth shut, but she couldn't help it. "And our date at The Bay…were you pumping me for information?"

He stayed silent a moment. Then he said, "Yes and no. I wanted to encourage you to get the hell out of the coach house." He paused and then continued softly, "But I also wanted to be with you. I enjoyed our time together, Claire. You must know that."

Was he bullshitting her, or was he for real? She wanted to believe him, but felt tied up in knots. She changed the subject. "Whatever," she murmured. "So why are you telling me all this now? Why the clandestine meeting, the disguise, the burner?"

He sighed. "Claire, they're watching you. It's essential they think you are unaware of their illegal activities."

"I still don't get it. Why tell me all this now?"

"Because you need to make a choice. Either you move out tomorrow and find another place to live, or you work for us."

Claire halted, dumbstruck. Work for them? What would that entail? Her mind hopped around like a scared rabbit. "Work for the FBI? Be a secret agent? You've got to be kidding!"

"You're an ideal candidate. You're living on the premises. And for now, you're not under suspicion." Another brief pause. "Look, I want you to decide whether or not you're in. Go home now. Act as you normally do. Tomorrow at noon, call me on the other burner. Don't call from your car or your apartment. Remember, they're listening in."

"Right." Claire felt light-headed. All this cloak and dagger business was unnerving.

"Are you near one of the fishermen?"

"Yes, I'm walking by the one closest to the house."

"Stop and talk to him. Surreptitiously, hand him the phone you're using. He'll get rid of it."

"Okay."

"We'll talk tomorrow." He rang off.

Chapter 49

At home Claire tried to act as she always did. She made herself eat half of the sandwich from O'Shea's but it tasted like sawdust in her mouth. She poured herself a glass of wine and drank half of it standing in the kitchen.

In the living room, she pretended to read *Commonwealth* but it was a futile effort. Should she accept Dax's offer to become a clandestine FBI agent? How dangerous was it? She could move out of Citrus Haven, find a room or apartment away from the ocean and be free of danger. But what about all the people who might die from RBBs? She could help destroy the gang that was preying on their hopes and dreams. When she finally went to bed, she slept fitfully.

The next morning, she had an appointment in Panama City Beach. The meeting went well and she landed a small order of yellow, green and hot pink bags. At noon Claire pulled into a parking spot along the beachfront. She got out and walked along the promenade. Then she pulled out the burner and called Dax.

"Hi," he said. "What have you decided?"

In that moment, she made her decision. "I'm in. What do I do next?"

"Good. Meet me at two o'clock at the Surf and Sand Shop in east Panama City Beach. It's on Front Beach Road. Go past Ripley's Believe It or Not Museum and The Upside Down House."

"Is it safe to meet there?"

"Yes. The shop is closed in January and February, and we've appropriated the locale for the afternoon. Anyone following you will think you're making a business call. Bring a box of purses in with you. See you at two." He rang off.

Claire had two hours to kill. She walked down to the Pier Park entrance and up the street to the Starbuck's where she'd first met Amy. Inside the café she ordered a latte, then brought it outside and sat down at the same table she'd sat at that day. It seemed so long ago now. The sun was warm on her back and a light breeze ruffled the palm fronds. At a table nearby, two elderly couples were arguing over Elvis Presley's most popular song: *Love me Tender* versus *Heartbreak Hotel*.

She remembered Amy and the laughs they had shared. Then she thought of the lonely spot on the beach where Amy had died. She owed it to Amy to find her killer—who could very well be the enigmatic boyfriend.

Claire took out her own cell phone and pulled up the picture she had taken of Amy's list. With her fingers, she enlarged the print. Then she went through the list slowly. She didn't recognize any names on the first page other than Reginald Brim's. She scrolled over to the next page and drew in a sharp breath as two more names jumped out: Françoise Lambert and, near the bottom, Celestina Villanova.

Claire looked blindly across the street. Reginald, Françoise and Celestina…three artists plying different crafts. Reginald was dead. Last Friday night she'd seen Françoise and Celestine whispering together. She remembered the feeling she'd had of interrupting their private conversation.

A chill went down her spine. She needed to talk to Dax.

Chapter 50

As Claire drove through Panama City Beach she glanced in the rearview mirror at the traffic behind her. She didn't think anyone was following her. The Surf and Sand Shop turned out to be a run-down affair. The display window held a sign indicating the store was open, along with some beach toys, buckets and Panama City Beach tee-shirts. She got out of the car and retrieved a box from the trunk, then locked her car and went up to the door of the shop.

A young woman stood behind a counter piled with bric-a-brac. The green apron she wore sported the shop's logo on the pocket. Her blond hair was tousled, her blue eyes friendly. For a moment, Claire wondered if they'd made a mistake and this woman was an actual employee.

"Can I help you?" the woman said.

"Hi, yes. I'm…uh…here with some merchandise to show you…purses and leather bags…"

The woman gave a little laugh. "Oh, you want to talk to our manager. He's in the back. Come this way." She led Claire through a doorway and into a small office. Dax was there, sitting on the edge of a desk, in a black suit and striped tie. He had blond hair and a matching mustache this time, but she recognized his eyes. Claire heard the door close behind her. It was probably safe to talk now. "Hi!" she whispered.

"Hi!" Dax whispered back.

For a long moment they looked at each other. Then Dax said, "I'm glad you're willing to help us out. Hopefully, what we're asking you to do won't be dangerous." He gestured to a chair. "Please, sit down."

"No thanks, I prefer to stand." She was too nervous

186

to sit. She bent over and put the cardboard box of purses on the floor.

"Okay, let's get down to business. I have several items for you." He gestured to the desk. Three small boxes were laid out along with a revolver.

Wide-eyed, she looked at Dax and then back at the gun. "You want me to shoot someone?"

"Of course not...well, hopefully not. The gun is for your protection. If you have to shoot someone, it's there for you."

Claire shook her head. "I don't know, Dax."

"Listen, you're a great shot. You won the Indiana State sharp-shooter contest when you were a kid."

"How do you know that?" As a child and teenager, she'd spent summers on her grandfather's farm. He'd taught her and her brother to shoot. She was a better shot than Timothy, which made him jealous. When she was seventeen, Grandpa had entered her in a state-wide competition and she'd won. But that was with a rifle, not a handgun.

"I know a lot about you, Claire. It's not as though you've been living a secret life."

"Still, you could have asked before delving into my past."

He ignored her irritation and went on. "I want you to take the Ruger, just in case. Put it in one of those fancy purses you sell. Here's a box of ammo."

Claire folded her arms across her chest. Maybe she should pull out of this deal now.

Dax continued, seemingly oblivious to her feelings. "In these boxes are three listening devices, similar to what they've put in your car and your apartment. Is there a way you can install them in the main house without being observed?"

Claire thought for a minute. "Yes. When I went down to the first floor the other day to get the vacuum, I noticed a vent near the ceiling in the utility room. The storage rooms are on the other side of the wall. I could slip a bug under a shelf with no problem." She frowned, remembering. "As a matter of fact, I thought I heard a voice coming from the storage room that day."

"Good to know. We think there must be a crew working in there to produce the capsules," Dax said.

Claire chewed her lip. "I could put one somewhere in the entryway. But that might be more difficult if there's a camera or sensors hidden there. Did I tell you there are sensors everywhere in the main house? The lights come on in the hallways as you pass."

"What about the third listening device?"

"How about the great room on the second floor? I know people have been in there. I've heard voices."

Dax nodded and picked up another oblong box. "This is an all-in-one detector. It'll detect all kinds of surveillance equipment: bugs, phone, GPS and spy-cams. You can locate the bugs in your apartment but don't remove them. We want our man to feel comfortable listening in on you."

Claire shivered. "All this gives me the creeps."

"To elude them listen to music in the car. When you're home, turn up the TV; or listen to a podcast with multiple voices. That will make it extremely difficult for them to listen in on you. Believe me, I know." He smiled ruefully.

The last item on the desk looked like a black Fitbit watch. Dax bent over and took her hand, startling her. His hand was warm and his fingers long. He slipped the gadget onto her wrist. "This is made to look like a Fitness watch but it's actually a listening device, cell phone and an SOS

188

transmitter. We call it an Exphone. You push down to open the hidden screen. Look at these buttons." He pressed on a small panel and slid it back. "Red for SOS, green to activate the listening device and blue to phone, which will connect you with me. We'll get rid of the burner you used today."

Claire slid the panel back until it clicked in place. Then she pressed down and opened it up again. "Red SOS, green listening, blue phone."

"Wear it at all times," Dax said.

Claire looked up into his eyes. He held her gaze. She leaned in towards him, but then he stepped back. Feeling rebuffed she said, "How long is this going to last?"

"Only a few days, Claire. With your help we'll be able to listen to them plot and plan. We need to get the name of the ringleader." He began to pace the small room. "In only ten days, the Art Festival will take over 30A. Artists, musicians, poets and writers will be pouring into the Emerald Coast region, ripe for the picking."

Claire nodded. It was horrendous to think of other artists dying of heart attacks. That reminded her of Françoise and Celestina. "Dax, I've already started on my spy mission."

"How's that?" He stopped pacing.

"On Tuesday, when I found out Amy died, I went over to see Aunt Irma. That's Amy's landlady, practically her surrogate mother. I asked Irma if I could check out Amy's room. I couldn't believe she committed suicide. I wanted to see if there was anything that suggested she was depressed, like a diary or a self-help book."

"And?"

"And I found a list of names on a legal pad. One was Reginald Brim, and two others are a painter and a jewelry designer I know. I think they're all artists or writers. I took a picture of the list with my cell phone."

Dax's eyes lit up. "Text it to me, okay?"

Claire nodded. "Anyway, I remember Amy said her boyfriend wanted to go out to different bars every night to meet people."

"Who's the boyfriend?"

"That's the thing. I never met him. She said he didn't want to meet me. It was all very mysterious." Claire sat in the padded desk chair. "She said he wanted her to introduce him to everyone she knew. Amy was super-friendly. She grew up around here and she'd been working at Beach Mania for several years. So she knew lots of people in Seaside and other towns up and down 30A."

Dax was listening closely.

Claire pulled out her phone and found the list. "These people might have been writers and artists she introduced him to. I only recognize three names." She handed the phone to Dax.

He scrolled through the names. "We'll get on this right away and identify these people."

"I'm convinced Amy was murdered," Claire said slowly. "We know now that she was involved with tracking down artistic people."

"Right."

"Was she killed because she got too curious? Because she figured out what they were doing? Did she confront the boyfriend? I owe it to her to find the answer." Claire realized she had grabbed Dax's hand and was squeezing it hard.

Chapter 51

On the way home, Claire stopped off to see Aunt Irma. The woman looked strung-out. Her hair was in disarray and she had on the same clothes she'd worn two days previously. A neighbor was sitting with her in the darkened living room. Claire learned that no funeral had been planned. The authorities were looking for Amy's mother. Her last known address was somewhere in Texas.

"Amy and her mother weren't close. But she needs to make all the decisions," Irma said. She spoke without inflection like a fatigued robot.

"Did they look for an address book upstairs?" Claire asked.

"I don't know what went on upstairs. Leo was up there the other evening looking around. He came down with a notepad of Amy's. Maybe he found an address for her mother. I don't know."

Claire thought Leo had probably seen the list she'd seen. He probably knew who the people on it were. But he didn't know about the FBI investigation. Wouldn't they normally inform the local sheriff's department? What had Dax said…they were keeping it under the radar.

#

At home, Claire closed the garage door and then removed the large box she'd brought into the Surf and Sand Shop from the trunk. She'd hidden the gun, the listening devices and the detector under the bags. She carried the box upstairs, then went back for her computer and purse.

Back in the coach house with the door shut, she felt as though she was on stage. She had to perform for her wire tapper. Humming softly, she went into the bathroom and changed into her running clothes. If things were supposed to be normal, she should go for a run. She put on the fanny pack and slipped the gun inside. That afternoon, Dax had worked with her so she'd become familiar with the weapon.

In the late afternoon light, the sand glowed gold. As she jogged, Claire went through everything she'd learned that afternoon. Dax had been patient and kind with her, but all business. Except when he took her hand to put on the Exphone, there had been no glimmer of romance. The closeness she'd felt after their date had probably been all in her mind.

Up ahead she saw a fisherman casting his line into the surf. Was he an FBI agent on surveillance, or a member of the gang who had her under observation? She felt incredibly vulnerable in spite of the Ruger bobbing in her fanny pack. From now on, she would suspect every stranger she met. Was he a secret agent or a mafia hitman? She felt like her world had been split into good and evil, with no gradation in between.

Back in the coach house, Claire turned on the TV and turned up the volume. Then she removed the detector from the box, slipped it from the casing and switched it on. She moved around the kitchen, but the red light didn't flash. In the living room, the red light blinked as she approached the sofa. She bent down and found the listening device under the coffee table in front of the sofa. The rest of the room was safe. She continued into the bedroom. Within minutes she found another bug under the bedside table. Claire smiled. Whoever was listening in was probably hoping for the sounds of hot sex. Instead, they heard her snoring.

Finished with prospecting for bugs, Claire headed back to the kitchen and set the detector down, then took out a frozen dinner and popped it in the microwave. She ate at the counter as she worked her way through her emails. After she cleaned up, she went over to the sofa, removed her shoes and plopped her feet on the coffee table. Hopefully, the sound jarred her wire tapper friend. She watched TV mindlessly with the volume turned up. Every few minutes she checked her phone. The time crawled by. She couldn't concentrate on the sitcoms in her heightened state of anxiety.

At long last it was nine o'clock. Claire figured any action that took place downstairs usually happened during the day or late at night. She should be able to sneak down without being caught in the evening. Soundlessly, she lifted her feet from the coffee table and tiptoed over to the kitchen, where she tucked one of the listening devices and a small flashlight in her pocket. Then she tiptoed over to the door that led to the main house, carefully disengaged the locks, and opened it. She crept along the hallway, hugging the wall. At the stairs, she switched on her flashlight, crouched down low and walked softly down the stairs to the entryway. At the bottom, she stopped and listened. All was quiet except for the throb of a motor. Crouching low again, she slipped across the entryway. With great care, she opened the door to the utility closet. As soon as she entered the small room, she heard muffled voices. Claire stood stock-still. If she could hear them, could they hear her?

She looked up at the vent. The top of the shelving beneath it would be the perfect place for the listening device, but it was beyond her reach. She shined her flashlight around the closet. A yellow plastic bucket sat in a corner. She could use it as a stepladder. As she bent down and turned the bucket over, she dislodged a broom. Her hand shot out, and she managed to catch the broom handle before it hit the floor. Again, she froze. Had the conversation stopped? She could hear her heart beating like a kettle drum. No, they were still talking in the storage room. Taking great care, she propped the broom back against the wall, moved the bucket over and stepped up onto its wobbly surface.

She reached up and placed the bug on the top shelf. She was about to get down when she heard a scream, and then the muffled voices again.

"Hold him still," a man said. She heard a crack, like the sound of a whip. Then another scream.

A muffled voice seemed to say, "You will do what I say."

Claire heard sobbing and then a reply: "Please, please...it's like being in prison. I'm alone and..."

Another whip crack and another scream. The muffled voice said, "Shut the fuck up."

The prisoner was moaning now. Another, deeper voice gave a vicious, sneering laugh. "You call this prison? You've got a TV, food shipped in, a little dope when you've done a good job. This ain't prison."

The moaning continued, but the other two voices grew unintelligible. The men must have moved away from the vent. Claire stepped down from the bucket and shone the flashlight around until she found the doorknob. She was about to leave the utility room when she heard a door opening down the hall, followed by the jangle of keys and the snap of a lock. She switched off the flashlight and stood paralyzed, barely breathing, her gaze glued to the utility closet's narrowly, open door.

Heavy footsteps came down the hall. "He's going to crack. We've got to get rid of him," the deep-voiced man said.

She peeked through the narrow opening as the two men walked by. In that brief second she glimpsed a ski-jump nose and a heavy beard. Taken aback, she recognized William, the man she'd met at the Zen meditation session.

The other man was not visible.

Claire waited for what seemed an eternity, pondering what she'd seen and heard. William was one of the gang. That nose along with the beard was instantly recognizable. She needed to tell Dax. But she couldn't call him from her coach house. They'd overhear. She would have to wait until tomorrow.

Slowly, she opened the utility closet door and peeped out. The men had gone. Resonating silence filled the hallway. Hugging the wall, Claire made her way back upstairs.

Once in her apartment, she carefully closed the door and slid the locks in place. The TV was still blasting. Hopefully, her listener hadn't noticed her absence. She turned off the TV and the lights and went into the bedroom, where she climbed under the covers without bothering to change or brush her teeth. Once in bed, the realization of what she'd just witnessed flooded her senses. Downstairs, a man was being held prisoner. He must be manufacturing the RBB capsules. He was being controlled by William and someone else. What was William's last name? Had she ever learned it? She didn't think so. And what about Zen meditation? The pursuit of self-realization and studying the nature of existence seemed totally out of character for a criminal.

Who was the other man? He seemed to be the boss but she'd been so shocked to see William, she hadn't caught even a glimpse of him.

Chapter 52

In the morning, Claire felt groggy and out of sorts. This spy life took its toll. She wanted to talk to Dax and tell him what she'd learned. Talking in the apartment was out of the question and so was a discussion from her car. She decided to walk to yoga. She could call Dax on the way.

After a quick cup of coffee, she pulled on her yoga outfit and headed out the door. The morning felt unusually warm and muggy. She slammed the gate and started off at a fast clip. Considering that there were cameras filming the entryway to the house, she waited until she had rounded the dunes to click on her wrist phone.

"Do you have your gun? I see you're outside the house," Dax said.

She'd forgotten he could track her by means of her spy watch. "No, where would I put the gun during yoga?"

"Claire, you're not being smart. You must protect yourself at all times."

Annoyance washed over her. "I didn't think about it, okay? I'll try to be smarter like you."

"Calm down. I'm concerned about your safety. I'm sorry. I used the wrong words. Good work last night, by the way. We're listening to the poor slob in the storage room now. He's currently snoring. We heard most of a discussion with the boss. It sounded as though they were whipping him."

"I know. I was stuck in the utility closet next door. I heard it all."

"You were still there?" He sounded concerned.

"I listened to the beating and the dressing-down. It was scary. Then two men came out and locked their prisoner in."

"Did you see them?"

"Just a glimpse. I recognized a man I met at a Zen meditation session. Searching for inner peace seems out of character for a thug, doesn't it?"

"Who's the guy?"

"His first name is William, or at least that's what he goes by. I don't know his last name. He sports a heavy black beard and has strabismus of the left eye. One eye looks at you while the other is looking somewhere else. He's also got a large ski-jump nose."

"I'll look through FBI files and see if we can identify him. Though if we missed somebody that distinctive-looking, he may be new to the drug scene. Whatever the case, I'd bet his real name isn't William."

"This afternoon I'll set up the other two bugs in the entryway and the great room. I don't want to sneak around at night. I'll pretend to do a load of laundry and trigger the sensors on purpose. Then I'll figure how to place the bugs."

"Where will you be today?" Dax asked.

"I'm going back to Destin. I've got a couple of appointments in the morning. I'll be home early. My friend Beth from the book club invited me to go with her and her buddies to Stinky's tonight. These girls go out every Friday together."

"Be observant. Pack your gun and the wasp spray. While you're gone this morning, we'll be watching the house."

Claire's morning went by fast. She made one good sale and then wasted an hour listening to a frustrated mother outline the issues she had with a local preschool. In the car, Claire was acutely aware of the fact she was being tracked and wiretapped. She found a talk show on the radio and let it blast, while she thought over what she had witnessed last night. Were these the men who had killed Daniel and maybe

Amy? Realizing she'd been only two feet away when they walked by her hiding place freaked her out. She could have been number three on their hit list.

At home she went for a run, geared up with gun and wasp spray. She ran into the couple with the chocolate lab, who told her they were back for ten days.

"We never miss the Artist Festival," Lenore said.

George laughed. "My wife here is a collector of arts and crafts. We've got more junk on the shelves of our house. It could be a museum."

"Now George, what I buy is fine art. You don't appreciate valuable artwork."

George rolled his eyes at Claire.

They talked for a few more minutes, then parted. As Claire walked away, she realized she was glad to have some neighbors nearby, however briefly.

Back at home, she collected laundry and put the two tiny transmitters into her pocket, then opened the door into the main house and walked purposefully down the hallway towards the stairs. Anyone listening or watching would know what she was up to. In the laundry room she started her wash and then went out to the entryway. She pretended interest in a stack of towels and several spray cans of sunscreen. Crouching down, she held a bright orange can in one hand while she slipped the listening device under the shelf. *One down, one to go.*

Upstairs, Claire stepped into the great room. Instantly a Bach cantata filled the expanse while the ceiling lights lit up every corner. Claire imagined she was on stage. This was the debut of her acting career. She walked over to the massive Subzero fridge and pulled open the door. Inside were several bottles of beer and cans of soda. She selected a Diet Coke and popped open the top. Then she wandered around the kitchen, pulling open drawers and inspecting the cupboards. In the living room area, she studied the pictures on the walls and then flopped on the sofa. Idly, she picked up a magazine off the coffee table and flipped through the pages. It was six months old. Then she leaned forward, put the magazine back and slipped the last transmitter under the coffee table. After another look around the room and a long sip of Coke, she ambled back to her apartment and slammed the door shut. Inside she smothered a giggle of relief.

#

Beth came by to pick Claire up at seven o'clock. "Wow, this place is ginormous," Beth said as Claire got into the car. "Who lives here?"

"Just me. I've got the coach house over the garages on the left."

"The rest of it is empty?"

"Yes. but I imagine they'll rent the main house starting in March."

"Aren't you a little spooked being out here by yourself?"

"I've gotten used to it. I fell in love with the apartment. It's beautifully furnished and the views are stupendous. Plus, the rent isn't over the moon."

Beth looked back through the rearview mirror. "I don't know if I could handle living on my own. I grew up in a big family and I have two roommates currently. I like company." She glanced over at Claire. "I like your tunic."

Claire was wearing a slightly fitted jade-green tunic and black leggings. Beth was dressed in jeans and a jeans jacket. She had a slim-hipped boyish figure and jeans looked great on her.

Stinky's Fish Camp was hopping. Louise and Olivia were already there and greeted Claire and Beth with hugs. Claire felt herself relax. It was good to be surrounded by people. She realized how on edge she was, knowing that someone was constantly eavesdropping on her.

They ordered wine and some appetizers: fried Brie with pepper jelly and firecracker shrimp. Claire ate her share and laughed with the rest of them. They ordered another round of drinks and dinner. Claire tried the crawfish pie, which was delicious.

As she polished off the last bite, she looked across the room. Leo Martin was there with another guy she didn't recognize. Feeling on top of the world, with all the wine and good food, she excused herself and walked over to Leo's table. He got up, as did the other man. Claire encouraged them both to sit down. "Sorry to disturb your dinner."

"Claire, let me introduce Josh Owens. He's the man behind the Artist Festival taking place next week."

Mr. Owens had sandy blond hair and a matching goatee. His eyes roamed over her body and settled on her breasts. She gave him a brittle, fake smile. "How do you do? Please sit down." She pulled out a chair and sat down herself, then turned to Leo. "I just wondered if there was something new in Amy's investigation."

"It's closed. The only fingerprints on the hypodermic needle were Amy's." He took a sip of beer.

Claire shook her head. "I just can't believe it." She wanted to mention the list of artists she'd found among Amy's magazines, but she stopped herself. Dax had said that the investigation didn't include the local police.

"She had a history of drugs. You didn't know her that well," Leo said.

"What about the boyfriend?"

Leo smiled patiently as though dealing with a child. "Claire, it's over. I'm sorry. I know Amy was your friend." He glanced over at her table across the room. "But it looks like you have some new ones."

Abruptly, tears stung her eyes. Did he think people

were dispensable—out with the old, in with the new like a pair of old socks? She knew she should stop there, but instead she said, "What about the Bartholomew Group? Anything new there?"

Leo looked irritated now. "We're stymied. The tech guys are still pursuing different leads."

Owens glanced from one of them to the other. "What's this about the Bartholomew Group?"

"Just part of an investigation. They own property in the area," Leo said offhandedly.

"I've heard of them," Owens said. "Big money."

"I'm sure Claire wants to get back to her friends."

"Right." Claire stood up, smiled briefly and headed back to her table. Her previous effervescent feeling was gone.

"Hey, y'all, Claire caught Mr. Josh Owens' eye," Louise drawled as Claire sat back down. Louise flipped her long blond hair and rolled her eyes.

Olivia raised her eyebrows. "My-oh-my."

"So what's the big deal?" Claire asked.

"The big deal is, he owns the Claremont Golf Resort along with a bunch of other real estate," Beth said.

Louise raised her wine glass. "And honey, Mr. Owens is super rich."

"Well, rich or not, I don't like someone who mentally undresses me in the middle of a restaurant," Claire said.

They all started laughing hysterically. "You're just too much, Claire." Olivia said, as she blotted her eyes with a napkin.

Chapter 53

Saturday morning, Claire went for a run east towards
Grayton Beach. She spotted several fishermen and some
families with children. It was reassuring to see vacationers
along her route, although she could feel the revolver's
weight in her fanny pack. After running all out for a couple
of miles, she turned and started back home at a leisurely
pace. Then she called Dax on her Exphone.

He sounded concerned when he answered. "Hi, how
are you?"

"All right. Why?"

"There was a lot of action at your place last night
while you were gone. And then again in the early morning
hours."

She slowed to a walk. "What do you mean?"

"We heard lots of conversation and observed several
vehicles coming in to pick up boxes."

"I don't see why you don't just arrest them all.
Someone would spill the beans under interrogation and tell
you who the big boss is."

"Listen, the minute we close down their operation,
the guy would take off and set up somewhere else. We've
got to get him. Sooner or later, he'll appear on the scene.
We found William, by the way. His name is William Shots,
better known as Slick Willy. He works as a bartender at the
Happy Parrot in Panama City Beach, which puts him in a
perfect position to sell RBBs. He's got a long rap sheet:
robbery, auto theft and burglary, to name a few. He's new to
drug running, though. The night you saw him in Citrus
Haven, he could very well have been with the big boss.
Neither one of them were seen at the house last night."

Claire stopped suddenly. "Dax, I told you I saw

William at the Zen meditation session. Oh, my God, do you think the Zen master could be involved in the operation? His name is Seijun. I remember seeing him in a tête-à-tête with Slick Willy."

"Good thinking, Claire. We'll check him out." Dax fell silent briefly, then said, "Where were you last night?"

"I went to Stinky's with the girls. By the way, I saw Sheriff Martin at the restaurant. I asked him about the investigation into Amy's murder. He told me the case was closed. They found her fingerprints on the syringe, and that was all the proof they needed." Claire looked over towards the dunes. She was nearly at the spot where Amy's body had been found.

"I know you liked this girl, Claire, but you probably didn't know her very well. She might have had demons you didn't know about. Maybe she wanted to end it all."

"I'm positive she did not kill herself." Claire sighed in frustration. "Oh, and I met Josh Owens last night, too. They said he runs the Artist Festival. Do you know him?"

"Yes. We've looked into his involvement with the festival. There are questions about his financial dealings up and down the Emerald coast."

"Could he be involved with the RBBs? Is that why he organized the festival?"

"It would be nice to talk to him about it. Listen, I've got to go. Take care of yourself. Don't go into the main house. Keep your gun at the ready." Then he was gone.

A minute later, Claire's cell phone rang. She pulled it out of her fanny pack and looked at the screen. It was a local number but not one she recognized. It could be a boutique that she hadn't yet entered into her contacts list. "Hello. Claire Hall here."

"Hello, Ms. Hall. This is Josh Owens. We met last night."

Claire stopped walking and looked out at the sky-blue water. Seagulls floated on the gently rolling surface. She felt as though her life was like them, in suspension. "Yes, I remember."

"I wondered if you'd like to come out to my club for dinner tonight. I could show you around. Sheriff Martin mentioned you might be looking into a new place to live. We have some apartments available on the property."

Leo had a nerve talking to Josh Owens about her living situation. She hadn't liked Owens last night but Dax had said the FBI wanted to learn more about the man. A dinner date offered a chance to pump him for information. The idea of spending time with him made her skin crawl, but she suppressed her revulsion and said, as brightly as she could, "I'd like that. Maybe I should think about moving, although I love my current home."

"Great. My driver will pick you up at seven."

"Thanks, but I'll drive over."

"Are you sure? It's no problem to swing over to Lemon Cove."

"Thank you, Mr. Owens. I'll be there at seven." She hung up. What was she getting herself into? Tonight she would have to be on her guard, but it could be fun. She was beginning to like her new role as spy queen.

Chapter 54

That night Claire dressed in a royal blue sheath. It fit perfectly. She'd lost weight with her increased exercise routine, as well as the fact that she'd been running on nervous energy. She took a long moment to check herself out in the mirror. Her hair was streaked with gold from the Florida sunshine and her skin had a rosy glow. With the addition of silver earrings and a necklace to match, she was ready for her fact-finding dinner with Josh Owens. She pulled out a new evening purse she'd borrowed from the collection. It had an inner pocket where she could stash the gun.

In the car, Claire typed the address of the Claremont Resort into her GPS. It was a fifteen-minute drive from Lemon Cove. The entrance to the resort took her breath away. Sheets of water cascaded down rocky formations on each side of marble pillars. A parade of tall palm trees and flowering bushes lined the drive up to the main entrance. Impressed despite her misgivings, Claire gave her name at the gate and then followed the drive up to the main building. A handsome young man in a dark blue uniform and white gloves came out to open the car door as she pulled up.

"Welcome, Ms. Hall. Mr. Owens is expecting you. Let me park your car." He gave a slight bow.

Claire got out and handed him the keys, then walked around her car and up a short flight of stairs to the heavy oak door. It was whisked open by another good-looking young man in a blue uniform.

"Welcome, Ms. Hall. Please follow me to the dining room. Mr. Owens is waiting for you." The entrance hall was enormous, boasting French period furnishings and an over-sized crystal chandelier hanging over a round mahogany and ormolu table. The doorman led her down a wide hallway, ornately decorated with gold-framed tapestries and a thick Persian carpet. Along the walls were marquetry tables and gilt Louis XV armchairs. Claire found the décor on the far side of good taste.

Through a doorway, they entered an expansive dining room decorated with heavy silk curtains, abundant gold leaf and more Belgian tapestries depicting hunting scenes and harvest tableaus. Mostly elderly couples were seated at several tables.

Claire spotted Owens in a far corner, intent on his phone at a table overlooking a pond with the golf course beyond. Fairy lights twinkled among the trees, creating a magical vista. He looked up from his phone, placed it on the table and came over to greet her. He wore a Brunello Cucinelli suit enhanced by an elegant blue patterned tie and matching pocket square. "You look fantastic," he said, inspecting her dress—and her curves underneath. Then he slipped his arm around her waist, leaned over and kissed her cheek. "May I call you Claire?" His lips were uncomfortably close to her ear. "Please call me Josh," he whispered, then let her go.

Claire stepped away. Had she made a major mistake accepting this invitation? This guy would be all over her if she wasn't careful. A waiter pulled out a chair opposite Owens, and Claire sat down.

"I've taken the liberty of ordering a special meal for the two of us." Owens clapped his hands, like some kind of medieval despot. Instantly, a sommelier appeared and poured a small amount of wine into Owens' glass. He took some time, swirling the liquid around in his mouth before giving the go-ahead. Then Claire was served. The elegant dinner began with a velouté of asparagus, followed by roasted pheasant with baby vegetables. Dessert was a decadent chocolate cake in a pool of raspberry coulis. Claire enjoyed every bite, though she couldn't say the same about the company. As it turned out she didn't have to pump Owens for information. He talked about himself throughout the meal; his childhood in New York, his success in school and in business, his superiority in assessing the stock market. Claire bobbed her head up and down like a kewpie doll, smiling and saying, "uh-huh" at appropriate moments. With luck, she could turn the conversation toward subjects useful to Dax.

When the waiter had cleared away their dessert plates, Claire leaned forward. "Tell me about the Artist Festival. I've heard so many great things."

Owens beamed. "Oh, that was one of my greatest coups. Things die down around here for a couple of months in the winter. The festival brings artists and masses of collectors and patrons down to the Emerald Coast for about a week. You'll see, it's amazing."

Claire nodded and smiled encouragingly. Owens drank wine and kept talking. "Local restaurants, shops, boutiques, all benefit from the action. Of course, I fill up the resort too. While the wife is buying paintings, books and baubles, the husband plays golf here at the club and everyone's happy. During the day artists display their work at a couple of outdoor venues in Seaside and Rosemary Beach. There's entertainment every night: concerts, poetry readings, art and craft demonstrations."

"That must take a lot of planning." Claire gave him her best innocent look. "Is that what you and Sheriff Martin were talking about last night?"

He nodded. "I always get together with Leo to talk about logistics. With all the people pouring onto 30A, we have to plan parking and traffic movement."

Claire gripped her purse tightly under the table. She

could feel the weight of the gun. Owens stared at her expectantly, as if awaiting a gushing compliment. She drew a silent, deep breath and took the plunge. "So…do you foresee any problems this year?"

He cocked his head and frowned. "Problems?"

Claire swallowed. "Like…problems with alcohol, pot, or…maybe other drugs?"

"Drugs?" He narrowed his eyes as though evaluating her.

"Yeah, you know, bohemian artists drinking absinthe, smoking pot…" She laughed nervously.

He glanced across the room and then back at her. His good humor was gone. "We run a clean operation. This isn't some druggie Woodstock reenactment."

"Right, I'm sure it's not." Claire wondered if he was lying or if he truly knew nothing about RBBs. Clearly she wasn't going to get anything more out of him. Maybe she wasn't cut out to be a spy queen after all. "Well, thanks so much for dinner. I probably should get going."

Owens stood up and came around the table. He pulled back her chair and reached for her hand. "I'd like to show you two apartments in the new wing of the resort first. Great views of the golf course, and you could enjoy the resort's amenities. You did say you were thinking of moving?"

She didn't have a good excuse to refuse, although she had no intention of moving into the Claremont Resort. She didn't want to be alone with this jerk, either, given the way he'd looked at her all evening and last night. She was in pretty good shape, though, and could handle herself if he tried anything. And there was the gun, if necessary. Maybe she could get him talking again and he'd let something slip, if he *did* know anything about the RBB ring.

She nodded, and Owens led her through the

restaurant and down the hall to the majestic foyer. From there they turned left and went down another impressive hallway. Halfway down, there was an elevator. He pushed a button and the doors opened. The elevator walls were covered with blue moiré, the floor with Persian carpeting, and the control panel was covered in gold leaf. Claire wondered how much it had all cost. They entered and went up two floors. As the elevator car ascended, Owens bragged about how he had designed the entire resort and how exclusive it had become. Claire wanted to clap her hands over her ears. She couldn't get a word in, about the Artist Festival or anything else.

When they left the elevator, he led the way down the corridor and through some heavy doors into another hallway, decorated in a spare, modern manner completely different from the gaudy style of the main building. Five doors lined each side of the corridor. Owens pulled a key from his pocket and opened a door on the left. Inside the room he reached around and switched on the lights.

They were in the large living room of a furnished apartment, decorated in grey and burgundy tones. A kitchen with an eating area lay to the right. Ahead of them, large windows gave on to a balcony.

"You can't see it now, but the view is stupendous. There's the Gulf in the distance, and the golf course is spread out below." Owens walked over and opened a set of French doors that led outside.

Claire looked out at the moonlit landscape. "Yes, I can see the water shimmering in the distance. Very nice!" She turned back and wandered around, looking in the kitchen cabinets and checking out the wall art, which reminded her of insipid hospital prints of nonexistent flora.

"Check out the bedroom. You'll love it." Owens walked over to a set of double doors and threw them open, revealing a grey and yellow bedroom. The bed was king-sized with a shiny grey comforter and a pile of lemon and grey patterned pillows. "Go ahead. Take a look."

Reluctantly, Claire went in. She peeked in the walk-in closet and checked out the granite and pearl-grey bathroom. Owens stood by the bedroom doors, looking inordinately pleased with himself, bobbing up and down on his toes. "It's great, isn't it? Everything is brand new. You could move in tomorrow."

Claire cocked her head. "I couldn't afford this place. There must be membership fees and other expenses."

"We could make arrangements about those."

He was still in the doorway. She'd have to pass him to leave. Her sense of danger went off like an alarm. "No, I don't think so."

A predatory light flashed in his eyes. He propelled himself across the room, grabbed Claire by the arms, and pushed her backwards onto the bed. Then he fell on top of her. The sudden motion sent her purse sailing across the room, and it landed with a thud. She tried to wiggle out from under him but he pinned her arms with his hands. He found her mouth and forced his tongue between her lips, then groaned and pressed her harder into the mattress. She turned her head to avoid his mouth. He reared up and slapped her face. Momentarily stunned, she felt blood on her lip. Then his hand slid between their bodies as he reached down and pulled up her skirt. His hand burned on her inner thigh.

Revulsion and fear gave her sudden strength. As he balanced his weight on his left side and fumbled with his fly, Claire braced herself with her elbows and shoved her left knee into his crotch. He screamed and rolled on his back. "You bitch! You little bitch!"

Heart pounding, Claire rolled off the bed. She landed

on all fours and crawled over to her purse, fumbled with the clasp, pulled out the Ruger and cocked it. Then she stood up and aimed the pistol at Owens. She was breathing hard. "If you come after me, I'll blow you to smithereens."

Owens lay on the bed, curled in a fetal position. "You little cunt. You could have had this place for free, if you just delivered."

Claire shuddered. "You're an arrogant asshole and a rapist. Don't ever come near me again."

Chapter 55

Downstairs, the doorman called for her car. He avoided her eyes. When the car jockey brought around her vehicle, he glanced at her and then looked away. She drove down the long driveway to the main road. Then she pulled over to the side and looked at herself in the mirror. Her mouth was swollen and her hair was in disarray but other than that she didn't look too bad. When she analyzed the reaction of the Claremont employees, she guessed they'd seen a parade of girls who'd gone through the same experience. Undoubtedly, she wasn't the first woman Josh Owens had tried to rape.

Claire needed to talk to someone, but she couldn't talk in the car and she couldn't go home. She felt caged in. Without thinking she drove over to 30A. A few minutes later, she was coming up on Watersound. To her left was The Hub, a large open-air restaurant, jumbotron and bar. A few people were sitting at tables under the lights. She braked fast and turned into the parking lot. When she stepped out of the car, she felt the chill of the evening air. She reached into the back seat and pulled out a black pashmina. Then she walked over to the bar and ordered a soda water with lime. She didn't need any more alcohol.

Claire sat at a distance from the other tables. Four guys were discussing football and scarfing barbeque. At another table two couples were drinking wine and talking quietly. She turned her back on them and pushed the blue button on her Exphone. It rang several times before Dax picked up. He sounded out of breath. "Claire? Are you all right?"

"Yes and no." She sounded firm and steady. She took distant note of that fact, as if her voice belonged to someone else.

"Where are you?"

"At The Hub on 30A. I just had a close call. I'm decompressing currently."

"What do you mean?" He sounded worried.

"I had dinner with Josh Owens at his resort. He's a pompous ass, by the way."

"Right. So what went wrong?"

"He...he..."Now she felt tears in her eyes, "He...he tried to rape me...but I escaped."

"Shit, Claire. How are you?"

She gulped her soda water. "Pretty shook up. But apart from a swollen lip, I'm all right."

"Do you need help? I could send someone over."

"No, I'm fine. I just needed to talk to someone."

"Why in hell did you go out with him?" Dax sounded angry now.

Her own temper flared to match. "Because I thought I could grill him on the Artist Festival and the RBBs."

In the brief silence, Claire could hear Dax gritting his teeth. Finally, sounding tightly controlled, he said, "So what did you learn?"

"Nothing much. When I mentioned drugs at the festival, he got defensive. He had this look in his eyes...I'm not sure if he's involved or not. But I won't be talking to him again. That's for sure..."

"Do you feel comfortable going home?"

"Yes, I'm just sitting here having a drink. Then I'll drive home."

"Okay. We'll be close by tonight if you need us."

Claire didn't want to hang up but she had nothing else to say.

"Claire?"

"Yes?"

Dax spoke softly, like a caress. "Take good care of yourself."

Chapter 56

When Claire got home, she stripped down and took a long, hot shower. Although nothing actually happened with Josh, she still felt dirty. The fact that he'd offered a free apartment for sex was appalling. Did he really think she was that kind of girl? Or did he think he was irresistible and she would do anything to be in his orbit? Probably the latter.

It took her a long time to fall asleep but amazingly she slept well. It was nine o'clock when she awoke. Outside, the sky looked misty, blending with the gray water of the Gulf. The line of the horizon had disappeared, and the murky air deadened the sounds of the waves. Claire felt as though she was enclosed in a cotton cocoon.

She got up and peered at herself in the mirror. In the morning light, her lip didn't look that bad. With a little make-up and lipstick she'd look fine. She fixed herself a cup of coffee and brought it back to bed. Propping herself on the pillows, she gazed out at the gloomy world. The weather mirrored her current life: murky. How close were they to uncovering the identity of the drug lord running the RBB business? Why was Amy killed? Why was Daniel killed?

As she lay there in bed sipping coffee, she remembered that another human being was being held prisoner downstairs. Who was he? And why had they rented this apartment to her, if Citrus Haven also housed a drug factory? Who was the Bartholomew Group and why couldn't Leo's techies uncover the owner of the house? So many unanswered questions. Lastly, what about Dax? Had he been concerned about her last night because he cared about her, or because she was useful to his investigation?

To distract herself, she snatched her phone off the night stand. No one had called or texted. Claire tried calling her parents but the phone rang and rang. They had probably gone to church and then out for brunch. She called Irma next, hoping to find out if a date had been set for Amy's funeral, but Irma wasn't home either.

#

On Monday, Claire went to yoga and then rushed home to shower and change. That morning after the Zen meditation session, she had an appointment with Maura, the owner of Tokimeku, the shop in front of the Kōfuku gardens. Mandy, the cute redhead, had given her a call when Maura returned from her trip.

When Claire arrived for meditation, she parked on one side of the store and walked around to the garden's side entrance. Through the high bushes, she saw Seijun deep in conversation with William and another man she didn't recognize. As she approached, the conversation broke off. The three men looked over at her.

Seijun nailed her with his gaze and gestured to a cushion on the stone bench inside the gazebo. "Welcome, Claire."

Claire murmured hello but avoided eye contact with William. The thought of sitting anywhere near him filled her with alarm. She would have to play her most convincing role yet. And what about Seijun? Was he part of all this— and if so, why had he taken such an interest in her?

"We have a new member in our little group," Seijun said. "This is Sean Sandler. He's a poet and journalist. He just moved to the area. William has offered to show him around."

Claire cleared her throat. "How nice," she said, thinking, *another lamb to the slaughter*.

#

Mandy was arranging scarves on a rack when Claire entered the store from the back garden. As she crossed the

216

threshold, Maura came sweeping down the rear staircase. She was a tall woman with blond curls piled on top of her head. That and the full-length, diaphanous gown she wore, reminded Claire of a Greek goddess. Her sharp blue eyes roamed around the shop, inspecting every piece of clothing. When they landed on Claire, Maura frowned and then smiled.

"You must be Claire, so very nice to meet you." Maura glided forward and took Claire's hands in hers. "Mandy told me all about you and your lovely handbags."

Claire felt engulfed in this woman's aura. "So...nice to...meet you," she stammered.

Maura asked Mandy to bring tea, and they sat down together at a little round table in the corner under an enormous ficus tree. As they drank the green tea, Maura quizzed her about her life and her move to the Gulf coast. Her charming manner drew Claire in, and she managed to extract every bit of personal data short of Claire's social security number. When they got around to the Letízia products, Maura agreed to purchase a line of warm beige and cream-colored bags. "They'll blend in perfectly with my shop's color spectrum.

Was this woman for real, or just floating on the periphery? A sale was a sale, though. After they completed their business, Maura asked if she enjoyed the meditation sessions.

"I do. Since I moved down here, I've been stressed. Meditation seems to calm me down."

"Yes, Seijun works miracles, but—" Maura broke off.

Claire leaned forward. "But what?"

"Oh, nothing." Maura yawned and stretched her arms over her head. "There's just more to him than you might think."

As Claire left the building, she wondered what Maura meant by that comment.

Chapter 57

Claire took Friday off, and with Olivia and Louise, wandered through the art fair in Rosemary Beach. The Artist Festival was in full swing. Each artist had put up a white tent, topped by a colorful flag. Claire bought a print depicting a summer beach scene and a pink and black, geometric silk scarf. At noon, Beth escaped the bank and joined them for lunch. That evening the four of them attended an outdoor concert, a Zydeco band Louise knew and loved since she'd grown up in Louisiana. For Claire, the rhythm and sounds were something new and delightful.

Saturday morning, Claire tried to shop at the farmer's market in Seaside, but the crowds made it impossible to park. Highway 30A was jammed with vehicles sporting license plates from Texas, Georgia, Alabama and other Southern states. She'd given up and driven over to the Publix grocery store where the workers were in a tizzy because someone had dropped a bottle of oil. One elderly lady had fallen in the slippery mess and the paramedics were carrying her to an ambulance. Claire was glad to escape the chaos and spent the afternoon at home working on the computer.

That night Claire dressed in black linen ankle-length pants and a black and white patterned tunic. She slipped her wallet, the gun and the wasp spray in a black cross-body handbag. She was meeting Irma and Françoise in Seaside at Bud and Alley's at six o'clock. She had offered to pick them up but Irma said she might want to go home before the evening's entertainment was over. Irma had sounded dull and lifeless. This would be her first outing since Amy died.

Claire left the house in the late afternoon. She was lucky to find a parking spot in Smollian Circle, in front of the Assembly Hall where the book club had met. For a moment she sat and stared up at the second floor, remembering Reginald Brim holding forth on *Mothering Sunday*. Although book club had taken place barely a month ago, it seemed like years. She'd lived a lifetime since then.

Claire got out of the car and walked through the covered passageway between two buildings and into the central square. A string quartet was playing in the amphitheater. Later a cover band, The Red Doors, would be playing music from the Sixties. After dinner, Irma and Françoise wanted to sit under the stars and listen to the familiar music of their youth.

Claire had a half hour before she was to meet them. She wandered through the artist stalls that lined the street. Every medium seemed to be represented: pottery, painting, wood carving, stone sculpture and jewelry. At the end of one row of tents, she stopped to admire an exquisite necklace made of lapis lazuli and silver beads.

"Hi Claire. That would look lovely on you."

Claire looked up, surprised to see Celestina standing behind the display table. In her long-tiered skirt, off-the-shoulder peasant blouse and dangling earrings, she looked like a beautiful gypsy.

Claire smiled hello. "I love it. The stones are gorgeous."

"Buy it. Make yourself happy." Celestina rubbed her hands together. She seemed on edge.

"How have sales gone? Has it been a successful show?"

"It's been going great, I'm pleased." Celestina smoothed back her hair and shoved her hands in her pockets. "But I need to make a decent profit if I want to stay in the business. I've got so many ideas and I need to keep on producing." She yanked her hands free and started rubbing them together again.

"Your work is unusual. This piece is exquisite."
Claire fingered a bracelet of highly polished green stones
and etched gold beads. Keeping her gaze on the glimmering
stones, she said, "It must be difficult to constantly come up
with new ideas…"

"It was," Celestina said, her voice low. "Now I'm
finding it easier, you know, to come up with something
new. I—"

Claire looked up. Celestina was staring down the
alleyway between the tents, pale, eyes wide. Claire turned to
follow her gaze. All she saw were the backs of three men.
Had they grabbed Celestina's attention, or was it something
else?

"Are you all right?" Claire asked. "You look like
you've seen a ghost."

"No, I'm fine. Just a little nervous."

"Nervous, why?"

"Nothing, Claire. It's nothing. So, do you want to
buy the necklace? I'll give you a special price since we're
Zen buddies."

Claire bought the necklace and then hurried over to
Bud and Alley's. Irma and Françoise were just arriving
when she walked into the restaurant. The waiter led them to
a table with a view of the Gulf.

They had a quiet but friendly dinner. Françoise
ordered a bottle of French wine, which was light and dry.
They shared the house smoked tuna dip followed by
scallops with creamy grits and mushrooms. All three of
them made an effort to keep the conversation light.

Across the candle-lit table, Claire studied Françoise.
She looked exhausted. Dark circles ringed her eyes and her
skin had a sallow tone. She was twitchy and tense. Claire
thought of Celestina, skittish and anxious when she'd

purchased the necklace earlier in the evening. Was it RBBs, wreaking havoc on their nervous systems?

"How are you doing, Françoise? You look tired," Claire said.

"Ah, I work too much, many hours. But I can't stop."

"What do you mean, you can't stop?"

Françoise didn't answer. Instead, clearly agitated, she asked Claire unrelated questions about her childhood, her favorite music and her job. Anything to keep the conversation away from herself, Claire thought. Troubled, she let it go. She'd definitely tell Dax later.

After dinner, they strolled over to the amphitheater and sat on a blanket on the grass. About halfway through the concert, Irma went home, pleading fatigue. Claire remained for a while longer, trying to put worry for Irma, Françoise and Celestina out of her mind, but it was a wasted effort. She might as well head for home, too. She wound her way among the concertgoers and crossed the street. She was halfway through the darkened passageway to the exit on Semolina Circle when she heard voices ahead. Three men stood outside the tunnel, talking loudly. She froze in place as she recognized Slick Willy's profile, the distinctive nose. He was gesticulating with his fist. Facing her was the hitchhiker, who she hadn't seen for weeks. The third man was hidden in the shadows. She could see little of him, beyond the impression that he was tall.

Claire shivered. She didn't think the hitchhiker could see her face, just her silhouette illuminated by the light from the central square. She turned and hurried back the way she'd come. At the exit, she glanced over her shoulder. The three men had turned to face her direction: Slick Willy, the hitchhiker and someone else.

Chapter 58

Claire stumbled into the crowd watching The Red Doors. She wove her way among the listeners, slid down the slope and sat on a patch of grass amid a noisy group. In the dim light, it would be difficult to spot her.

A man to her right leaned over and put his arm around her. "Hey, babe, how about a kiss?" He tried to nuzzle her neck but she pulled away. He smelled like beer and sweat. The band was playing their version of "I Can't Get No Satisfaction". Claire glanced over the guy's arm at the top of the slope. She thought she saw three men outlined there, looking down into the crowd. She turned back around and leaned into the man next to her. He brought up his right hand and turned her face to his. Then he kissed her, a slow slobbery kiss. Claire let him do it. When he pulled away, she extricated herself from his hold. People around them were getting to their feet and clapping. Claire stood up and began clapping as well. The man next to her tried to stand but he kept falling down.

This was The Red Doors' final number. As the song ended, people picked up their blankets and hampers and headed to their cars. Claire moved with the happy, raucous crowd through the central walkway between Heavenly's Shortcakes and The Great Southern Cafe. She looked nervously from right to left, but saw no one she knew. Slipping between parked cars and concertgoers, she found her way to her car. Before getting in, she snuck around to the back of the Assembly Hall, where she called Dax on the Exphone. It rang and rang but he didn't pick up. She considered using the SOS option but decided against it. She wasn't actually in grave danger. She tried calling on her cell phone next but there was still no answer.

Back inside her car, she turned on the engine and pulled out. The drive home along 30A was slow and tedious. As she drove through Watercolor and Grayton Beach at a crawl, she analyzed what had happened that evening. If Slick Willy was in cahoots with the hitchhiker, that meant they were both involved in the sales of RBBs. But who was the other man, the tall one she hadn't clearly seen? Was he the ringleader the FBI was after? She shivered, hoping they hadn't recognized her. If they had, did they know where to find her? Was she safe in Citrus Haven or should she get away?

At last she arrived in Lemon Cove and turned onto Lemon Drive, following another car. Through the trees, she noticed lights in several of the big houses. People had come back for the Artist Festival. The car ahead turned into a driveway. She passed it, followed the road to the right and drove along, parallel to the Gulf and around the dunes. Citrus Haven looked dark and menacing in the moonlight. A premonition of evil flooded her psyche. She shouldn't have come home. She should turn around right now, go find a motel, someplace safe.

Stop it, Claire. She drove up to the gate and then into the garage beneath the coach house. Fumbling in her purse she pulled out the Ruger and then exited the car, holding her gun ready. She eyed the recesses of the garage and under the metal stairway. No one was there. *Come on Claire, you're getting paranoid.*

Once inside her apartment, Claire double-locked the door. She tucked the gun back in her purse and left it on the kitchen counter. After turning on all the lights, she stood still in the middle of the living room. She felt wrought up and feverish. Was living here really worth it? The fear and insecurity were driving her mad. She looked around at the pretty furnishings and out the windows at the moonlit waves. This beautiful apartment wasn't worth the personal anguish. She'd been stubborn—no, pig-headed and stupid—because she wanted to handle life her way, with no one telling her what to do.

She walked into the bedroom, pulled down her suitcases from a closet shelf and opened them up on the floor by the window. In the morning she would pack up and leave Citrus Haven. If necessary, she would move into a motel for a few days until she found a place to live. Dax would have to find another undercover agent. She didn't have the grit for the job.

In the kitchen, Claire opened a bottle of wine and poured herself a glass. She took it into the living room, where she kicked off her sandals and curled up on the sofa. Leaning back, she gazed out at the silver-topped waves nibbling at the shore. She sighed deeply. Now that she'd made the decision to move, she felt a sense of relief. Tomorrow would be a new beginning.

What about Dax? He'd said he would always respond to the Exphone. She needed to try him again to tell him her decision.

She got up and walked over to the sliding door that led out to the deck. After pulling the door shut behind her, she walked to the far end. Surely, the listening device under the coffee table couldn't pick up the signal out here. She called Dax again, but the Exphone registered no signal. She frowned, uneasy, and tried her cell. No signal there, either. Her breath came faster and her heart pounded. Something must have gone wrong. Had they cut her off somehow, the gang that was watching her? No, that was crazy. But this wasn't good.

She hurried back inside and into the bedroom. Frantically she started throwing clothes into the suitcases. She would move out tonight.

Chapter 59

As Claire took a pile of shirts from the dresser, she heard banging on the kitchen door. Who could have gotten through the gate and into the garage? Claire scurried into the kitchen and listened. The banging came again, and someone rattled the door knob.

"Open up, Claire. We've got to talk."

She knew the voice. It was Leo Martin. She reached out to open the door, then hesitated. "How did you get through the gate and the garage door downstairs?"

"I have my ways. Open up." His voice was hard, an unfamiliar tone.

"Why do you need to talk to me?"

"You're messing in my business."

"Business?" Oh God. Leo was involved. Leo, whom she had trusted from the start. She tiptoed over to the counter and pulled the gun out of her purse.

"Don't be coy. We've seen you sneaking around. The game is up." He banged on the door again.

"I don't know what you're talking about."

"I'll shoot off this lock if necessary. Open up, *now*," he yelled.

"Okay, okay. Just a minute. I'm not dressed."

Claire looked around the kitchen. There was nowhere to hide. She needed to escape. He'd break the door down any minute. Her gaze fell on the bottle of olive oil on the counter. She remembered the slippery mess she'd seen at the Publix, the elderly woman flat on the floor. She slipped the gun back into her bag and slung it over her head.

"Just a minute, Leo. I'm pulling on my sweater." She picked up the oil bottle, unscrewed the top and ran to the door that led into the main house. As quietly as she could, she pushed back the chain and turned the bolt, then eased the door open. The corridor was empty. She poured oil across the sleek stone floor behind her and then raced barefoot down the hallway to the staircase. All the lights came on and Nirvana's "Smells like Teen Spirit" blasted through the space. Behind her, she heard a splintering crash as the kitchen door burst open.

She started down the stairs but halted as she heard someone coming up from the entryway below. She turned, hurried around the elevator and started upstairs, taking it two steps at a time. She emptied the rest of the olive oil on the floor behind her and tossed the glass bottle over her shoulder. It smashed into a thousand pieces.

A crash and a lot of swearing cut through the air. Leo, angry and in pain. He must have slipped and fallen in the hallway. "Fuck, fuck, *fuck*. Willy? Where the fuck are you?"

She heard another thud as Slick Willy tumbled down the stairs behind her. He yelled out in anger as something clattered away. "Damn, what's on the stairs?" Willy shouted over the pumping music.

"Some kind of oil. Fuck, my knee is killing me." Leo groaned.

Claire flew up the stairs to the third floor. With the music pounding, she couldn't hear her pursuers. Then suddenly, silence fell. They'd turned off the music somehow. For a second she stood still and considered her options. Where could she hide? The bedrooms on the third floor had no hiding places. She continued up to the fourth floor, two steps at a time.

Now she could hear heavy breathing coming up from below. Panic shot through her. There was nowhere to go. The two bedroom suites on this floor offered no escape. What about the sitting area on this floor that opened to the great room? Could she slip behind a sofa. She remembered the rope tied to the safety railing. Daniel had suggested it was an escape hatch in case of fire. She ran from the open hallway between the bedroom suites, to the sitting area that opened onto the great room below. Moonlight, flooding through the immense windows facing the sea, gave enough light to see by. She walked over to the steel pipes that served as a railing along the edge of the balcony. No one was down below in the great room. She didn't see the rope at first, but then spotted the thick white coil beneath a nearby end table. As Claire crouched down to pull out the rope, Slick Willy came around the corner. He was limping and had a gun in his right hand.

"There you are, you little bitch. Thought you could escape. But we've got you." He started towards her, one eye on her and the other on the floor.

Claire pulled the wasp spray out of her bag. She leaped up and moved forward, aiming the spray at Willy's face. He screamed in pain and dropped the gun as he reached up to claw at his eyes. Then he staggered away from her, toward the low railing. She reached out to pull him back, but his shirt-tail slipped through her hands. He stumbled forward blindly towards the low railing. Claire screamed out and then watched in horror as he hurtled over the balustrade. He screamed for what felt like a lifetime. Then there was a horrible splat. And then silence.

Claire stood shivering. What had she done? She'd killed a man. She was a murderer. She covered her face with her hands. In her mind she saw Willy go over the railing and heard his final scream. Guilt paralyzed her. Then, distantly, she heard Leo's voice. "What have you done, Claire?" His heavy footfalls trudged up the stairs.

"I didn't mean to," she whimpered. "It was an accident."

"I'm going to kill you. You've been a problem from the start." He was getting closer. He *would* kill her. She knew that. She had to get away. The thought of joining Willy was frightening, but she had no choice. She crouched down and pulled out the rope. It was tied to the top rung of the railing. She threw the heavy rope over the side just as Leo appeared around the corner, gun drawn. "Stand still, Claire." He seemed enormous, illuminated by the light from the hallway.

Claire grasped the rope. Her hands slid down to a knot. She swung her body over the railing, held the rope between her legs and with her bare feet felt for another knot. The rope swung back and forth under the sitting-room overhang. She slithered down the rope from knot to knot. The rough surface chafed the skin of her palms. Above, she heard shots and a bullet pinged past her ear. She kept climbing down, swinging back and forth beneath the balcony. Leo fired again and missed. She reached the last knot and dropped to the floor.

She landed a few feet from what had been Slick Willy. A pool of blood oozed from underneath his crumpled body. She jumped back under the balcony overhang. From above she heard swearing, then Leo's footsteps on the stairs. He would be here in just a few moments.

Claire ran to the stairwell and started down to the ground floor. If she could make it outside through the back door, she could hide in the woods. Broken glass from the bottle of olive oil cut into her feet. She yelped in pain but kept going. Gripping the banister to keep from sliding on the slick surface, she raced down the stairs. Leo was close behind.

Chapter 60

Claire jumped down the last few steps and raced towards the back door. Then someone grabbed her from behind in a powerful grip. She cried out as her arms were wrenched behind her. "You're not going anywhere," a voice said with a sneer.

Then Leo was there, breathing heavily. "You've got the little bitch." He came around and looked down at her. Then he brought up his right hand and slapped her back and forth across the face. Her head whipped from side to side and she tasted the salty tang of blood.

"Stop, stop." She was crying, and she thought he'd split her lip. Leo, the symbol of law and order. How could he be beating her? "Leo, what are you doing?" She spluttered.

"Shut up." He plunged his fist into her stomach. She doubled over, all the air knocked out of her.

"Bring her into the lab," Leo said.

Claire tried to breathe. She felt dizzy and disoriented. The man who held her kneed her in the back to propel her forward. She tripped, and he yanked her upright by her hair. Leo, limping from his fall on the olive oil, went ahead to the storage area door. He pulled out a key, unlocked the heavy padlock and swung the reinforced door open.

Claire's captor thrust her forward into an enormous room, as large as the great room upstairs. It looked like a make-shift laboratory. Bright fluorescent lights illuminated the room. Stainless steel equipment rested on heavy wooden planks placed on reinforced crates. A machine whirred in a corner like a massive centrifuge. Bottles of green liquid and metal canisters covered one of the makeshift tables. On another, small medication bottles without labels were lined up in rows.

A man emerged like an apparition from an alcove on the far side of the room. He was dressed all in white. His bald head gleamed under the lights. His dark eyes flitted around the room like those of a frightened bird. His morbid pallor and shuffling gait reminded Claire of a ghost. He looked at her and then glanced up. Claire followed his gaze and saw a row of TV screens above the equipment. They displayed the video feeds from the cameras inside and outside the house. Undoubtedly this man had seen her often.

"Get some duct tape," Leo demanded.

The ghost floated towards a tall shelving unit and brought back a roll of tape. Leo reached down, yanked her purse away from her and threw it under the nearest table. The gun inside made a loud clunk, but the men seemed oblivious to it. Not that it would do her much good now. Leo removed the Exphone and tossed it aside as well. Then he tore off a long piece of duct tape. "Hold her arms," he said to the man behind her. Claire tried to move her shoulders, but the man wrenched her arms tighter and she felt the duct tape being wrapped around and around her wrists. Then someone pushed her down, first on her knees and then flat to the ground, her face smashed into the cement floor. She cried out and turned her head to the side, her cheek resting on crumbled cement.

"Ronny, hold her feet," Leo said.

Claire wrenched her head around for a look. Revulsion and fear shot through her as she recognized the hitchhiker sneering down at her. As he reached for her legs, she kicked out, knocking him off balance. He fell back a step.

"Shit, you little bitch." He pulled himself up and grabbed one kicking leg and then the other. With a vicious twist motion he brought her legs together. Then he sat on her thighs while Leo bent down and taped her ankles.

Why was Ronny, the hitchhiker, working with Leo? She remembered when he'd accosted her at the gas station in Alabama and Leo stepped in. "Leo, was that some con game at the gas station when I first met you?" she blurted out.

He looked down at her. "What…Ronny? I hired him that night. I figured he'd be a good foot soldier." He turned to Ronny. "Watch her. I've got to make a call."

"So you didn't know each other before?" Claire remembered the times she'd called Leo when she'd seen Ronny in the area. He must have gotten a big laugh out of that.

"Not till that night," Ronny said with a snide chuckle. "Leo drove me down and put me in that motel where you were staying. What a joke."

Claire remembered seeing him when she drove away from the motel that first day. She looked up at Ronny, who was rubbing his shins. "Were you Amy's mysterious boyfriend? Françoise told me his name was Ronny." Claire went on, thinking out loud. "And Amy introduced you to all the artists she knew, so you could sell them RBBs."

"You are fucking smart." He kicked her in the ribs with the toe of his boot.

Across the room, the ghost floated on the edge of their conversation. Leo was rooting through boxes, his phone to his ear. "Right, we're going to clear out the place. I've got a truck coming. Should be here any minute."

Claire needed to know more. "What about Amy? Why did you kill her? She helped you find customers. I don't get it."

Ronny looked at her with contempt. "It was a mistake."

Claire tried to change her position. It felt as though her arms were being torn from her shoulders. "A mistake?"

"Yeah, I was supposed to kill you."

"Me?"

"I'd watched you run on the beach wearing that pink hoodie. That night it was cloudy and I couldn't see so well, just the flash of pink. I stuck the needle into the wrong girl." He leaned against the wooden counter, crossing his arms. "I was getting tired of her anyway. She was asking questions."

"Why did you want to kill me?" Claire choked out.

"Because you shouldn't be here and you wouldn't move, and you kept asking questions."

Claire pulled her knees to her chest. "What are you going to do with me?"

"Whatever the boss says." He pulled a knife from its sheath on his belt and began cleaning his nails.

Leo walked back across the room, tucking his phone in his pocket. "Hand me the tape." Ronny obliged. Leo tore off a short piece and stretched it across her mouth and cheeks, catching loose strands of hair. "Help me pick her up. We'll put her in the back room." Ronny put away his knife and reached down to grab her legs. Leo picked her up by the shoulders and they carried her through the doorway into the rear alcove. They dropped her on a pile of rags in a corner hidden from the main room. Her head hit a hard object and the world started to spin.

As she descended into darkness she heard Leo say, "Get over here, Lazarus. We've got to disconnect the equipment and pack it away. Hurry up. We're moving out tonight."

Chapter 61

Claire slowly opened her eyes. She didn't know how long

she'd been out. With care, she moved her head back and forth, pushing away from the hard object hidden under the stinking rags that had smashed into her skull. At the slight movement, pain shot through her head.

She lay on the floor, trembling. The duct tape across her face filled her with fear. What if she couldn't breathe through her nose? What if she choked? She would suffocate. She mustn't cry and fill her nose with mucus. She needed to breathe. The stench of the rags under her head brought bile to her mouth. She swallowed it. Then, applying what she'd learned in meditation sessions, she concentrated on her breathing: in and out, in and out, one, two, three, four...It didn't work.

Her arms ached and she felt as though she had lost circulation in her legs. From the other room she heard men packing boxes and taping them shut. They'd unplugged the equipment and it was eerily silent. The men grunted and swore as they worked. Leo kept yelling at Lazarus, who said nothing. After a while she guessed the truck had arrived, because she heard other voices. More grunts and swearing in English and Spanish as the new arrivals picked up boxes or equipment and trudged out the door. Claire gave in to her woozy feeling, and slipped in and out of consciousness.

A loud bang brought her back. Then it was quiet. Was she alone? Had they left her here to die? No, she mustn't cry: *breathe in, breathe out, breathe in, breathe out.* Her heart fluttered in her chest and she had a massive headache. Everything hurt: arms, legs, stomach, face. She thought back over the evening. Why hadn't Dax returned her calls? Where was he? He'd sworn she could always reach him, but that wasn't true. She was totally alone. A sob filled her throat. She choked it back. No crying. She closed her eyes and concentrated on her breathing.

Then she heard a slight noise and felt acrid breath on

her face. Her eyes flew open. The ghost was there, his face inches from hers. He looked down at her with pity.

"Help me, help me," she tried to say, but the duct tape muffled her words. She pleaded with him with her eyes: *Help me*. Those deep set, dark eyes in his unnaturally white face stared back at her.

He stood up abruptly and shuffled into the other room. She heard rustling paper and the bumping of boxes. What was he doing? Would he save her or kill her? All he had to do was cover her nose and she would die. She closed her eyes again. *Breathe in, breathe out.*

A few minutes later, she heard shuffling feet again and was aware of the ghost looking down at her. He held a box cutter in his hands. "I will free you. Hold very still." His voice was low and whispery, probably from lack of use. He gently rolled her over. Holding her hands still, he sawed at the layers of duct tape. It took a while. He was being careful not to cut her. Eventually the tape loosened, and then her hands were free. She felt a brief, sharp pain as he tore the tape off.

Claire rolled back over and pushed herself into a seated position. She felt dizzy as she rubbed her hands up and down her arms and around her wrists, trying to restore circulation. Lazarus held out the box cutter and gestured to her feet. "Do you want to do it?"

She shook her head. As shaky as she felt, she didn't trust herself. He bent down and sawed at the binding around her ankles. Claire reached up to her ear and felt for the edge of the duct tape across her mouth. Steeling herself, she yanked hard and felt the tape rip across her face, pulling her hair and stinging her skin. She hurled the strip of tape into a corner and gulped deep breaths of air through her mouth. Her lip had started to bleed again, and her bare feet throbbed where slivers of glass had cut them.

235

Lazarus had managed to free her legs. As he pulled the tape from around her ankles she gave a yelp, then panted, "Thank you, you saved my life."

"Not for long. They'll be back." His tone was grim.

"Where did they go?"

"To a new site. We've only been here a month and they're moving the lab."

"So they'll be back to get you?" Claire said.

"I think they've decided they don't need me anymore. Someone else will run the lab."

Claire inspected her feet. The cuts didn't look too bad. Hopefully, no glass was embedded in them. They hurt, but she could deal. She braced her hands behind her to push up off the floor, and felt the hard object that had knocked her out. She turned and pulled the rags away. Hiding underneath was a hammer. She had fallen on the rounded head. It had probably given her a concussion. Claire shoved it aside, reached over to brace herself against the wall and tried to stand up. Lazarus reached to help but she shook her head. On her feet, she felt woozy and leaned into the wall. "We have to get out of here."

"There's no way out. Don't think I haven't looked." He rasped.

"There has to be." She stepped away from the wall and walked towards the main room, wincing with every step.

The room was a mess. Discarded boxes, plastic containers and other trash littered the floor. They'd removed the wooden tables and shelving. Everything had been dismantled and carried away. Claire scanned the room from floor to ceiling. There had to be a way out. In the far corner she spotted her purse, thrown there when Leo taped her arms. She hobbled over to the bag and picked it up. The gun was still inside. She pulled it out and waved it around. "Hey,

Lazarus, look what I've got! I can shoot off the lock and get us out of here." She hobbled toward the heavy metal door.

"It won't work," he rasped. "It's a reinforced steel door. You can't hope to shoot through and hit the lock."

"But we have to get out of here." She looked around again, holding the gun in both hands. There were several heating and air-conditioning vents about five inches from the ceiling along the longer wall. On the short wall was one vent. It had to be the air hole into the utility room. The listening device she'd installed was on the other side. She hobbled over to it and yelled, "Dax, Dax. Help. I'm locked in the storage room. You need to come *now*."

Lazarus looked at her as if she'd lost her senses. "What are you doing? Who are you talking to?"

"I placed a listening device on the other side of that vent up there. The FBI should be listening to our conversation right now." She yelled again, "Dax, help us. I'm locked in the storage room in Citrus Haven. Help!"

Lazarus shook his head. "No one will hear you. They turned on the firewall bubble."

Chapter 62

"Firewall bubble? What are you talking about?"

"Look at the TV screens. They're dead. The camera feed is off. Leo has someone switch on a firewall that stops all communication with the outside world. We're in a vacuum. Nothing gets in or out."

Claire limped over to the side wall, where Leo had tossed her Exphone. She pushed on the green button, but there was no sound. She tried the SOS button, but it was dead too. Feeling desperate, she retrieved her cell from her purse and turned it on, but was met with a blank screen.

"What are we going to do?" She looked frantically around the room.

Lazarus held his hands out, palms up, a sign of helpless uncertainty.

Claire shook her head. "We've got to think. The only opening is that vent." She gestured up at the grate. "If we could enlarge it by a couple of inches, I could get through. Then we'll figure a way to get you out."

Lazarus continued to look at her with quiet resignation. He had given up fighting. But Claire hadn't. She sized him up, guessing his height at six feet or so. That should be enough… "I know what we'll do." She walked gingerly across the room and into the alcove. When she came back she was carrying the hammer in one hand and her gun in the other. She bent over, retrieved her cross-body bag and slung it over her head and shoulder. Then she placed her cell phone, the Exphone and the gun inside.

"Okay, Lazarus. You let me sit on your shoulders and I'll reach up and enlarge that hole in the wall with this." She shook the hammer.

He still looked uncertain. "I don't know if it'll

work." He glanced up at the twelve- by five-inch vent. "My name isn't Lazarus by the way. That's what Leo calls me. I hate it. My name is Walter, Walter Remus, and I'm wanted by the police." His voice had grown stronger as he identified himself.

Claire groaned. There was no time to talk. "I'm sorry, Walter. At this point I don't care if you're wanted by the police. Okay? Let's get out of here." She walked over to the wall under the vent. "Come on, bend down. I'll climb on your shoulders." She handed him the hammer.

Looking dubious, he crouched down. Claire wasn't sure how strong he was but balanced on his shoulders, she knew she could reach the air vent. She climbed onto his shoulders and he slowly hoisted her up, steadying himself with his hand against the wall.

With Walter at his full height, Claire could touch the ceiling. She flipped her purse over against her back so it was out of the way. "Hand me the hammer, would you?" He passed it up, and she used the claw to leverage off the grate covering the vent. It came off easily and she tossed it over her shoulder. Then she banged on the edges of the opening. The first crack revealed two layers of drywall with space in between. She made more cracks and used the claw to tear off pieces of drywall. With her hands she pulled off larger fragments and tossed them down, taking care not to hit Walter.

"How are you doing down there?"

"All right," he said. "But I'm weakening."

"It shouldn't take much longer." Claire kept hammering, clawing and pulling the drywall. At last she made a jagged hole she could probably slip through. "Walter, I'm going to crawl through here. Then we'll figure out how to pull you up." She thought of the sturdy rope in the great room. Would she have time to run up there and cut a piece off?

First things first. Claire poked the hammer through the hole and let it go, then reached into the utility room and grasped the metal shelving unit beneath the vent. Groaning with effort, she slowly pulled herself through the opening. From below, she felt Walter push her feet upward. Suddenly she was balanced on the ledge of the hole she'd made. Her cross-body bag was snagged on the ragged edge of the vent. She freed it and wiggled her way into the utility room, ripping the fabric of her tunic. She managed to swing one leg over the ledge, dislodging more drywall. Good—Walter wasn't a big man, but he'd likely need a wider opening. She snatched the hammer from the top shelf and banged off a few more pieces, then set it down and gingerly placed her foot on a shelf. Bottles of cleaning supplies crashed to the floor. She pulled her other leg over and pointed downward with her toes until she felt another shelf. The unit trembled with her weight. She jumped blindly to the floor, dislodging more boxes and bottles. Feeling around with her hand, Claire found the light switch. Slowly she opened the door to the hallway and peered out. The hallway was dark and silent.

Claire stepped back into the utility room. "No one's around. We need to hurry and get you out," she called.

Walter's response was muffled. Claire inspected the utility room. Her gaze fell on the heavy-duty vacuum cleaner, with its thick black cord wound up and down along the side of the shaft. Was it strong enough to carry the weight of a man? Quickly, she unwound the cord.

"What are you doing?" Walter sounded panicked, like he thought she was leaving him in the lurch.

Claire yelled up at the opening in the wall. "I'm going to toss over a cord. You'll have to shinny your way up the wall. I'll try to counterbalance your weight." She made a lasso with several feet of cord. Then she climbed onto the upturned bucket, carefully set one foot on a shelf, and tossed the lengths of cord upward. Her first try missed, but on the second, the cord went through the hole.

"Got it," Walter yelled.

Claire stepped onto the base of the vacuum. She braced a foot on each side of the shaft and grasped the cord in her hands. "Okay!"

There was a quick pull on the cord as Walter started his climb. After a few seconds, the cord ripped away from the vacuum. Claire reached out just in time to grab the end. She heard Walter crash down on the other side and a series of swear words.

"The cord came off the vacuum. I'm tying it onto the shelving unit. Let's hope that will work." She climbed up on the bucket and reached up, winding the cord around a metal post and then around her hands. "Okay, try now."

She braced herself and held on for dear life as Walter pulled himself up the wall. The cord cut into her hands and the metal shelving wobbled from Walter's weight. Within thirty seconds he had reached the opening. "Grab on to the shelving inside and use it as a ladder," she said. Walter's hands grasped the top shelf and he snaked his way through the hole. One leg came through and he felt for a shelf with his foot. The unit couldn't handle his weight and toppled over. Claire flattened herself against the door as Walter crashed down beside her. He landed on his back, the shelving on top of him.

Blood dripped down Claire's cheek where a corner of the shelving had scraped her. She reached up and felt a cut under her hair line. Walter dragged himself upright. Together they pushed the shelving back in place. The floor was littered with cans, bottles and rags.

Claire looked over at Walter. "Are you all right?"

He looked over at her and smiled, in spite of the blood streaming from a cut on his face. His cheeks were suffused with color. He looked almost human. "Am I all right? I'm fabulous. For two years I've been a prisoner and a slave." He beamed at her. "Let's get out of here."

Claire handed him a clean rag and he dabbed at his face. Then as she reached for the door to the hallway, another door whooshed open down the hall. They looked at each other. Walter's face had gone white. She switched off the light and they stood still, barely breathing as heavy footsteps approached.

Chapter 63

"Let's each take two cans. You start upstairs. The living room furniture, curtains, bedding; drench everything that's flammable. This place will go up like a powder keg. I'll do the garages."

Claire recognized Leo's voice. He'd undoubtedly returned with Ronny. They were right outside the utility room door. She held her breath. If he opened the door, she and Walter would be dead. She felt as though she could hear Leo breathing on the other side.

She listened as Leo walked down the hall toward the garages under her apartment. For a moment she thought of all of her belongings as well as her car that would go up in flames. Ronny's steps echoed as well, trudging up the stairs. She whispered to Walter, "We have to get out of here. Now."

"How?" he whispered.

Silently, Claire debated their best plan of action. "We'll go out the front door and make a run for it. Follow me. Careful where you step. There's junk all over the floor." Slowly, Claire opened the utility closet door. All the lights were on, and the glare momentarily blinded her. Down the hall, she saw the open door to the garages. She gestured to Walter to step out into the hall. His foot hit something that clinked. They froze and looked at each other. The odor of gasoline permeated the air.

Claire gestured to Walter to close the door behind them. She tiptoed down the hall toward the entranceway. The front door was partially open but when she got near, she heard voices. Someone was out in the driveway. Panicked, she turned and bumped into Walter, who was right on her heels. "Back door," Claire murmured. "We'll go out through the garden and into the woods." She spotted the oars leaning up against the wall beside the cubbies, grabbed one and handed it to Walter. He questioned her with a look. She turned away and took the other oar. Then she gestured for him to follow.

She led the way down the short hall toward the back garden. Silently, she pulled open the door and they ran across the expanse of grass to the back gate. She fumbled with the cover on the panel. For a moment her mind went blank. She couldn't remember the code. After some trial and error, it came to her and the gate swung open. They went through and she closed the gate behind them. Were they safe and away? It all depended on whether Leo checked the storage room before setting the house on fire.

Claire looked back at Citrus Haven. Light streamed from the windows on the first floor where Ronny was emptying cans of gasoline. She thought of Slick Willy's dead body and shivered. Leo planned to obliterate all evidence of the lab and incinerate three people.

She turned and headed through the forest, Walter following closely. The clouds had dissipated and the moon cast just enough light through the branches to illuminate the path. They jogged for several minutes. Claire's feet were raw and bleeding. In the tension of the last few hours, she'd almost forgotten the glass on the stairway that had cut into her bare soles. Now the pain was acute each time she took a step. Her cross-body bag, heavy with the gun, thumped against her hip as she ran.

Walter's breathing was labored. After a few minutes he hissed, "Stop." He wheezed and tried to catch his breath. "I can't keep up. I haven't run for two years."

"Okay, we'll walk. But we have to keep moving."

She strode swiftly ahead but Walter had trouble keeping up. He was hobbling as though his knee hurt, using

244

the oar as a cane. It should be a fifteen or twenty-minute walk to Lemon Cove, but he was slowing them down.

"Maybe you should go on ahead," he gasped.

"It's only another five minutes. You can make it."

He didn't answer. The oar thumped on the ground, followed by the soft slap of his bare foot. Thump, slap, thump, slap.

"We're going to the rowboat on the cove, aren't we? I've been in it."

Claire turned and looked at him. "When was that?"

He took a deep breath. "A month ago, they had to move the lab. Before, it was in an old warehouse in Mobile. When Leo figured the Feds were on to us, he moved the lab by boat down the coast. It took a couple of nights. They used a fishing boat and a rowboat."

"That's ridiculous. Why didn't they use a truck?" Claire recalled the sounds she'd heard at night those first few weeks after she moved in.

"They thought... they would be...stopped on the highway." He wheezed between phrases, but kept walking.

After what seemed like ages, Claire heard water lapping gently against the shore. They were almost there. Far away, she thought she heard voices. She touched Walter's arm to stop his progress and listened. Male voices yelled in the distance. Leo had probably opened the storage room and found them gone. He and Ronny were surely coming, and maybe some other members of the gang as well. Her heart thudded in her chest. How far away were they? It was hard to judge.

She gripped the heavy oar with one hand and yanked Walter forward with the other. "Come on, it's not much further."

They moved painfully onward, Claire walking gingerly on her bleeding feet and Walter protecting his knee. The voices in the distance grew louder. Leo, and whoever else, was gaining on them.

At last they arrived at the cove. The moon shone brightly, but a layer of mist blanketed the water. There, under the tree, was the rowboat. Claire ran forward, leaving Walter to make his way across the beach grass. She unzipped the purse swinging at her side and pulled out the Ruger, cocked it, stepped back and aimed at the lock that tethered the boat to the tree. Two shots reverberated through the air and the lock exploded. If Leo hadn't heard them before, he knew where they were now.

Claire gestured to Walter. "Help me flip the boat over and we'll get it into the water. We can row over to the other side and make it up to Route 98."

He looked at her and shook his head. "I don't know."

"Walter, we don't have a choice. Come *on*."

Propelled by her energy, he hobbled over. Together they reached down and heaved the heavy wooden boat right side up. They dropped the pins of the oars into each oarlock and propped them inside the gunwales. Then they pushed the boat across the footpath that led around Lemon Cove. There was a drop of two feet or so down into the water. Claire held the chain as Walter pushed the boat into the cove with a loud splash.

"You hop in first, then I'll follow," she said.

Walter turned his back to the water and reached down with one foot, holding onto tufts of grass. As he brought down his other leg, he lost his balance and fell backwards into the boat. There was loud splash and the boat bucked up and down. He pushed himself up and pulled himself on to a seat. "I can't swim," he said, his voice tense.

Claire didn't respond but pulled the boat close to the bank of the cove and stepped down into the bow. The boat rocked up and down. She pulled in the chain and seated herself between the oars. She could make out Leo and Ronny's voices in the stillness. They were getting closer.

"Can you row?" Claire asked.

"I don't know how. I've never been around boats."

"Okay, sit in the stern."

Walter crawled to the back of the boat, clearly fearful of falling into the water. Claire used an oar to push away from the shoreline, turned the boat around and headed across the cove. She hadn't rowed since that time in the Poconos. At first, she chopped the oars into the water and didn't make much headway. Then she picked up the rhythm and the boat began to move smoothly through the water. The mist swirled around them. Claire could still see the bank and the gazebo where she had sat talking with Dax. She needed to try calling him again. But first they had to escape.

"I want to go straight across the cove," she said. "Can you keep the gazebo in sight and guide me?"

"I'll try. Pretty soon, we won't be able to see anything with the fog," Walter said.

They were silent for a moment. The splash of the oars cutting through the water was the only sound.

Claire broke the silence. "Walter?"

"Yes?"

"What about Daniel—Boone Williams? Do you know what happened to him?" She held her breath, not wanting to know the answer.

"Leo beat him and shot him."

Claire swallowed hard. "Why?"

"They never got along. They fought about everything. Boone wanted a larger cut of the profits. He was the front man in a lot of deals because Leo wanted to stay out of the limelight. Then Boone thought bringing Ronny in was a mistake. They argued about that." He paused and said more quietly, "They fought about you. Leo didn't want to rent the coach house, but Boone said it would add credibility to all the comings and goings."

Claire thought about how she had fallen for Daniel's fake persona. He'd seemed like a nice guy. In fact, he had been a superb con man. She pulled hard on the oars. Then she heard Leo's voice, calling from across the water as he emerged from the forest.

"I can see you, Claire. It's over. Turn around or I'll shoot."

Chapter 64

Claire kept rowing. Just a little bit further and they would be lost in the mist.

"Walter is a murderer. He's dangerous. You don't want to be alone with him. Turn around and row back here," Leo yelled.

Claire pulled harder, trying to maintain her rhythm. She looked back at Walter. His face was ashen.

"I gave you plenty of chances to get out of the house but you wouldn't listen to anybody."

A shot cracked next to the boat. She crouched down and pulled on the oars. There was another crack, and Walter gasped and fell forward. She propped the oars on the gunwales and hunkered down. A volley of shots echoed. Claire lay low as the bullets flew past. Then there was silence.

"Walter. Are you all right?" she whispered. He didn't move. She reached out and touched his arm. "Walter?" He slumped lower. Gently, she lifted his head. Blank eyes stared into hers. Above them was a hole in the middle of his forehead.

Claire fought down nausea and let Walter's head go limp. She sat up briefly and glanced back at the shore. The gazebo was a mirage in the distance. Had they given up? She squinted, trying to see better across the water.

"Man, you're a stubborn little bitch," Leo shouted. Another volley of shots peppered the cove. Bullets zinged past. As she crouched back down, she felt a searing pain in her upper left arm. She fell sideways and hit her head on the gunwale. For a few seconds, she blacked out. When she came to, her arm was burning, and she felt warm blood oozing down her forearm.

In the distance she heard more muffled shooting, but no bullets were coming her way. The mist was a thick blanket muting sound. She'd lost all sense of direction. Claire sat on the floor of the boat, propping her injured arm on the seat. She needed to get up and start rowing but her arm was throbbing in pain. Rowing with only her right arm would send the boat spinning in circles.

Did Leo think he'd shot them both? Then why did she still hear muffled gunshots? Her brain was moving at a snail's pace. She rested her head on her knees and closed her eyes, feeling woozy. Minutes later, she came to again, cold and wet. She realized she was sitting in an inch of water. Leo had managed to puncture the side of the boat and it was taking on water.

Awkwardly, Claire pulled herself up onto the seat. She looked over at Walter's inert body and for a brief moment felt like laughing and crying at the same time. This was an unimaginable nightmare. She was in a sinking boat with a corpse; not just any corpse, but the body of a murderer. She imagined Jeremy saying, "Claire, you've got yourself into one hell of a mess," shaking his head in smug superiority.

Gradually she realized the boat was moving too fast. She glanced to the left and saw the outline of the dunes along the seashore. The boat had floated towards the mouth of the inlet and was drifting out to sea. The tide must be going out and her boat along with it.

The water at her feet was deeper now, the boat going faster. She was going to drown, if she didn't come up with a plan. What could she do? Her mind was slower than molasses in January. As the rowboat moved out into the Gulf, Claire realized the fog was gone. The stars were visible and the moon was low in the sky. Far off along the beach, Citrus Haven glowed from within as if alive. Its spirit whirled up to the heavens in gyrating smoke. The vision was horrifying and weirdly beautiful. Leo had destroyed the house and all it contained. Mesmerized by the sight, she felt oddly relieved.

The boat kept drifting on a strong current. Gently rolling waves surrounded her. She had to do something, quick.

Don't panic. Think logically. The Exphone. It might work out here. She still had the cross-body bag slung over her right shoulder. With cold trembling hands, she unzipped the bag, pulled out the gun and laid it between her thighs. Then she reached in and felt around inside for the Exphone. She extracted it and slid back the panel, held it up to the light and pushed the red SOS button. Was there a connection out here? Would the agents pick up the signal? She didn't know. She pushed the red button again and again.

The water in the boat was rising fast. Claire shivered in the cool air. Her feet were cramping from the frigid water. She moved her legs without thinking and the gun dropped into the water. It didn't matter. The weapon was useless out here. She pulled her feet up onto the seat and wrapped her right arm around her knees, cradling her left arm. It was pulsating painfully. Claire tried the Exphone again. No answer.

Walter's head, down between his knees, was partially submerged. Claire gazed down at him. Had he been such a terrible man? Was he really a murderer? He hadn't seemed like an evil person.

In the distance Citrus Haven had shrunk. It had lost its grandeur and glowed red and black like an enormous lump of charcoal. She was beginning to feel sleepy. It had been an impossibly long night already. Then it hit her that nobody knew where she was. Only Leo and Ronny, and they wouldn't notify the authorities. Heck, Leo was *the authorities.* That was how he'd become a successful drug lord. The man who was supposed to hunt down the dope peddlers was one himself. He had wanted her dead and now her body would never be found out here, far from the shore. She pushed the SOS button on the Exphone again and again. Hoping against hope.

The water was up to the seat now; the boat was going down. She watched Walter's head and shoulders disappear. With her good arm, Claire pulled one oar from its oarlock and then the other. She lay down on top of them and pushed off from the boat as the water gurgled around her. The shore in the distance seemed like an impossible swim, but she began kicking, propping her body on the oars.

Minutes, hours, centuries later, Claire heard the chopping of a helicopter. It flew overhead, flashing a bright beam down into the water. She tried to raise her right arm, but the left one couldn't handle her weight. She flipped over, losing an oar in the process. The helicopter circled again and again. Had they seen her? She yelled, but who would hear?

Then in the distance she saw a large vessel coming towards her.

Chapter 65

"Claire, Claire."

She was stretched out on the chaise lounge in her bedroom. Amy's throw was wrapped around her and she felt incredibly warm and cozy. She looked down at the beach that stretched into the distance. The sand was snowy white and the water a brilliant blue. Puffy white clouds glided through the sky. She felt as though she was floating through the air bolstered by billowing pillows.

"Claire."

She wanted to burrow down into her warm cocoon and never wake up.

"Claire, can you hear me?"

Yes, she thought but the word didn't come out of her mouth.

"Claire, I need to know you're all right." There was a catch in the voice. "Please wake up."

Slowly she opened her eyes, blinking at first in the semi-darkness. It must be night time. She was in an unfamiliar room, attached to some wires and tubes, and something kept beeping somewhere.

"Hello, darling Claire."

Who was speaking? She turned her head slowly. It felt heavy and seemed to be wrapped in scarves.

Dax sat there beside her, smiling at her, his eyes moist. He reached over and took her hand in his large and warm one. She squeezed his palm and he squeezed back. Then she drifted into sleep.

Hours later, she woke up again. The hospital room was bright and sunny. Irma sat placidly in a chair near Claire's bed, knitting a multi-hued afghan and humming to herself. When she became aware of Claire's gaze, she glanced over and beamed. "There you are," she said. "I knew you'd wake up for me. How are you feeling, my dear?"

"Let's see," Claire croaked. "Everything hurts. My head aches, my arm throbs and my feet sting. How long have I been here?"

Irma laid her knitting on her lap. "Two days. You were in a bad way when they brought you in."

Claire nodded, then winced, and tried to think back. She didn't remember much after they'd pulled her from the water.

"We were all worried, I can tell you." Irma frowned. "Would you like a drink? There's ice water here."

"Yes, thank you."

Irma poured a glass of water and added a straw. She brought it to Claire's lips. The water tasted cool and delicious.

Irma sat back down. "They treated you for hypothermia and concussion. Then they operated on your arm. Luckily the shot was a simple through-and-through with no structural or vascular damage. Your arm will be just fine."

Claire wiggled her toes. "Why are my feet all wrapped up?"

"You cut them pretty badly...on broken glass. They picked out the shards."

The memories came flooding back: the olive oil, the broken bottle, being pursued through Citrus Haven by Leo and Slick Willy. She shut her eyes and tried to forget. Moments later she floated out of consciousness.

#

When she came around again, the room was dim and Dax was there. He looked tired, with dark circles under his eyes. "Hi," he said.

"Hi. Have you been here long?" Her voice came out in a scratchy whisper.

"A couple of hours. We've tried to have someone here all the time. Seijun left a while ago."

"Seijun?" She remembered seeing him talking to Slick Willy. "Wasn't he part of the gang?" she whispered.

Dax smoothed her hair back. "No, he was working with us. I approached him after you told me Slick Willy attended the meditation sessions. It turned out Seijun was suspicious of the man. When Reginald Brim died..." He trailed off, looking at Claire. "What's the matter?"

Claire felt tears pooling in her eyes. "Dax, I killed him," she blurted out.

"What do you mean?" He grasped her hand. "Who did you kill?"

"Slick Willy." She pulled herself up to a sitting position and told him all about Leo and Slick Willy pursuing her through the house, and about the wasp spray and Slick Willy's fall over the railing. At the end she was in tears.

"Claire, you were defending yourself. You're not guilty of murder." Gently, he pulled her into his arms. "Those guys were killers. It was you against them. You had no choice." He kissed her forehead.

When she was calmer, he helped her lie back down. But she wanted to keep talking, and told him everything. It was a long story. From time to time she paused for a sip of water or to calm down. Dax didn't stop her. He knew she had to get it out.

At the end, when she described watching the destruction of Citrus Haven from the sinking rowboat, her eyes widened and she clenched her fists. "Where's Leo? He'll be hunting for me. I'm not safe." She scanned the hospital room as though Leo might be lurking in a corner. She tried to sit up again but Dax gently pushed her down.

"It's over, Claire. Leo Martin is dead. He'll never hurt you again." He grabbed her hands in both of his and murmured, "You're safe. I'll protect you."

When her eyes refocused, she said quietly," What happened to him?"

"I shot him. While you were out floating in the Gulf, we had a gun battle on land. There were six of us against four of them. Leo Martin was killed, Ronny was shot in the leg and the other two gave up. We have Ronny and his pals in custody. They're all singing like a canary chorus."

Chapter 66
Six Months Later

Claire gazed out at the sparkling blue water. She was lying on a chaise in her white bikini. Dax lay next to her, their hands loosely entwined, his fingers curled against her thigh. The red beach umbrella overhead gave a rosy glow to their skin. She glanced at Dax. He was asleep; a smile on his lips. She sighed contentedly. Life was good.

As often happened, her mind went back to the previous winter, focusing on her relationship with Leo Martin. There were several glaring events that should have tipped her off. All in all, he'd been pretty unresponsive to her calls for help. The fact that he'd taken her statement about Boone Williams at The Wine Bar instead of the police station should have been a red flag. Then the way he behaved when he came to the apartment after Amy died, acting as though he'd never met Claire before. And he'd never told her a thing about the Bartholomew Group. He'd strung her along instead, lying through his teeth.

Claire clenched her free hand into a fist as she remembered the time they'd run into each other for lunch in Rosemary Beach. He'd said he'd seen her car, but her vehicle had been hidden between two vans. It must have been the tracking device that led him to Rosemary Beach. The worst thing was how stupid she felt. She had confided in him when all along he was plotting her demise.

She shivered, although she knew she didn't have to worry about Leo anymore. She felt Dax stir beside her and looked over at him. His eyes were open and he was studying her. "Hey, beautiful. Penny for your thoughts."

She smiled. "Oh, you know, the usual. I was going

over everything that happened."

He gave her hand a squeeze. "You've got to let it go."

"I know."

He sat up and gently kissed her lips. "It's over. You're safe." He looked into her eyes. She reached up and laid her palm against his cheek. They kissed again, slow and deep.

When Dax lay back down, keeping hold of her hand, Claire said, "So what's the latest with Josh Owens?"

"He's being held on rape charges. Several girls came forward. We've yet to nail him on his financial dealings with the Bartholomew Group but it's only a matter of time."

"I still think about Walter Remus," Claire said.

"Yeah, he got a tough break. He was a scientist who made a deal with the devil. When Owens got wind of Remus's research, he funded the lab with the promise that Remus would own the formula. Poor Remus had no clue about business dealings and he wanted the money to continue his research. He developed the drug that enhances creativity but when he saw the side effects, he wanted to stop the program."

"And Owens wouldn't let him," Claire said.

"Right."

"And Josh Owens and Leo Martin convinced him he was a murderer."

"Yes. Apparently, Martin claimed Remus was on the government's most-wanted list because of the people who died taking the drug he created."

Claire shivered again as she remembered that terrible night when she'd met Walter. "So they imprisoned him and forced him to continue production."

Dax nodded. "Owens and Martin were making a huge profit. They needed their golden goose."

He fell silent as they looked out at the waves breaking on the shore and ebbing away. The rhythm was hypnotic.

"I stopped by to see Celestina this week," Claire said. "She's doing great and has hired two assistants to work with her. They create the pieces she designs. Several online companies are carrying her necklaces and bracelets." Claire paused. "She told me that at first she missed the RBBs. But then she realized the fountain of creativity was within her, that by believing in herself she could make it happen." Claire sat up, the sea breeze ruffling her hair. "Dax..."

He was smiling up at her. "Yes?"

"Isn't that true for all of us? Believing, having faith in yourself, is really the secret to success and happiness."

"I think you're right..." he chuckled, "...along with an ounce of good luck." Then he stood up and held out his hand. "Come on, let's go for a swim and then home. I'll make you a fabulous pineapple margarita."

Claire held out her hand and he pulled her up. They raced across the white sand and plunged into the turquoise water.

Dear Readers,

The Girl on 30A takes place along the Emerald Coast and most of the towns, restaurants and shops actually exist. However, the village of Lemon Cove is a figment of my imagination as well as the Beach Mania shops, the Baby Beach Bunny shops, Kōfuku and the Claremont Resort.

I invented the February Artists Festival, but you would probably enjoy the **30A Song Writer's Festival** that takes place in January or the **Seaside Writer's Conference** in May.

I participated in several Zen Meditation sessions in a lovely little garden called **Monet, Monet** which is a small replica of Monet's Garden in Giverny, France.

Enjoy the Sunshine,

Deborah Rine

Made in the USA
Columbia, SC
24 July 2021